# WIELDING AN
# HOURGLASS

# WIELDING AN HOURGLASS

## THE CHRONOS PARADOX • BOOK 1

## HUNTER BLAIN

Podium

# WIELDING AN
# HOURGLASS

"Trying to comprehend time travel is hard.
Coming up with new methods of it is bullshit."
—Hunter Blain

# PROLOGUE

**D**addity!" Alison cheerfully cried out as I stepped into the kitchen, where she was helping her mother prepare the salads for our dinner. Little hands clutched at the air as I approached, and I lifted my beautiful baby girl up above my head.

"Whoooaaa," I let out, as I rested her on the side of my hip. "You're getting heavy!"

"The steaks are ready to go on," Sylvie said with a smile as she moved the freshly washed spinach from the colander to the salad bowl.

"You hear that, Ali?" I said in a breathy, overly excited voice typically used with small children.

"Eeeeewwwwww!" she let out while squirming where I held her in place with my right arm. "I don't want steak!"

"Well then, what *do* you want?" I asked with a quick tickle of her tummy using my free hand.

"Chickie nuggies!"

"No, honey. You had that for lunch," Sylvie said as she added the cheese and croutons to the mix.

"Chick-ie nugg-ies. Chick-ie nugg-ies!" Alison chanted over and over, emphasizing her point with little fists that pounded in protest.

"You heard your mother," I said in my normal voice, keeping a soft tone to it.

To show her dissatisfaction, Ali dramatically sighed and went limp while leaning backward, almost slipping from my grip.

"Be careful!" Sylvie told me with a half smile.

"Uh! She's the one . . . " I trailed off while pointing at the theatrical child. "You trying to get me in trouble, Ali? Huh? You trying to get me in trouble?" I playfully asked while vigorously tickling her belly again, which did the trick because she stiffened right back up while batting my hands away.

Tiny giggles escaped her mouth, followed by a play scream and protests of, "No, Daddity! Stop!"

"Besides, you want a *special* dinner for a *special* day, don't you?" I asked as I pulled out a wrapped box that I had kept hidden in my back pocket.

A squeal of excitement nearly ruptured my eardrums as Ali reached for the rectangular box covered—poorly—in pink gift wrap with a stick-on blue bow.

Within seconds, the wrapping was floating to the ground, and Alison was opening the box with little, clumsy fingers.

Inside was a silver necklace with a black marble in the middle, dotted with different colored specs.

Ali gasped, her large eyes seeming to sparkle while staring at the gift.

"What's this?" she asked in awe.

"The universe, baby."

"You *would* give your daughter the universe," Sylvie spoke with pride in her words.

"Happy birthday, sweetie," I said, voice spilling over with love, and then leaned my head over and kissed her little nose. Normally, Ali would squirm and fight against kisses to her face, but at that moment, she was transfixed.

"Are you going to put it on?" Sylvie asked just before our eyes met and I saw the happiness contained within.

With little pants of excitement, Ali snatched the necklace from the box and quickly slung it over her neck without even having to unclasp the chain first.

"She'll grow into it," Sylvie assured me with a wink, apparently noticing how I was looking at the length of the necklace, realizing my oversight.

"But what about Mommy? It's her birthday too!" Alison exclaimed, and I couldn't help but feel a tinge of pride in my heart at seeing how selfless my sweet girl was.

I feigned a gasp and pulled out an identical box from my other back pocket.

"It is?" I playfully teased before holding the gift out to my gorgeous wife who had given me a perfect child.

"We said no gifts this year!" Sylvie protested, but with a smile that she couldn't hide.

She took the box, unwrapped it, then moved to throw away both her wrapping paper and Alison's, which had been strewn on the floor.

"Mommy! Hurry!"

"Yeah, Mommy! Hurry!" I mimicked, though I was actually eager for her to open it.

"Okay, okay!" Sylvie placated as she opened the white box to reveal a platinum necklace with an angel pendant at the center holding a raw, uncut diamond.

"Oh my God," Sylvie said with an inhale as she placed one hand over her heart. "It's beautiful."

"You like it?"

"It looks just like the one my mother used to have."

"It *is* the one your mother used to have," I said with a wide smile. "I had the lady at Tiffany's add the diamond."

"I . . . I thought she'd lost it!" Sylvie exclaimed as she unclasped the chain and put it around her neck. I was about to set Ali down to help her, but she easily got it on by herself.

"Remember when I went to help them with the Wi-Fi boxes to extend the signal?"

"Yeah?"

"I found it in the attic while running an Ethernet cable. And when I showed it to her, she said she wanted you to have it."

"Oh, Andrew," my wife said as she rushed over and wrapped her arms around us.

"Where's your present, Daddity?" Alison asked. "It's your birthday too! 'Member? ASA-Day!"

"You are my ASA-Day present, baby," I replied as I kissed the side of her head, then did the same to Sylvie. "You both are."

My wife leaned closer before whispering, "I'll give you your gift later tonight," and then playfully bit my ear.

"Oh, um . . . uh, heh. Oh my . . . " I stammered, feeling the weather get a little warm all of a sudden.

"What does, um, A-S-A mean again?" Alison asked, slowly enunciating the letters.

"It's our names, silly girl," I replied as I gave her hair a quick tussle.

"Daddity! Sto-hop!" She giggled. After I did, she thought for a moment, then said, "But-but-but your name is *Daddity*! And Mommy is *Mommy*!"

Sylvie and I looked at one another as we both stifled a laugh at how absolutely adorable our baby girl was being.

I feigned a gasp, then said, "You're right! It should be ADM-Day, huh?"

"More like AMD," Sylvie countered over her shoulder, moving the letters into a better order, probably stemming from who was in charge of the house, starting with Ali.

"Steaks, please," Sylvie let out in a singsong as she moved across the kitchen to place the cooking sheet into the preheated oven with fresh, homemade garlic butter slathered across a split loaf of French bread.

"Yes, ma'am!" I replied, squatting to set Ali down.

"Nooooo!" she whined before locking her arms around my neck.

"Whoa! When did you get to be so strong?" I asked while gently pulling myself free from her tiny death grip.

"Ali, can you come help Mommy set up the table?" Sylvie distracted her before giving me a wink indicating that I was clear to proceed. One of her hands was resting over the angel pendant, and I knew I had done good.

I winked back while our daughter switched her attention and gave little hops over to where Sylvie was holding three dinner plates and salad bowls.

"Now, be careful, okay?"

"Okay, Mommy!"

I opened the fridge and grabbed the Ziploc bag that contained two-and-a-half steaks soaking in low-sodium soy sauce and our favorite seasoning which only the butcher shop up the way sold. It didn't even have a label on it, but damn, was it good!

Pulling out the meat, I set them on a small rectangular pan that Sylvie had left out for me and moved toward the backyard where the grill awaited.

Holding the tray, I looked at the half-empty bag of mesquite coals, the long red lighter, and an empty spot where the starter fluid should have been.

"Ah, damn it," I mumbled, lifting my face to the sky in frustration at my oversight. But as I thought about it, I *knew* I had just pulled it out of the shed and set it next to the grill. Or maybe I had just been really hungry.

With a long sigh, I stepped back into the kitchen, shutting the door behind me in defeat and drawing the attention of both of my girls.

"That was quick," Sylvie said with a slightly wry smile, knowing the expression on my face meant I had forgotten something.

"I need to run to the corner store and grab some lighter fluid," I admitted while setting the pan of meat on the countertop.

"In the fridge, please," she playfully indicated, and I moved to put the tray into the refrigerator.

"Need anything while I'm there?"

"Candy!" Alison excitedly cried out while jumping up and down.

Sylvie looked at me and shrugged.

"We don't have any dessert."

"Candy it is!" I said, feeling more at peace for my oversight considering now we were going to benefit from the mistake by having dessert of the chocolate bar variety.

"Can I go with you, Daddity?"

"No, honey. It'll only take me ten minutes to run there and back. Fifteen tops."

"What if you . . . you-you-you um . . . don't get the one I like?" she protested, using every bit of her developing brain to formulate an argument as to why she needed to go with me.

"I know which one to get," I replied with a warm grin. "The peanut butter chocolate one."

"You can help me out here, baby," Sylvie told our daughter.

"Okay, Mommy," Ali conceded before holding up her index finger and motioning for me to come to her, mimicking the same thing her mother did on occasion.

I moved toward her, and when she continued to waggle her finger, I leaned down further, allowing her to grab either side of my face.

"Daddity, I need you to listen, okay?"

"Okay, sweetie. What is it?" I inquired with an amused chuckle at how grown-up she was trying to be.

She turned to look at her mother before returning her focus to me and pulling my face even closer while forcing my head to pivot to the side.

Whispering into my ear, she said, "I want two. Okay?"

"Two?!" I mock gasped, turning to look her right in her adorable eyes.

"Yes, two." She nodded with abandon, as if the wild motion would somehow accentuate her point.

"You got it," I whispered back while giving her a little wink. "Anything for the center of *my* universe." As I spoke, I lightly touched the marble around her neck with my index finger.

"Two?" Sylvie asked with crossed arms and a playfully arched eyebrow.

"How could I argue with that?" I chuckled as I straightened my stance and pointed at the stoic little girl standing her ground.

Sylvie rolled her eyes and uncrossed her arms while she returned her attention to the food she was preparing, but her smile gave her away, giving me all the permission I needed.

"I'll be back in a few," I told my family as I began making my way toward the garage. "Love you, girls!"

"Love you too!" they repeated in unison, with Alison almost yelling it to be heard.

In my Honda Accord, I turned on the radio and drummed the steering wheel to the music, eager to taste the homemade meal for our special day—our ASA-Day.

At the corner store, I got out of my car, leaving the engine running because the neighborhood was a safe one, and made my way inside with a pep in my step. The lighter fluid was closest to the door on the wall, so I grabbed the only size they had, mumbling at the inflated price as I did.

Next was the candy aisle, where I made sure to grab not one, but *two* of the chocolate peanut butter candies that Ali liked, as well as a bag of cherry licorice for Sylvie. She hadn't specifically told me to grab some for her, but I knew my wife. For me, I snagged the first dark chocolate bar that looked good, then whistled as I made my way to the counter.

After paying, I returned to my car with a white bag in hand and plopped down in the driver's seat.

A few minutes later, I was home.

Shutting the door to the garage behind me, I sauntered toward the kitchen, calling out in a singsong, "I got the dessert!"

A bitter, metallic smell tickled my nostrils, giving me pause for a moment before my feet blurred the rest of the way to where I had last seen my family.

Sitting at the dining table were Alison and Sylvie.

Their heads were lolled back with white dishrags covering their faces. But the squares of cloth weren't solid white anymore. Crimson stained the centers, spreading outward in a Rorschach that cut at the threads of my sanity like a razor blade of untold agony and sorrow.

"S-Sylvie? A-A-Ali?" I mouthed as darkness gripped my heart and squeezed while anxiety wrapped tendrils around my throat, choking me.

The white plastic bag dropped to the floor, sending the candy sliding away as if to flee the mind-breaking scene.

There they sat, as motionless as two faceless store mannequins.

My vision spun as my legs gave out, and even through the closed doors, my scream could be heard throughout the neighborhood, prompting a cascade of dog barks and howls that spread outward like a shock wave of unimaginable anguish.

# CHAPTER 1

Coffins.

Beautiful and terrifying all in the same cold breath.

It'd never occurred to me that coffins for children would simply be smaller versions of those made for adults. I'd just always thought they were a one-size-fits-all scenario. I mean, I'd been to a few funerals in my time, and even those who could barely fit through a door seemed to be stuffed into a normal sized coffin.

But not my daughter's.

Hers . . . hers was half the size of my wife's.

Did you know they sold them with cute pink unicorns or baby blue dinosaurs? Because I didn't . . . I didn't . . .

" . . . leaving behind a grieving father and husband, Andrew . . ." the priest rattled on with his cookie-cutter eulogy. So generic. So vague. So bullshit.

I hated him.

I hated him for all the things he hadn't done to deserve my wrath. I hated him for being a stronger man and speaking in place of me to these— these *pretenders* who had come to mourn my family.

The air was rich with the aroma of flowers, creating a permanent association with the smell that would probably haunt me for the rest of my life. If I decided to live, that is.

With a head weighed down with a near lethal dose of prescription drugs, I managed to turn my gaze to my in-laws.

Sylvie's parents noticed the awkward movement, and both shot blurry eyes toward me.

Her mother gave a single sympathetic nod before turning back to the stage.

Her father, on the other hand, glared at me with an intense, hot loathing that could melt the layer of permafrost in the most frigid ice lands on this planet.

His expression said it all: you let them die. You. Let. Them. *Die.*

I ripped my gaze away from them and let my head hang low—no longer able to muster the strength to face judgment from the people who had entrusted me to protect their daughter and granddaughter.

Seated next to me, my mother grabbed my cold, lifeless hand, and rested her forehead on my shoulder. I could smell the coffee on her breath as she silently cried, and it disgusted me.

I wanted to yell at her and demand to know how *anyone* could drink coffee on a day like this.

Her sobs felt like a mixture of sorrow outlined with a palpable relief that it hadn't been me, and I pulled my hand from hers. She didn't notice. Or if she did, she at least didn't acknowledge it.

My father, who had been blinking back his tears for the last twenty minutes, reached over and patted my upper back a few times, just to let me know he was there.

But *I* wasn't.

I was drowning in a pool of anguish inside my own head, not even caring to try and stay above the surface.

I wanted to be with my girls again.

A pathetic speck of water resembling a tear attempted to roll down my cheek, only to be absorbed into my skin from how small the drop was. Hell, even my own tear ducts were too depressed to function properly.

To make up for the lack of water flooding from my eyes, my gaping jaw let loose with a strand of drool. I hadn't even realized my mouth was hanging open, but I also didn't care. Moving an arm that felt like it weighed as much as a cinder block, I managed to wipe away the saliva, and looked up at the caskets which contained my family.

Ten years with Sylvie, the unequivocal love of my life and high school sweetheart, who had given me a perfect daughter, Alison, five years ago.

Like a forgotten box of old memories that had been discarded in the corner of the attic, the coffins now held ten years of love with my wife, and five years with my sweet baby girl. So many years of happiness . . . so many memories . . . now locked in these boxes which were to be buried in the dirt this afternoon.

"They can't breathe!" a deranged man screamed, but everyone ignored him.

I looked around to see who had dared yell at my family's funeral and why no one was stopping him, only to realize that I was now standing with an outstretched hand reaching toward the coffins.

Embarrassment, who had always had limitless authority on when I acted, asked my drugged mind if it should just take the day off. My mind agreed, and I felt nothing as I looked around at all the faces trying so desperately to not make eye contact with me.

The priest cleared his throat, then continued.

"We do not know why evil exists, or why our flock is sometimes accosted by the wolves of the world. But we know that God has a plan, and that he loves us immensely. Sylvie and Alison are now embraced in God's love. So let us rejoice as—"

"Love?!" I screamed, this time aware it was me. "*God* let my family be murdered! Where's the love in that?!"

"Er, um . . . I, ah," the priest fumbled at the predicament I had thrown him into. It wasn't his fault. He was just doing the job Sylvie's father had paid him to do because *I* didn't have the mental capacity to arrange payment to cover the funeral expenses.

Waving my hand dismissively, I turned and half ran, half stumbled out of the cathedral. No one followed. Not even my loving parents who knew when I needed to be alone.

Once I was through the white wooden doors that led out of the parlor, I grabbed the back of a chair in front of the receptionist's desk, gasping for breath as the tears decided now was their time to shine.

I could see from the corner of my eye a young administrator covering her mouth as she looked around in hopes that someone *else* might come and comfort the grieving man.

After several seconds, I managed to mend my crumbling mind long enough to give orders to my body: grab keys from pocket, get in car, and go home. My body would have to rely solely on muscle memory, as I had already begun to lose grip on my sanity.

"Mister, ah, Frost?" the female receptionist asked, and I had just enough cognitive ability left in me to turn and look at her.

She had a package for me with a letter under the binding. But that wasn't what caught my eye.

The wrapping was a brown paper type which my wife loved to use on special occasion gifts, like for our anniversary. To me, it was just brown paper, but to her, it was an elegant poetry which embraced the gifts contained therein. Something about tradition that I'd never really understood.

I stumbled to the desk and reached for the package.

"Who brought this?" I demanded as I tried to slide the letter out.

"I . . . I don't know. It was just here!"

She must have thought she sounded crazy because she tried to further explain.

"Th-th-the phone rang, and when I picked it up, no one answered," she said as she pantomimed turning in her office chair toward the phone, then swiveling back again. "Then it was just there!"

I was going to tell her to throw it in the trash when I saw it was also wrapped in twine.

I took the package, mentally guessing the contents were some sort of collection of papers. Maybe a will or something like that. But the wrapping . . .

Pushing through the doors outside, I scowled up at the hot sun and cursed it for disrespecting my family's funeral by shining. Didn't it know that it was supposed to be cloudy with light drizzles? The singing birds appeared to mock my torment, and at that moment, I fully understood Edgar Allan Poe's *The Raven*.

Stomping to my car with a drugged mind barely able to acknowledge I wasn't just a sack of potatoes, I fumbled with the key fob until the doors unlocked.

Plopping down in the seat with a grunt, I turned on the car, set the AC on high, and groaned as the heat from the sitting vents hit me directly in the face.

I set the package down in the empty passenger seat . . . which would always remain empty now . . . and stared down at the letter under the twine bow with my name on it.

*Daddity*, was all it said.

My heart skipped a beat as I sucked in a breath at reading the nickname my sweet angel, Alison, had given me. But that wasn't what made my guts start to churn with unease.

The name was written in *my* handwriting.

# CHAPTER 2

I hesitantly reached for the letter as if it were a cobra waiting to strike, and slowly pulled it free from where the twine held it in place pressed against the brown paper wrapping.

*Daddity* stared back at me, and my moist, pliable throat all of a sudden became as dry and stiff as concrete, threatening to separate my lungs from the hot air blowing from my car's vents.

I tried to swallow, but the muscles required completely ignored the command, and I had a coughing fit from the saliva that had been positioned at the back of my tongue, ready to hydrate my arid throat.

A knock on the car door made me yelp right as I coughed, clearing my airway.

I rolled down the window and saw my father looking down at me, the position of the sun casting a long shadow across his face to personify the damper mood.

"Come on, son. They are taking Sylvie and Alison to their final resting place."

Heavy eyes looked past him to see the caskets being loaded into the hearse while my mother and in-laws climbed into the awaiting limo.

"I'll . . . I'll meet you there," I replied, setting the letter back on top of the package. "I just want to be alone right now."

My father, sensing a change in me from the time I had been sitting in the parlor to that moment, nodded once and turned toward the limo. He paused after one step, shifted his gaze to look over his shoulder at me, and said, "You have to be strong . . . for *them*." Then he walked away, leaving me alone with his words.

I continued to stare after him while I rolled the window back up, right as the AC began blowing cool air.

"Strong?" I grumbled, watching him disappear into the limo to sit with my mother and Sylvie's parents. "Why should I be strong? I wasn't strong enough to save them. Why do I have to be *strong* now?" I said the word as if it tasted bitter across my tongue.

Throwing my Honda Accord in reverse, I followed after the limo just behind the hearse while an army of pretenders took up the rear. Neighbors. Acquaintances. Work colleagues. Anyone masquerading as being close to my family made up the cavalcade of people who had called in to work for a convenient funeral held on a Friday.

None of my friends showed up because she *was* my only friend . . . my best friend . . . my everything.

The sun glinted off of the white envelope, and I peeled my gaze off the slow-moving parade to stare at it, wondering at the secrets contained under the sealed flap.

An impact threw the package to the floorboard while I cursed through my teeth and forcefully straightened my arms to push against the jolt. The limo seemed surreal with how close it was, and I sat frozen in place, pressed against the back of my seat with enough force that I was surprised the steering wheel wasn't bending or even breaking entirely.

With a sigh to lower the spiked adrenaline, I let my hand smack against the shifter, threw it in reverse, and pulled back a few feet before putting it in park.

The limo driver got out, trying his best to remain professional and not show how flustered he was—or maybe I was projecting.

"What on Earth was that?" a smooth, male British voice asked from somewhere in the car.

"Ah!" I yelped, looking all around. My eyes, sensing something that my brain couldn't fathom, latched onto the package lying sideways on the floorboard.

"Were we in an accident?"

"Who's talking, please?" I panted with heaving breaths of disbelief as I continued to gawk at the box wrapped in brown paper and twine.

"That depends."

" . . . on *what*?" I hysterically asked, briefly wondering if I was experiencing an overdose on my prescriptions.

"You are Andrew Frost, yes?"

"Ye-yes."

"Excellent!" the voice exclaimed happily. "We'll chitchat later. First, go lay your family to rest. Oh, and don't mention me to anyone," the voice instructed before mumbling, "Not that anyone would believe you in your current state, that is."

There was a knock on my window, and I nearly jumped out of my skin.

My father moved out of the way as I opened my door, my eyes still the size of Mars's twin moons.

I glanced back and forth between the package on the floorboard and my concerned dad.

"I'll pay for it," I heard my father-in-law tell the driver. Then just above a whisper, "Just like everything else."

Rage, fury, and wrath all banded together in some sort of synonym gang which asked my brain if it was okay to, over a series of days or even weeks, beat the man to death with a metal spoon.

I managed to suppress the desire and shove it waaaaay down into my guts to where it was sure to develop into some sort of tumor.

Shaking my head to clear the cloud of confusion, I looked back at the box and determined that I had, indeed, experienced a hallucination. Or perhaps I'd hit my head in the minor fender bender. Either way, I could deal with that problem later.

People were staring as they left the line of vehicles and walked toward the large green canopy set up in front of two holes in the dirt. Seeing the graves made the world around me melt as if the cemetery were nothing more than a painting and the canvas was being power washed with paint thinner.

My heart lurched like it was trying to punch out of my chest, and I had to take a step forward to drunkenly catch myself.

Good ol' Dad did what dads do and shot his arms forward with blinding dad speed, catching his son before he fell face-first to the dry dirt and stiff grass.

"Thanks, Pop," I whispered to my father as I recentered myself, sucked in a long breath, and attempted to be strong, just as I had been advised to do.

As the coffins were placed on the platforms, ready to be lowered into the ground, I could hear or see nothing but the containers that separated me from my entire world. I didn't even think about the hallucination I had just experienced or the letter that had my handwriting on it. All that existed . . . were the coffins.

My father had his arm over my shoulders, but I think it was to make sure I didn't fall over, or maybe so I didn't burst from my seat like I had done in the parlor. My sweet mother, on the other hand, clasped one of my hands in both of her shaking ones. Her skin was dry, and I could feel the folds in her wrinkling flesh.

I looked at her as she silently cried, and I realized she probably didn't have much time left on this planet. Time took us all, eventually, unequivocally, unescapably.

Something tickled the back of my brain, and I dared a glance over my shoulder toward my car. The limo driver was mean mugging me, evident even through his typical aviator sunglasses.

But I didn't care about him.

My eyes glided to my car, and I had to wonder if insanity had taken me. Which, if I were to be honest with myself, I probably wouldn't mind at a time like this.

The priest/pastor/funeral home director—whatever he was—finished up with the final prayer.

"We therefore commit these bodies to the ground, earth to earth, ashes to ashes, dust to dust; in sure and certain hope of the resurrection to eternal life."

At that, I stood, walked to the mound of dirt as they lowered the caskets into the ground, and gawked at how unnerving it was that they were so brightly illuminated by the happy sun above.

Grabbing a handful of the surprisingly warm earth in each hand, I moved to the foot of the graves just as the caskets reached the bottom, feeling a surge of grief that swarmed over the disorienting haze left over from having my sanity questioned by a talking box. This *was* happening.

My throat did an impression of an armadillo and curled in on itself, choking me so that only shallow breaths seeped past.

The world became blurry as I stared down at my whole world, my lips quivering while I tried to say something, *anything*.

The letter with the word *Daddity* flashed across my mind, and I whispered, "I'll see you again, soon. I . . . I promise," as I dropped the handfuls of warm dirt on the reflective caskets. I didn't know *why* I said that, but I knew the words to be true in my gut.

My parents and in-laws approached next, each dropping their own handfuls of earth into the holes. Phil, who stood on the other side of his wife from me, couldn't help himself and grumbled, "Why weren't you a man and saved them?"

My head rocked back as if I had been struck by a brick right between my eyes, and I nearly passed out at the words.

"How *dare* you!" my dad snarled as he powerfully strode the two steps toward my father-in-law and awkwardly punched him in the mouth by bringing his fist up next to his face—his elbow pointed forward—and then launching his hand like a trebuchet.

My pop wasn't a trained fighter and had probably never even been in a physical altercation before, judging by the punch, but it sure as shit was satisfying to see the look on Phil's face as he took a shocked step backward and cupped his hands over his bleeding lip.

The audience gasped while the funeral director just shook his head as if to convey, *I knew this was going to happen.*

Phil recovered after a few seconds, balled his thick hands into fists, and prepared to pummel my dad just before Claire, my sweet mother-in-law, placed a firm hand on his chest and sharply said, "You *deserved* that, Phillip. Now walk away before you make an even bigger ass out of yourself."

Phil's wild, rage-filled eyes flicked between my dad and Claire before something in his face registered that he should probably listen to his wife. I had to give him credit for that.

As my father-in-law walked away, Claire sighed, turned to face me with a look of apology written on her face, and told me, "He's misplacing his anger, Andrew. Because they didn't catch the . . . " She choked off, unable to say the words.

"The murderer," I finished for her.

She nodded, wiping away a tear as she gracefully recomposed herself, and finished with, "Because we don't know who it was . . . he's placing all his hurt on the next closest person."

I looked at the graves as the audience murmured to themselves, with some starting to get up and head toward the line of cars.

"I understand," I whispered. "I blame myself, too."

"Hey!" my dad barked out, jabbing an index finger into my chest. "This wasn't your fault. You can't control the actions of someone with the intent to kill. You hear me?"

My mom patted him on the shoulder a few times, prompting him to yank his finger away, cross his arms, and turn to face the cars.

"I think what your father is trying to say is that we know you, and we know how much Sylvie and Alison meant to you . . . " my mother started to explain before she trailed off, not wanting to finish where the thought was taking her.

"I'm not going to kill myself, Mom," I assured her with words that I didn't believe.

She looked up at me, her weathered eyes flicking back and forth between mine as she forced a smile that suggested she wanted to believe me, and then nodded. Turning to link her arm with my father's, I watched as my parents made their way back to the limo.

"Ed and Mary are right, you know," Claire spoke, drawing my attention. I had to admire how strong she was at that moment, reminding me of Sylvie. I wanted to burst into tears at seeing the resemblance to my wife, but I held it in, the emotion being choked by my throat for a change. "This wasn't your fault. And I pray you don't do something that Sylvie and Alison wouldn't want you to do." She paused for a second, looking me in the eyes, and finished with, "They are watching, you know. So make them proud."

With that, she grabbed both my hands, lifted them a little, and squeezed before dropping them again.

I watched as Claire went to have a discussion with Phil, who was standing with crossed arms and a slightly bleeding lip. He was a smart man who knew not to mess with his wife, especially when she was right, which was probably most of the time.

Two workers in blue overalls stood nearby with shovels and a look of mild impatience directed at the last man standing at the gravesite. The funeral director held his Bible in both hands at his waist as he watched me with more understanding eyes than the other two employees.

Looking back down at the holes, I wiped away a tear and managed to use every ounce of my will to turn toward my car. The simple action of not facing them felt like the final nail in the coffin, as it were, and a part of my heart withered and died as I walked away.

# CHAPTER 3

The drive home was both electrifying and numb. Only the oddity that was the package kept me awake enough that I didn't pass out from the cornucopia of pharmaceutical narcotics that seemed to be trying to make a comeback now that the traumatic ordeal of the burial was behind me.

Looking at the floorboard where I had left the mysterious box, I asked, "He-Hello?"

Only the hiss of the AC and hum of the road provided any sound.

With a shake of my head at talking to a damn box, I turned on the Bluetooth and played an energetic metal album. The chugging guitars, machinelike drummer, and screaming vocalist helped mutate my sorrow into aggression as I let the music flow through me.

"Can you turn that garbage down, please?" a muffled voice called out, just beneath the decibels of the music.

Pressing the button to turn the Bluetooth off, I narrowed my eyes and looked down at the box.

"So you *are* here?" I drawled, almost as if I were accepting, even welcoming, of my insanity.

Silence was my answer.

"Okay," I said to the empty car. "If no one is here, then they won't mind if I turn my music back on."

As I reached for the power button once more, the British voice blurted out, "Okay, okay, okay! I'm here. Just . . . just please don't turn that trash back on."

"Ha! I knew it!" I victoriously cried out while shifting my gaze from the road back to the box. "I'm *not* crazy!"

"Well, that is a subjective term, isn't it? Relative to the user in much the same way as time."

Pulling into my driveway, I clicked the garage door opener and sat with my foot on the brake while waiting for the door to fully open.

"What are you?" was the only question I could think to ask.

"I was hoping to wait until we were inside. Alone."

"Why?" I asked as I eased off the brakes and let the car roll into the garage, parking next to the SUV that Sylvie mostly drove.

"For one, I didn't want you getting into another accident, especially while traveling at highway speeds."

I threw the car into park and clicked the button to lower the garage door again.

"You're really *real*, aren't you?" I was in disbelief as I reached down to grab the box off the ground and pull it to my lap. Realizing there might be a sentient being inside of the package, I moved it to rest on the center console.

"Of course I'm real," the voice answered with indignation dripping from his words at the absurdity of the question. "Now, are you going to turn your vehicle off? Or is this going to be my shortest mission yet?"

"Mission?" I repeated before registering the first part of his concern and turning the car off before I could asphyxiate. It clicked and clacked as the engine cooled.

"Shall we discuss this inside?"

Shaking my head at talking to a damn box, I grabbed both the package and letter, and made my way inside.

I set the box on the quartz of the kitchen peninsula which had several cabinets on one side, and a row of black stools on the other. The room was lit by under cabinet lights as well as the afternoon sun spilling in from the windows of the open concept home—the home Sylvie had designed herself.

Stuffing the thought into the darkness for now, I grabbed a pair of scissors from the junk drawer, cut the twine, removed the paper, and slit the tape that held the lid together open.

"Careful, *careful*," the voice said.

Setting the scissors on the white stone countertop, I opened the box to see something from a sci-fi movie. Picking it up, it was some sort of smooth metal cylinder that was hollow in the middle and had what looked to be padding lining the inside.

A floppy-eared Cairn Terrier puppy appeared in midair above the device, standing about six inches tall and scaring the shit out of me with his sudden appearance.

I dropped the cylinder back into the box, and the dog cried out before falling over as if I had picked him up and let him go again.

"Don't do that!" we both yelled in unison, but for completely different reasons.

"Oh my God . . . I'm talking to a . . . a *talking* dog," I hissed out, reaching up with both hands to grab my hair. "I've lost my mind."

"You haven't lost your mind, Andrew. Crazy people don't realize they are crazy," the dog said as he stood up from where he had fallen.

"Are you going to tell me who you are and what the hell is going on?"

"Oh, right. Please, forgive my manners. I always forget to introduce myself," the dog replied before taking a little bow and announcing, "I am Tim."

"Tim? Just . . . just Tim?"

"I believe I was named and modeled after a canine in one of my creator's favorite book series."

"So you are a machine?"

"What did you think I was? A puppy ghost?" he asked as his fully colored image went pale and see-through with wispy edges.

"As if that would make me any less insane right now?"

"Andrew . . . as I said, you are *not* insane, I assure you," Tim repeated with an exasperated breath as his body returned to its fully colored shape, no longer see-through.

"Good to know that a machine can get annoyed."

"Oh, please believe that this is a reflection of you rather than me."

I waved my hand in the air at the fruitless direction the conversation was quickly sliding toward.

"Besides," Tim continued, "I'm not just *any* machine. I'm a Clepsydra."

"A clep-what now?"

"A clep-suh-dra," he said, sounding out the word phonetically. "Latin for hourglass. At least I *think* it's Latin."

"Clepsydra," I repeated, trying out the proper pronunciation. "What the hell is that?"

"It's what *I* am. Or, more technically, the vessel that I use to function. Think of it like how your brain relies on your body to live, and vice versa."

"What do you want, Tim?" I asked, disregarding the minutiae of the conversation.

Tim looked at me with his alarmingly intelligent puppy eyes, and said, "I want to help you see your family again . . . and take vengeance on their killer."

# CHAPTER 4

I stood completely dumbfounded as I stared at the hologram puppy who was staring right back at me.

"H . . . How are you going to help me see my family again?" I croaked with a throat that had less moisture than the entire planet of Mercury.

"I think it's best that you read the letter," Tim answered, gesturing with his snout toward the envelope.

I glared at him for a moment before the call of the unknown overtook me and I snatched up the letter with *my* handwriting on it.

"This better not be a trick," I grumbled as I opened it and began reading.

Confusion at seeing the words written by my hand seeped in before being deflated and replaced by a dark sense of purpose mixed with dread. The letter read:

*D-Frost,*

*Hey, man. I know you think it's your fault that Sylvie and Ali were taken from you—from us. And I'm not here to try and tell you any different. I mean, we are the same person, so I know exactly what is going through your head. And if I couldn't talk myself out of believing it wasn't my fault, then what hope do I have of convincing you? But I digress.*

*Tim is exactly what you need in order to see them again. Do what he says, and he can help make things right . . . for everyone.*

*Most importantly, enjoy the ride. Not everyone gets to freaking go through time.*

*—Drew Frost*

*P.S. To prove this is really me—I mean you—and not the self-aware AI trying to trick you, I'll leave you with a memory of ours that only you and I would know: when you were in your early teens, you and a group of friends would crawl through the newly constructed drainage system, starting at the bridge, and then crawl out of one of the drain ditches. You had to stop once you couldn't fit as easily through the narrow ditches, unlike your skinny friends.*

"Heh."

"What's so funny?"

"He used my nickname."

Tim just looked at me and tilted his puppy head.

"Something my friends in high school called me. D-Frost."

Tim tilted his head to the other side.

"Andrew Frost . . . Drew is . . . is short for Andrew? Drew Frost? You see where I'm going with this."

"Is that supposed to be clever?"

"Said the hologram named *Tim.*"

"Monty Python had a character named Tim. Do you dare question their genius?"

I ran a hand down my face as I let out a long breath.

"I can't begin to tell you how creepy it is to have an AI with a preference for Monty Python."

"Whatever you say, *D-Frost.*"

"Okay! That's enough!" I blurted out, slamming my hand on the quartz counter. "The letter said you could help me see my family again."

"And I can," Tim affirmed, his tone softer than before.

"How, exactly?" I demanded as I crossed my arms over my chest.

"Put me on your forearm, and I'll show you."

I stared at the hologram for several heartbeats while I considered his words.

A scene from a memory played in my head.

I sat down for breakfast on a weekend morning. Alison had helped her mother prepare waffles that were somehow crispy on the outside and doughy on the inside. Sylvie had worked on the bacon and eggs by herself while keeping Ali distracted with various tasks.

We had forgotten the syrup, so had to make do with dry waffles. That is until Alison had the brilliant idea of packing her eggs and bacon on top, and then trying to fold the concoction like some sort of hot dog. Sylvie and I laughed, but followed the leader, stuffing and folding the waffle until it was about to burst. It. Was. Delicious.

Seeing how well her idea had worked, Alison grabbed the container of ketchup and spewed a thick layering on top before holding the bottle out to me.

"Oh," I chuckled. "None for me, thanks."

There was an unmistakable look of disappointment from my daughter, one I wasn't going to allow. So I grabbed the bottle, forced the ketchup to fart out a comical amount, and made Alison laugh as I produced silly faces at the sounds.

My mind zipped back to the present, where a dining room sat empty and my head felt like it had been replaced with a balloon. I had to grab the counter to keep from falling over as the wave of emotion from the memory washed over me.

"Andrew? Are you alright?"

"Huh? I . . . I . . . " I stammered, unsure of how to speak at that moment.

His words flooded my mind and played back on a loop, informing me that he could help me see my family again. Without telling my hands to do so, they stripped off my black suit jacket, tossed it on a chair at the dining table, and rolled up both sleeves.

I locked gazes with the hologram puppy, set my jaw, and gave a fierce nod before picking up the apparatus. The metal was cool beneath my fingers, and it felt expensive, for lack of a better term.

I slid my hand through, feeling the soft material of the padding glide across my skin, and felt a sort of click as the device was set in place. I winced at a small pinprick of pain at my wrist, feeling as though an ant had bitten me.

"Good," Tim said as a floating chart appeared in front of him. The puppy was now standing on his hind legs while wearing a white doctor's coat; he even had glasses on his little nose. "Your vitals look strong, even with all the medications flowing through your system as we speak."

Tim pawed at the air, and flashes of what appeared to be square buttons briefly lit up where he touched before fading from sight again.

"Now let's see about cleaning you out, shall we?"

"Cleaning me out of wh—" I started to ask before a more vibrant pain bloomed on the underside of my forearm near the elbow. "Ow! What are you doing?!"

"As I said, cleansing your body of all these pharmaceutical toxins," Tim explained as he regarded his chart once more. "Why you humans pump yourselves full of these harsh chemicals that do more harm than good, I'll never know."

"What other options do we have?" I asked, just before my body began to feel heavy.

I dropped to my knees, trying to hold myself up with my forearms on the countertop while a violent tsunami of emotions smashed into my psyche.

"Oh God!" I bellowed as my eyes, which had been kept at bay by the medications, let loose with everything they had been holding back like flinging open a dam and spilling out the floodwaters.

My mental capacity for thought was overrun by a cacophony of sounds and images, all stemming from happy memories with my wife and daughter. Each one reached out with ghostly fingers as they flew past, raking across my sanity and bringing me closer to a complete mental breakdown.

I could feel every hug all at once—every kiss, both given and received. Ali's smooches with overemphasized sucking noises caressed every inch of my face, and I returned the affection, much to her giggling protests. But Sylvie . . . I could feel her lips press against mine a thousand times over. It was then that I realized I didn't give her silly, playful kisses all over her face as I had done with Ali; at that moment, I wanted nothing more than to do just that.

In my vision danced a morphing, coagulated stream of incorporeal memories from a lifetime of events. Just behind, I could make out the textured ceiling, and the memory of Sylvie and me working on the house after we'd bought it. That scene swallowed all others.

It had taken us months to do most of the work ourselves because we didn't have the money. And I swore that I never wanted to see a popcorn ceiling again for as long as I lived.

"Oh dear," Tim said from somewhere far away as blackness swarmed my vision. I thought I heard the blaring of alarms like what was attached to hospital monitors, but it, too, seemed miles away.

Sylvie stood in front of me in a T-shirt and yoga pants that had countless splotches of gray paint on them. *Agreeable Gray* was the exact color; I remember because every time it dripped on me, I would think to myself, *This isn't very agreeable.*

She turned and looked at me with a smile that was brighter than all the stars in the universe . . . and then everything went black.

# CHAPTER 5

lear!" I heard an echoing Tim shout from somewhere nearby before white-hot pain shot up my forearm.

"UHHHHH!" I sucked in a deep, lung-stretching breath as I pushed myself up to a seated position . . . which I wish I hadn't done. Hot bile spewed from my mouth to splash on the laminate floors that were meant to resemble wood.

My left arm burned like it was inside of an oven, and I moved to unconsciously take the source of the pain off.

"No need for that," Tim spoke as he pawed the air, briefly illuminating the buttons once more.

A wave of coolness spread up my arm, stifling the burning sensation like pinching the wick of a candle between thumb and forefinger.

"What . . . what happened?" I heaved as I attempted to scoot back from the puddle of clear vomit on the floor.

"It would appear that you've been taking a heavy dosage of your medications for quite some time. As well as mixing them in what should have been a fatal cocktail."

"The funeral was almost two months after they died."

"Sixty days, hmm?" Tim said as he seemed to jot something down in a notebook that appeared in one of his paws.

"Some crap about extended family not being able to travel here until then." I spit on the ground, and I wasn't sure if it was to get rid of the taste of bitter bile from my mouth or because I had to wait two full months for closure due to people with bullshit excuses.

"I'm not referring to *why* the funeral was sixty days after their deaths, Andrew. I am simply extrapolating the idea that you've been on a heavy, and frankly *dangerous*, dose of antidepressants and SSRIs for two months." Then, under his breath, he added, "I've never had to deal with this before."

"What does that have to do with anything?"

"When I cleansed your system of all traces of the drugs, it . . . ahem, *basically* killed you."

"You mean *you* killed me," I responded as I reached up with my right hand and placed it over my pounding heart.

"Andrew," Tim spoke softly, "judging by the amount of medications in your system . . . I anticipate you would have passed away in the upcoming days."

"That was the plan," I said coldly, not meaning to say the words out loud. But even when I realized my mouth had worked on its own volition, I just mentally shrugged, letting the message hang in the air, unembarrassed.

"Hopefully, your attitude has changed now. Yes?"

"If you can really take me to see my family again . . . and if I can kill the bastard who took them from me . . . then yes."

"Excellent. We will get started in the morning. But first, you need to get a full day's worth of meals, and a good night's rest."

"I'm not hungry," I mumbled as I pulled myself up to my feet. Looking at the paper towel holder, I sighed, ripped off several sheets, and then dropped them on the puddle of bile.

"You are now," Tim declared as a ravenous wave of hunger exploded from my stomach.

My eyes went wide as I shot for the fridge and threw the doors open.

On the top shelf was a box of leftover pizza from sometime this week. Or maybe last. Either way, I was tearing into it before it even hit the countertop. There was a lot left, considering I had barely taken one bite from it whenever I had ordered it.

The cold, slightly wet slices went down faster than a pack of piranhas stripping a baby ox to nothing but bone.

I started to get hiccups from shoveling so much bread down my gullet, so I turned toward the still open fridge to yank free an expired gallon of milk. It was only slightly bitter as it went down, and I all but moaned in ecstasy at how amazing everything was tasting.

"Okay, maybe a bit much on that one," Tim said as he floated above my forearm and touched a floating square button.

My ravenous hunger subsided to a feeling of being not quite full, but not quite hungry.

I looked at the milk, feeling the cold liquid slide down the front of my shirt, and quickly set the expired jug on the counter.

"What the hell was that?" I heaved, feeling the pizza expanding in my stomach from the half gallon of milk I had chugged.

Looking down at the box, I realized I had eaten nearly an entire pizza in a matter of a minute or so.

"Sorry about that," Tim offered. "I'm still trying to acclimate to your unique body, and I'm having a doozy of a time doing so."

"Don't . . . do that . . . again," I burped as I reached behind me to shut the fridge door, all while the bread and liquid in my stomach continued to grow in size.

"I'm afraid I must."

An eerie feeling crept up inside me as I registered his words.

"Excuse me?"

"It's what is keeping you alive at this very moment."

There were a few seconds of silence before I asked, "How's that now?"

"I had to pump some of your ghastly medications back into your system to keep you from convulsing or going into cardiac arrest again."

"Whoa, whoa, whoa." I threw my hands out, which made Tim wobble back and forth as I moved, though I noticed he didn't make a big deal out of it like when I'd dropped him back in the box. "What do you mean, *again*?"

Tim sighed as he removed his spectacles with one paw and rubbed at his eyes with the other.

"The sudden removal of the drugs from your bloodstream—and bloodstream only, as I do not have access to the transmitters in your brain—resulted in a volatile spike in your blood pressure caused from the surge of suppressed anxiety that your body, frankly, doesn't know how to deal with anymore."

"Oh . . . "

"*Oh* is right, Andrew. You're beyond lucky that you didn't suffer from a stroke in your brief but intense manic state."

I had no words to convey, as I had intentionally been swallowing more pills than the doctor had prescribed. Whether I consciously knew it or not, I had been aiming to join my wife and daughter.

"So, what now?" I finally asked.

"Like I said, you need to spend the day fueling up for what is to come."

"And what is that, exactly?"

Tim reverted back to his normal canine self, doing away with the theatrical props such as the white coat and glasses. Looking me in the eye, he said, "We are going to open a portal between places in time and space, and pass through it."

# CHAPTER 6

I spent the rest of the day doing what Tim had suggested: eating, bathing, and even taking naps that I didn't seem to have a choice in taking. I would simply sit on my recliner as instructed, wide awake, and then *bam*, I was out as easily as flipping a switch.

After a while, I began to suspect that he was keeping me busy while he calibrated my baselines or whatever he called it. When I asked myself *why*, my thoughts flooded with Sylvie and Alison.

"I'm not upping your meds anymore," Tim announced after something on the wrist sleeve began to beep, like a fire detector with batteries that needed changing.

"I didn't ask you to," I said from the chair as I prepared for another forced nap.

"*You* didn't. But your body did."

"Nothing I can do about that," I replied, wiping at a single tear that had formed at the brief thought of my beautiful family.

"Replace the feelings of anguish with hope, Andrew. I promise, you *will* see them again."

"And I get to kill the bastard who took them from me?"

"Would it make you feel better?" Tim asked as he tilted his head to one side.

"It would," I answered coldly, prompting a different beep from the apparatus.

"Calm yourself, Andrew. Calm. We can't have you stressing your heart out anymore until I've had a chance to integrate."

"Integrate with what?" I inquired, lifting my right hand up and letting it plop back down on the chair's armrest.

"Traveling through the portal will not be an easy task, Andrew. I have to connect with certain systems inside your body to prevent potentially fatal side effects."

"Such as what?" I asked, feeling a sense of worry waft into my chest, similar to how the aroma of a Cinnabon at a mall or airport invades the nostrils from a hundred feet away, whether you wanted it to or not.

"There have been instances—from when time travel was first discovered, mind you—of people trying to remove their own flesh because their skeletons felt like they were made of fire."

"Jesus . . ." I drawled as I tried to picture how extremely odd of a sensation that would be. I had never thought about how my bones felt before, and it made a shudder run up the back of my neck.

"That's also after we figured out that the brain must be protected, otherwise the neural pathways could be rewritten."

"Should I even ask what happens then?"

"Complete psychosis, for one. That is, *if* the brain is even able to continue sending signals to the organs and keep the body alive."

"So, uh . . . h-h-how do you protect against that?"

"Let me worry about all the finer details, Andrew," Tim said with the tone of someone growing increasingly tired from having to explain themselves to a listener who wasn't even aware of how little they knew about the subject. I imagined doctors and nurses must feel that way every day.

I kicked out the legs of the recliner and leaned back, ready to let Tim put me under for another quick nap.

"Andrew?"

"Hmm."

"Hypothetically . . . if the person who murdered your family didn't have a choice . . . would you still want vengeance?"

"What, you mean like a crackhead trying to get a fix or something?"

"Something like that."

"Why?" I asked in a shockingly aggressive tone as I brought my left arm up to better look at the hologram. "What do you know?"

"As I said, it is hypothetical."

"Why even ask, then?"

"There are always two sides to every story, yes?"

I gritted my teeth, refusing to acknowledge his point because doing so felt like it would diminish what had happened to Sylvie and Ali.

"Look, all I am suggesting," Tim explained, "is the possibility that it might not be so binary. There's a space between the ones and zeros where the truth can often be found."

"I . . . don't . . . care *what* the truth is," I growled between my exposed teeth. "That bastard decided his fate whenever he pulled that fucking trigger. The cops even said it was a suppressed pistol, which means he had the intention to use it. So he made his choice."

"What if it was to save his own family?" Tim asked softly.

My mouth dropped open and my brow quivered as I stared at the talking dog.

"What do you know?" I finally demanded before closing my gaping mouth.

Tim took a lengthy inhale, which struck me as odd for a hologram to do, and said, "I am limited on how much I can tell you. My programming doesn't allow for a lot of wiggle room. But what I *can* say is the timeline is vast, and there are endless possibilities that one must consider."

"I . . . I don't understand."

Tim sighed in mild defeat.

"Which is why I'm even allowed to say what I've said. Now close your eyes so I can test my baseline."

"But I'm no—" I started to protest before sleep took me as quickly as yanking a rug out from under my feet and sending me tumbling face-first into unconsciousness.

# CHAPTER 7

I awoke in a haze, feeling like a colony of ants had burrowed a new home inside my brain. My hands felt heavy as I lifted them to rub at my face, and I was surprised at the darkness that filled my vision.

"Wha—?" I asked with a dry tongue and cracked lips.

"Sorry about that, old chap," Tim said as he blipped into view above my left forearm.

"What time is it?" I weakly asked while I reached down and pulled the lever for the recliner's feet to retract with a *thunk*.

"It's late. But I had to wake you for rehydration and waste removal."

"What now?"

"You need to urinate and then drink at least sixteen ounces of water so you can go back to sleep," Tim explained. "I'm almost done with my calibrations."

"Why does my head hurt?" I cringed as I tried to get to my feet, then grabbed at my pounding temples with both hands.

"Don't mind that. Just drink at least sixteen ounces of water, please. More would be better."

I finally pushed myself up to my feet, and black bugs swarmed my vision, causing me to begin losing connection with my legs.

"Take a deep breath in," Tim instructed.

I did, and the pesky vision bugs began to drop off in vast numbers as if I'd inhaled a fast-acting pesticide. My legs also became stronger with each molecule of oxygen that was injected into my bloodstream.

Once I was stabilized, I sauntered into the kitchen and opened the cabinet where the glasses were stored. It was empty except for Ali's cups made for a child's hands. Glancing with tired, crusty eyes at the sink, I saw that every adult glass had been left to soak in whatever liquid they had once contained.

Slamming the cabinet a little harder than I had meant to, I turned on the kitchen faucet and brought my face next to the falling water, slurping with pursed lips.

"Seven . . . eight . . . nine . . . keep going, Andrew."

He didn't have to tell me to keep drinking the most delicious water I had ever drank from in my entire life.

My tongue returned to feeling normal as my throat rehydrated. I could feel the collection of cool water building in my now empty stomach. I thought that was odd considering I had eaten more today than the past month.

"Aaaaand sixteen. Good job, Andrew."

I kept right on drinking.

"Oh, a thirsty boy, I see."

An entire minute must have passed while I sucked down enough water to bloom the Sahara Desert.

"O-kay . . . that's a tad odd," Tim said. "I, ah, think you've had enough, dear boy."

I ignored him, even as my stomach felt like it was going to rupture. Nothing had ever tasted better than the tap water flowing from my faucet.

"That's enough," Tim spoke a little more aggressively, and my desire to drink all the water on Earth vanished in an instant, like a semi passing through that-dude-you-know's vape cloud.

As the urge to consume disappeared, the feeling of regret manifested itself in my gut, making my insides resemble an overstuffed water balloon.

"Oh God," I lamented, keeping my head positioned over the sink as I shut the faucet off.

My mouth began to water, and I knew I was getting ready to vomit.

"Ah-augh," I gagged with my tongue out, feeling it about to happen.

"How about we not?" Tim mused, and the feeling subsided like a huge, unforgiving wave stopped by the seawall washing back out to the ocean.

I lifted my head from the sink filled with dirty dishes and held my distended stomach as if I were pregnant.

"Maybe throwing up wouldn't be such a bad idea," I moaned, leaning against the counter.

"And maybe next time you'll listen. Hmm?" Tim challenged. "Now go to your bedroom. It's time for the final calibration."

"Yeah, you keep saying things like *calibration* and stuff . . . and it doesn't give me a very pleasant feeling. Ya know?"

"Oh? I never thought about it like that," Tim said as he placed a paw under his chin in a gesture that conveyed thinking. "What about having your brain scrambled? Hmm? Or having your bones be replaced with molten lava? Would you like that?"

I could only answer by narrowing my eyes at him.

"That's what I thought," Tim concluded. "Now, please, go to bed."

With a roll of my eyes, I pushed off the counter and waddled to the bedroom with what felt like enough water in my belly to fill a bathtub, or maybe even the Pacific Ocean.

Sitting on the edge of my bed, which creaked under my weight, I dared a look to the side that was now unoccupied. I had taken the side closest to the door so that anyone who might break in to do us harm would have to go through me first. I almost had to laugh at the absurdity of the positioning, considering we hadn't been in bed when . . .

I peeled my eyes away from Sylvie's side of the bed, feeling a surge of sorrow bubbling up inside my heart. On cue, a mild alarm sounded, prompting a response from Tim.

"Alrighty, then. It's time for sleep. Get situated, please, Andrew."

This time I did what was asked without protest, wanting nothing more than to escape the pain that was rearing up to strike like a coiled cobra.

I scooted to my side, plopped my head onto my pillow, and was asleep before a sigh could finish leaving my mouth.

# CHAPTER 8

*est. Test. One, two, three,* Tim's voice said somewhere from just beyond my dream. *Is this thing on? Hellooooo.*

"Uhn," I moaned. Peeling my eyelids open, I was hit in the face by blinding sunlight. "Uhn!" I repeated with hands shielding my face.

*Andrew? Can you hear me?*

"Of course I can hear you. Why wouldn't I be able to?" I grumbled as I pushed myself up to a seated position.

*Because I'm speaking from inside your mind.*

"Huh?" I looked down at my forearm; the hologram was off. "You're *inside* my head?"

*It would appear the calibration was a success! Huzzah!*

"How . . . how did you manage that?" I asked. "And why do I have such a massive headache?"

"Oops. Let me take care of that," Tim said as his hologram popped to life.

After a few seconds, my headache dulled until the only thing that was left was the phantom pain.

"Oh, uh, you *might* want to go to the bathroom. I don't think I can hold your bladder back any longer."

"What are yo—OH MY GOD!" I leaped from the bed and sprinted to the bathroom. Luckily for me, the toilet was a straight shot. Unluckily for me, I used the drywall as a springboard; only . . . it wasn't very *springy.*

With my left shoulder embedded into the wall, I all but ripped my pajama pants off and let loose with the absolutely most satisfying piss of my life. I thought I was going to break the porcelain with how much pressure I was exerting, and I used the opportunity to power wash some of the, ahem, *other* stains off the bowl.

"Dear, sweet, merciful Jesus," I prayed as I physically felt my bladder deflating from something approximating the size of any of the moons of Jupiter.

"Yes, maybe next time you'll listen when I tell you how much water to drink."

I wanted to argue with the AI but couldn't pull myself from the pleasurable relief I was experiencing. At one point, I thought the toilet was on the verge of flushing on its own accord, given how much liquid I had added to the bowl.

After I was done, I washed my hands, splashed my face with cold water, then toweled off before brushing my teeth.

I watched myself in the mirror as the minty toothpaste foamed at my lips. The dark circles under my eyes had all but vanished, and my skin appeared healthier than it had been in years.

"What did you do to me?"

"Repaired the things that were falling apart. I swear, Andrew, some of the organs inside of you were barely hanging on, as if held by dollar store duct tape."

"Pfft." I choked out a single laugh as I pulled the toothbrush free, rinsed it clean, and put it back in its place before gurgling some water.

I looked at myself for a few seconds longer, and asked, "Why do I feel . . . okay?"

"What a strange question to ask."

"I just mean . . . I don't have th-th-the *darkness* inside my heart right now."

"Oh, I see. Well, I was able to help your, um, *body* produce more of the happy juice."

"How is that any different than the meds I was on?" My eyes flicked to the collection of orange, transparent bottles on the bathroom counter.

"It's different, Andrew, because your modern pharmaceuticals must first survive passing through your liver, which in turn damages the organ. After that, your body is unique when compared to that of your neighbors, and each drug affects the system differently. A lot of times, there are side effects that can lead to bigger problems than the ones for which the medicine was first prescribed."

My mind played back a vague summary of every commercial touting a pharmaceutical drug where the last half was comprised of all the known side effects.

"So . . . how did you manage to fix me?" I hesitantly asked, concern over the potential answer trying to silence my tongue.

"The details would bore you, Andrew," Tim replied. "Now hop in the shower and get ready for the biggest day of your life."

"Right. Time travel."

"Correct! Well . . . mostly correct."

I ignored his comment and walked to the shower. I set the temperature, then went back into the bedroom to grab some fresh underwear. My eyes looked at the eight long drawers, and I almost chuckled at realizing I only had two while Sylvie used the other six.

Sylvie.

"Tim," I said softly.

"Yes, Andrew?"

"Give me back the darkness . . . please."

"I, uh . . . you *want* me to allow sorrow into your heart?"

"I need it, Tim," I replied in a flat tone as I looked at the drawers belonging to my wife.

"If you say so," Tim relented. I could hear the headshake in his voice. "Let's start with ten percent."

A cold feeling spread from the center of my skull while a hand which had been holding on to a fistful of ice for too long grabbed at my heart.

I sucked in a breath, and the urge to sob rushed over me.

"Dialing it back to five percent."

The wave of sorrow diminished, leaving me with a dull hole where my heart was instead of an icy clutch. I wanted to say thank you, but my body forbid me from rewarding the AI for having filled my heart with deserved anguish, then taking it away again in an act of unwarranted mercy.

"Are you okay, Andrew?"

"I'm—I'm fine," I stammered as I opened my drawer, grabbed the underwear, and made my way back to the bathroom.

I let the warm water wash over me as I tried to hold onto the darkness that had been stolen from me while I slept. It wasn't that I was a martyr for pain; more like I felt I deserved the agony for letting my wife and child be taken from me. It wasn't right that the bulk of my heartache had been squashed before it could rot and fester inside of me until the day I died.

"Why do you try and torture yourself, Andrew? I can see all of your vitals; I know what you are doing."

I ignored the question, making quick work of getting clean, and stepped out to drip all over the bathroom floor. Sylvie hated when I did that, but that didn't matter anymore.

"Do you have any tough clothing?"

"Tough? Like what?"

"Jeans and steel-toed boots for one. Or maybe some overalls?"

"Overalls? Like redneck style? Or roughneck?"

"Whichever *neck* covers most of your body."

"Yeah, I might have something," I said as I went to my closet, opened the door, and stepped into the small space. On a hanger in the corner was a set of dark blue Dickies from when I had gone as Michael Myers for Halloween.

"Will this do?"

"That's perfect!"

"Want me to wear the mask?"

"The wha—" Tim began to ask until I pulled down the burnt version from the most recent train wreck that was a *Halloween* movie. "Oh . . . oh no. No, no, no. We will *not* be needing that."

I smiled as I put the mask back and grabbed a pair of hiking boots from the ground. They went above the ankle, were thick, and still had light brown dirt coating them from our last hike.

"These aren't steel toed, but they should be strong. They're even water-proof . . . I think."

"Yes, yes. They'll do fine," Tim said dismissively.

"Are you in a hurry or something? What's your deal?"

Tim didn't answer right away, so I walked to the bed, dropped the over-alls, and turned to the drawers again to grab a pair of hiking socks, along with a pair of gym shorts and a white undershirt.

"Tim?"

"I just would like to get going, is all."

I froze in place as I listened to his words and the tone being used by the calculating AI.

"What's wrong?"

"If we could get going, that would be greaaaaat."

A scowl crossed my face as I sat on the edge of the bed and began put-ting the shorts, shirt, and socks on, followed by slipping my legs through the overalls up to my waist. Next, I put on the hiking boots and laced them up nice and tight before standing and pushing my arms through the dark blue Dickies.

The hologram puppy disappeared, which made sense considering the metal sleeve was completely covered now. After zipping up the front of the overalls, I undid the clasp on the left wrist and pulled back the sleeve far enough to expose Tim.

"Now what?" I asked, looking myself up and down.

There was a screeching of brakes right outside.

"Shit!" Tim cursed.

"What?!"

"They're here."

# CHAPTER 9

They?! Who's they?!" I demanded as I strode to the bedroom window and slipped my fingers between the blinds, prying them open so I could see outside.

A single generic black car that appeared to be from the late eighties with fully tinted windows was positioned outside, blocking the driveway completely.

"Get back!" Tim cried out as men fully dressed in black suits, complete with wide-brimmed fedoras, stepped from the car. I could see they each had glowing left hands that gave off a slight blue illumination.

One of the men locked gazes with me and lifted his glowing fist in my direction.

"GET DOWN!" Tim shouted, and I stumbled backward right as an explosion of blue light ripped through the window, evaporating the blinds and sending a shower of broken glass spilling to the ground.

"Ah!" I gasped, crawling backward until I hit my bed, then crying out again, "Ah!"

I flipped over and continued crawling on the floor; I could hear the men outside calling out commands to one another.

"What's going on? Who are they?!" I heaved out with wide eyes and a gaping mouth while entering the hallway.

"Later!" Tim called back. "We have to do this *now!*"

"Do what?" I asked right as the front door exploded open, flinging the metal rectangle into the living room and taking the furniture with it in its momentum. "Ah! What the hell!"

Two men entered with determined, gritty faces. One was extremely tall and had to duck under the door's frame, while the other was squat and thick. Each held out their glowing left fists, and I realized they were weapons.

"HOLD ON!" Tim shouted as a surge of energy electrified the air, making every hair on my body stand on end.

The men pointed their weapons at me, and I brought my arms up to shield my face.

When nothing happened, I slightly lowered my arms to see the men were looking back and forth between one another with their fists lowered. The third man entered, standing between the height of the other two, and I could tell by the way they moved to the side that he was their boss.

Beneath the wide-brimmed black fedora was a cleanly shaven head. The bald man also had a thick, well-manicured, salt-and-pepper beard that fit perfectly around a frowning mouth.

The leader was looking at something near my feet. I followed his gaze right as something made a ripping sound.

With a scream that made it feel like my vocal cords were being shred apart, I fell *through* my floor, and into a world of streaking light.

# CHAPTER 10

A tunnel of vibrant light flew around me while I shrieked in terror with arms and legs flailing in a desperate attempt to find purchase. But it didn't feel like I was falling. Instead, it seemed the tunnel, roughly the size of what a train would ride through, was moving *past* me.

My mind played back YouTube videos of first-time skydivers admitting that, because of the wind resistance, it hadn't felt like they were barreling toward Earth.

I think Tim was trying to yell something at me, but I couldn't hear him over the sheer volume of my own screams. Even if it *felt* like I wasn't falling, my brain was interpreting the visuals that strongly enforced the idea I was, contrary to what my equilibrium was experiencing. Simply put, I *must* be falling.

"Andrew!" Tim shouted again, this time loud enough to be heard.

My cries of terror dissipated to whimpers as I forced my focus to latch on to Tim. A part of me knew he had put us in this mess, so he *must* have an understanding of how to get control. At least, I hoped he did.

*Andrew! Can you hear me?* Tim cried out inside my head.

"Y-Yes!" I replied in an accidental falsetto from having every muscle in my neck flexed in preparation for an eventual impact.

*I need you to relax, and trust that I have you,* he said in a calming tone. I could almost hear him holding up metaphorical palms to further try and calm me.

At his words, I didn't relax, but I did at least halt the runaway panic.

*Take in a long, deep breath. Can you do that for me?*

"Uh-huh," I let out as I tried to inhale, but the streaking lights disoriented me to the point where I couldn't expand my chest. Only quick, shallow breaths kept me from passing out.

*Close your eyes, Andrew.*

After three or four seconds of trying, I eventually was able to slam my eyelids together.

*Now breathe.*

Though I could still see the fast-moving lights as they passed through my eyelids, I was able to relax enough to snatch a long breath in.

*Good. That's good,* Tim praised. *Now, exhale, then repeat the process as I talk. Can you do that for me?*

I rapidly nodded my head, afraid to waste any of the precious oxygen on words.

*We are in a wormhole. What you are experiencing is completely normal, especially for a first timer.*

I nodded my understanding again, but with a slower motion, as I regained control and my fear began to dissipate.

*I didn't have time to lock in our intended destination, and because of that, I just sort of threw us into the wind.*

"That doesn't sound good," I managed to say while keeping my eyes squeezed shut.

*Um . . . it isn't. That's why I need you to relax so I can figure out wheren we are.*

"Wherein?"

*I assume you are using the only spelling of the word you just phonetically heard for the first time you know.* Wherein *is not the word I used, Andrew. What I said was* wheren. *Slightly different, you see?*

"What's the difference? I can't see them spelled out on a page, you know."

*We don't have time for this,* Tim sighed while still speaking inside my mind. *Hold up your arm and open your eyes.*

Fear tickled the back of my mind for a second before I forced it back down and did as told.

The tunnel appeared to slow, but it was still mesmerizing as it flowed.

"Ahem," Tim said out loud.

"Oh," I let out as I lifted my left arm to see Tim dressed in a professor's attire, complete with suede jacket.

"W-H-E-R-E-I-N, or wherein, is a pompous word that intellectuals use, especially authors. But W-H-E-R-E-N, or wheren, is a word from my time, which means both *where* and *when*, simultaneously."

"What, like asking for coordinates?"

"Exactly like that!" Tim said, impressed with my ability to catch on to the meaning of a new word so quickly.

"So *wheren* are we?"

"That's the problem," Tim answered as he glanced all around. "I don't know."

Panic opened glowing eyes on the recesses of my mind, searching for its opening to strike once more.

Perhaps sensing this, Tim quickly added, "Bu-but . . . I think I can figure it out!"

"Think?! You *think* you can figure it out?"

Panic set one predatory paw into the light, speeding up my heart and quickening my breath.

"Andrew, *you* control the wormhole. You must realize that!"

"But y-y-ou're the one who brought us here!"

The other paw belonging to the panic monster entered the light inside my mind, followed by a tooth-filled snout that led into two glowing eyes.

"Andrew, please don't make me fill you with narcotics to force calmness."

"Why not?!" I dry chuckled at how absolutely crazy the situation was. As if on cue, the lights of the tunnel began moving past me again, bringing with it a sense of vertigo.

"I need you clear and free from medications for when we jump through the wormhole."

Rather than argue, I closed my eyes again and forced in a deep breath. It was easier this time, and I was thankful for it.

"That's it, Andrew. That's it," Tim cooed in a soft voice. "*You* are in control."

"I'm in control," I repeated his sentiment, feeling the words manifest into reality.

The streaking lights outside of my eyelids began to slow again, and I dared to open them to verify that the tunnel was, indeed, easing up, like lifting your foot off the car's accelerator.

"Excellent!" Tim called out, surprising me as I kicked the rest of the predatory panic monster back into the shadows of my mind. "I am now able to get a fix on our wheren."

"What a weird word," I whispered to myself while I watched the wormhole continue to slow.

The streaks of light became oblong, like glowing eggs, and I gasped when I realized I was looking at the literal universe.

"Jesus . . . " I mouthed, wide eyes looking all around at the cluster of stars that made up huge swathes of expanding galaxies.

"Ah, yes. Welcome to the known universe."

At my awe, the moving scene came to a halt, and the glowing oblongs stilled to balls of flickering light.

I wanted to weep at the beauty of it all; at the purple clouds of one galaxy that seemed indifferent to the orangish-yellow disks of its neighbor. Everywhere I looked were more clusters of stars than I could possibly fathom. I would have better luck counting all the grains of sand on a beach rather than trying to do the same for the number of stars I could see at that moment.

"Why was the universe moving a second ago?"

"It wasn't."

I waited for the punch line. When none came, I waved a hand through the air I was somehow breathing, and sarcastically said, "Yeah. Right. It *wasn't* just moving at a blur a few seconds ago."

"Correct," Tim answered flatly.

"Then . . . then *I* was moving? But it didn't feel like it."

"More technically, you were moving *through* a wormhole, not the universe itself. And the reason it didn't feel like you were moving was because the bridge between space and time is fairly short, all things considered."

"What do you mean?"

"Imagine you were flailing your arms wildly while screaming as you casually walked across a footbridge."

My mind betrayed me and did exactly that.

I imagined onlookers gawking at a man shrieking at the top of his lungs while flinging his arms around him, all while his legs moved at a regular walking pace across the bridge.

"Yeah, but there wouldn't be a freaking tunnel of light from crossing a bridge, would there?"

"Stop thinking within the parameters of your lowly third dimension, Andrew. You just traveled across time and space in a wormhole."

"Heh . . . I . . . " I tried to find the words but could only shake my head in disbelief as my primitive human brain tried—and failed—to register the situation. Everything simply felt surreal.

"They found us!" Tim suddenly cried out right as a light began flashing on the metallic sleeve.

"Who?!"

"Not now, Andrew!" Tim excitedly replied; only, it was the wrong kind of excitement, like when you were watching a car crash about to happen and there was nothing you could do to stop it.

A pulse of boiling light zipped by me, narrowly missing my head but close enough so that I could feel how insanely hot it was.

"Jesus!" I barked. Following where the light had come from, I saw the bald man from my house holding up his left fist in my direction. Even from how far away he was, I noticed the bald man was wearing a metallic sleeve almost identical to mine.

His fist glowed, and another burst of light shot forward.

I flailed out of the way just as a small section of the shot burned away the cloth covering my right elbow, putting a smoldering hole in my overalls.

"Ah!" I cried out, feeling my skin inform me that it thought it was probably in contact with a white-hot stove at the moment.

"Hold out your left arm toward him!" Tim shouted.

I did, aiming my fist right at the bald man whose eyebrows shot up once he realized what was about to happen.

There was a muscle spasm in my left forearm, making me cringe in pain right as a blast of light erupted from my fist. Unfortunately for me, I had moved slightly at the spasm and missed the bald man by several feet.

He aimed once more, and I shouted, "Shoot again!"

"I can't! It needs to recharg—LOOK OUT!"

On instinct, I spun in place, and the streak of boiling light passed just over my back.

"Gah!" I blurted as I could only assume the skin down my back bubbled from the immense heat.

"Um . . . um . . . HERE!" Tim shouted, and a portal of light opened ten feet in front of me.

I reached for it, feeling what astronauts must go through when free-floating in zero-gravity. Realizing I wasn't moving, I relied on my gut instinct, pointed my fist toward the bald man again, and forced muscles that were still stinging from the spasm to fire.

"Wait!" Tim warned right as a huge explosion of light shot out from my fist, throwing me in the opposite direction.

The portal zoomed forward, and I had just enough time to turn my head and see the bald man point his glowing fist toward me once more . . . and fire.

# CHAPTER 11

landed in a heap, all the air in my lungs rocketing out of my mouth as my diaphragm convulsed from the impact. After what felt like an eternity, I sucked in a lungful of air and pushed myself to my hands and knees.

I was in a field with long grass waving in the wind and a line of trees a few hundred yards ahead of where I was catching my breath.

My lungs hurt, feeling like my diaphragm had collapsed them to the size of raisins before violently stretching them out again.

"Get up, Andrew! They'll be here soon!"

Without waiting for an explanation, I began stumbling forward through the tall grass, heading for the trees. I fell to my hands more than a few times as I struggled to find my equilibrium again.

Once I reached the tree line, I wrapped my arms around one of the trunks, moved until it was blocking my line of sight to the field, and collapsed to my knees with heaving breaths that burned.

There was a crackle from somewhere in the field, and I eased my face just past the tree to see a blur drop from a portal in the air.

The gateway closed, and I quickly moved back behind the trunk.

"What now?" I whispered.

*Run,* Tim said inside my head. *It'll take time for the Clepsydra to recharge so I can open up another gateway.*

"You want me to run?" I asked, moving my head just past the trunk again to look at the field. "But he can't see me here, right?"

In answer, a streak of light exploded a few feet above my head. Immediately, I *knew* he had been aiming where he thought my center mass might be had I not been on my knees.

*Andrew, RUN!* Tim shouted inside my mind.

I pushed off the thick trunk and sprinted deeper into the forest as the top half of the tree began falling. Daring quick glances over my shoulder, I mentally cursed at seeing the thing aiming straight for me, as if it were seeking revenge for its fate.

Even though I was seeing the tall tree falling in my direction, my body's instinct was to keep running forward.

Finally taking control, I darted to the left, just as another blast cut through the forest as easily as a tank firing through drywall.

"Fuck!" I cried out as I toppled to the ground and continued to move out of the way of the falling tree in an awkward scramble.

The ground seemed to shake beneath me when the old tree crashed down, shooting up leaves and broken twigs. A lizard the size of a dog leaped from the thick, fallen canopy, screeching as it darted away from danger.

Even with the bald man in direct pursuit, my mind couldn't help but latch on to the fact that the fleeing lizard was running on its hind legs. I knew of tiny reptiles that could do that, but none the size of dogs.

*Stay low and keep moving!* Tim mentally instructed.

Flipping from my butt to my hands and feet, I crouched low and moved as fast as I could away from where the bald man had been.

There was a muffled voice that I couldn't quite make out.

"What's he saying?" I whispered.

*I can only assume he's calling for backup on his wheren.*

"Should we try and stop him?"

*When did you turn into an action star? Hmm?* Tim chastised. *No, Andrew. We need to keep moving away until we are ready to jump again.*

"Jump?" I asked, easing down an embankment that led to a creek with flowing water less than a foot deep and four foot wide.

*Put the pieces of the puzzle together, damn it. I don't have time to baby-sit you.*

I could hear the stress in the AI's voice as I started to cross the creek.

*No,* Tim stopped me. *Walk with the stream for a couple hundred yards to hide our trail.*

"You think that guy is good enough to track us?" I asked as I turned and began shuffling down the creek—the water testing the limits of how sealed my hiking boots actually were.

*They are trained for this, Andrew. The Clockmen can hunt in most environments.*

"Well, isn't that fun . . . " I muttered just below a whisper.

From somewhere far behind, I could hear the crackling of air.

*Crap!*

"What?"

*The reinforcements are here.*

I froze as the surprisingly warm water tugged at my feet as if urging them to continue moving.

*Keep going, for 01's sake!*

I wanted to ask who or what 01 was, but I could extrapolate the meaning based on where I would have cursed with *God* in place of the numbers.

My feet swiftly moved as I scanned the water for any pitfalls or rocks that could trip me.

*Move faster!*

"I'm going as fast as I can!"

*Well, it's not fast enough,* Tim said right as something that felt like jet fuel flooded into my system.

Sucking in a breath, my eyes went wide, and my vision tunneled toward the end of the creek. My arms and fingers trembled as if they were being electrified, but my legs pumped faster than I'd ever thought possible.

The sound of rushing water and my clomping footsteps were replaced with what could only be described as the fast thumps of a diesel engine. I could feel the *thump-thump-thump* in my ears as my face and fingers went numb.

*Turn here! Use the roots to quickly climb up the embankment!*

I couldn't see what he was talking about with how narrow my vision was.

*To your right!* Tim shouted, and I managed to find what he was yelling about.

Within seconds, I was all but flying up a collection of roots with a relative ease that impressed me.

*Keep moving forward at a forty-five-degree angle away from the creek.*

I followed his directions deeper into the forest.

*The system is almost charged.*

"That's a . . . good thing . . . right?" I asked with heaving breaths as the jet fuel in my veins began to fade. My mouth was as dry as the inside of a black car sitting on an asphalt parking lot in the middle of summer.

*Not exactly,* Tim replied. *The more power I charge, the more accurate their tracking will become.*

"Well . . . can't you just . . . stop charging long enough . . . for us to get to safety?" I panted, feeling my muscles begin to fill with concrete.

*That's . . . not a good idea, Andrew.*

"Why not?" I asked, already not liking the answer.

We came to a clearing with a large lake that took up the rest of the horizon.

*Because of that!* Tim barked out.

I skidded to a halt while my sanity questioned itself as to what I was seeing.

A massive crocodile, at least thirty feet long, was resting on the beach. It turned toward the noise, locking reptilian eyes on me.

"Oh no," I mouthed as I slowly began taking steps backward toward the safety of the dense forest.

"He's this way!" a man called out from behind me, freezing me in place.

The crocodile rose on legs that looked like they belonged on a feline and lunged forward with incredible speed.

"NO!" was all I could shout as the hissing monster charged while time traveling hunters closed in from the rear.

# CHAPTER 12

*Hold on!* Tim shouted inside my head while the air around my feet crackled. The alarming sense of falling made me yelp as I passed through a portal—right as the ancient crocodile leaped for where I had been.

I looked up in horror at the creature sliding backward into the hole, unable to find purchase with his long limbs.

The gateway closed right after the monster began free-falling toward us.

"Um . . . TIM?!" I shouted, pointing my shaking hand toward the enormous reptile.

*That's not good.*

"No shit!" I barked. "What the hell are we going to do?"

*We need to wait precisely twenty-seven seconds, and then jump through the tunnel.*

"I don't think we can wait that long!" I cried out as the crocodile oriented on the sound and began slithering *through* the air. "He's gaining on us!"

*That's not good,* Tim repeated once again.

"Learn a new phrase!" I shouted as I turned away from the steadily approaching monster and began swimming in midair.

To my surprise, there was some purchase, causing me to move forward, but as in water, the crocodile was vastly superior in the swimming category. I looked over my shoulder and all but shrieked at seeing the monster had halved the distance between us in only a few seconds.

In that moment, I knew I was going to die.

Sylvie and Alison flashed through my mind, and the images of my family told me I would never see them again unless I stopped this creature somehow.

I set my jaw, pivoted in the air to face the crocodile, and pointed my left fist directly at its long face.

*We don't have enough of a charge!* Tim shouted inside my head as the reptile grew alarmingly closer with each passing second.

"What about a shield?"

*I, uh . . . I haven't ever tried before.*

"Well, try now!" I shouted as I gritted my teeth and, on instinct, opened my fist to point my palm at the lunging crocodile.

A brilliant bloom of light shot out from my open hand, and I rocketed backward.

The monster snapped at where I had just been, unaffected by the . . . the . . . whatever the hell that was.

"Some shield!" I barked, flailing in a pathetic attempt to try and recenter myself.

*Didn't I just say I had never done that before? Hmm? Didn't I?*

A portal formed several hundred yards behind the crocodile, and three men leaped in with expert precision, like a diver piercing the water so barely a wave was made.

The bald man was flanked on either side by his men, who pointed their fists toward me. I took note that the apparent leader didn't, and I quickly guessed he had been the one to open the portal, which required time to recharge.

"Do another blast!" I shouted, pointing my open palm at an angle to the tunnel wall.

Tim did as I suggested, and we rocketed out of the way as two streaks of boiling light crashed into the tunnel wall close to where we had just been. The quick burst from my palm had only been a fraction of the power that a fully charged blast would have produced, but just like in space, it didn't take much energy to create movement in the wormhole.

The crocodile had a few of his scales burned off, which he apparently didn't like, and turned toward the attackers.

"Go get them, Kermit!" I cried out as the monster began swimming back down the tunnel, much to the delight of the three—very surprised—men.

*Kermit?*

"Shut up. It's the first thing I could think of," I said in a surprisingly calm voice as I gleefully watched what was about to happen.

The enormous reptile opened jaws big enough to crush a car's engine block, and chomped down on the shorter, squat man that made up the left flank. From what I could tell, he went down in a single gulp, screaming as he was swallowed alive.

But that wasn't as alarming as watching the bald man's stoic face never show even a flicker of fear as he kept stern eyes locked on my position.

He lifted his fist toward me, and I could feel my stomach clench with sudden fear.

"Tim!"

*Jump!*

Not knowing what else to do, I pivoted to put my feet on the tunnel wall, and then leaped straight across rather than at the angle of the tunnel itself, making myself a harder target to hit in the process.

There was an explosion followed by a crackling sound, and I dared a quick glance at where I had been, just in time to see the wall dissolving into a creeping darkness.

*Shit!*

"What?" I cried out as I slammed into the opposite wall. The air rocketed out of me, and bugs swarmed my vision as I floated in place, stunned.

*I can't make you produce any more adrenaline without giving you a heart attack or, at the very least, making you pass out!* Tim replied from somewhere nearby. I just couldn't quite locate where.

I sucked in a breath, curling into a fetal position, and forced my eyes to look at where my attackers were quickly approaching.

The other goon that had been flanking the bald man pointed his fist toward the crocodile as it swam toward him. The prehistoric monster exploded into a mass of bubbling goo, along with the upper half of the swallowed man. Everything below his ribcage had been disintegrated, and I could see sheets of blood and dislodged organs floating freely.

"Wh . . . " I tried to say but couldn't get air past my throat. Using all my willpower, I tried again. "What are we . . . going to do?" I squeaked.

*We are almost done charging, but we aren't anywhere near where we want to jump.*

"I don't think we have a choice." I winced as the bald man checked his sleeve, presumably to see if he could fire again.

Something caught my eye, and I turned to see the blackness steadily spreading outward, swallowing large swathes of the tunnel as it grew.

The bald man gestured to his remaining associate, then pointed at the hole in space and time. The fact that the man broke off from his pursuit of me to address the damage meant it must be of incredible importance.

The leader pointed his fist at me once more, and I gritted my teeth in preparation for his strike.

*NOW!* Tim shouted inside my head, and a portal crackled to life in front of me, right as the bald man fired.

# CHAPTER 13

landed in a heap and was immediately confused as to why there wasn't a surge of pain from the impact.

"Oh God . . ." I wheezed. "I broke my back."

*No, you didn't.*

"Then why don't I feel pain?"

*Open your damn eyes and look, you fool.*

I hadn't realized I was squeezing my eyes shut, so I sent the orders to slowly open my right eye only.

A bright orange sun blinded me, making me quickly shield my face with both hands. Sand spilled over my face, and I began spitting the hot grains from my mouth as I rolled over.

"Huh?" was all I could say as I saw I was in a sea of sand.

The wind danced to the shape of the massive dunes that littered the landscape for as far as I could see.

*We have to move,* Tim urged.

"Where?" I said with a chuckle that tiptoed toward insanity.

*Anywhere! I don't think they'll be able to fix the rift in time to be able to track us, but it's worth putting as much distance between our landing point and future jump point.*

"So where do you propose I go?"

*Just walk, damn it! I'll charge the device again so we can get the hell out of here.*

I got to my feet, which started to sink a tad, and began walking down the dune I had landed on top of. It seemed smarter to walk with gravity than against it. Plus, the sharp peak of the giant mound provided a modicum of shade from the sun near the bottom.

"How long . . . do we have?" I asked, already out of breath. The adrenaline dump had pre-exhausted me to the point I was beginning to understand what a zombie might feel once reanimated.

*It depends on how quickly they can stitch the rift back together,* Tim explained with a tone that suggested he was expending most of his computing power on the Clepsydra.

A small portion of the dune gave way under my feet, and I didn't have the energy to try and stay upright, opting to fall to the soft, hot sand.

*Oh 01, help me,* Tim said to himself, but inside my head, which was odd. *Come on, Andrew. Get up.*

"I . . . I just wanna lie here for a little while. Just . . . just a little while . . ."
*Think about Sylvie and Alison.*

My gaping mouth began to shut like a soft-close cabinet as my eyes narrowed both in anger and determination.

With a grunt, I pushed into the hot sand and lifted myself on unsteady feet.

"I want to see them . . . *now!*" I demanded, a tad more harshly than I had intended.

*What do you think I'm trying to do?* Tim challenged with a sigh. *I swear, all you meat bags forget everything I say the moment it passes through your ears. Do you—do you have any idea . . . just how frustrating that is? Hmm?*

I took note that the AI had stumbled on his words, and the idea gave me a light sprinkling of worry.

Tim must have sensed my trepidations because he quickly followed up with, *I'll get you to them, Andrew. I promise. I just need you to do exactly what I say. Okay?*

I nodded once as squinting eyes glided over the sand canyon I was in. Looming dunes reached up on either side with a narrow, winding path that led away from where we had first arrived. Without waiting for Tim to tell me what to do, I just started walking, doing my best to stay in what little shade there was.

*The Clepsydra should be charged,* fully *charged I mean, within twenty-seven more minutes.*

I glanced down at the metallic sleeve that covered my forearm, half expecting to see a charging symbol like on a cell phone. There was none.

"I gotta walk for twenty-seven minutes . . . in this desert?"

*I suppose you could just stay in place and wait for certain death.*

"So, my choices are *death* or *death*?" I wheezed, feeling the dripping sweat on my forehead mixing with the sand.

*Would you prefer cake as an option?*

I brought my hands up and vigorously shook them through my hair, trying to get the pesky sand off like a dog scratching an itch.

"Cake or death?" I mumbled, confused at the contrasting choices.

Tim didn't respond, apparently still focused on whatever he was doing behind the scenes. So I did the only thing I could: I walked.

An eternity later, I collapsed onto a heavily shaded part of the sand canyon, being sorely disappointed when my skin informed me that the ground, though not in direct sunlight, was still hot enough to cook an egg—or an Andrew.

"How . . . how far . . . have I walked?"

*Less than an eighth of a mile.*

"Great . . . super . . ." I panted as I rolled onto my back and laid my right forearm across my eyes.

*But the good news is we aren't being followed, yet, and the Clepsydra is almost at a full charge.*

"That's good . . . right?"

*Very good, Andrew,* Tim replied with a grin evident in his voice . . . which was still inside my head. *And I've managed to program the apparatus to form a shield, just as you asked for. Honestly, I'm not sure why I didn't think of it sooner. Nor did any of the other meat bags.*

"What about water?" I asked with a tongue that had somehow been replaced with an extra-crispy strip of bacon.

*You'll be drinking your fill in less than two minutes.*

My mind flashed back to the kitchen sink incident and how much water I had managed to swallow.

"Just my fill though, right?"

Tim chuckled, and I let my right forearm slide off my eyes to smack onto the ground. Unfortunately, in doing so, I had also grated the sand across my nose and brow. *Fortunately* for me, I simply didn't care right then. My muscles were numb, mouth was drier than the inside of a . . . of a . . . *dryer* . . . and I couldn't even come up with a cogent simile.

"Tim?"

*Hmm?*

"Who was that bald guy?"

I could hear Tim take a long inhale, as if deciding what to say. After a few seconds, he answered. "His name is Commander Retnuh Ordune, lead field agent for the Clockmen."

"Right." I smacked my cracked lips, willing the air to somehow waft moisture into my mouth. "And what do the Clockmen want with me?"

*Well, heh . . .* Tim nervously chuckled, drawing my full attention. *They are the gatekeepers of the wormhole.*

"The same wormhole we've been using to jump through space and time?"

*Exactly.*

"All . . . right . . . " I let out as I thought about the situation. "Why are they so gung ho about protecting it?"

*Because we are altering space and time, Andrew.*

I had to lie there, staring at the cloudless blue sky, and think about his words.

"Then why are you helping me?"

Tim didn't answer for over twenty seconds. When he finally spoke, he said, *It is imperative that you stop the killer, Andrew.*

I tried to hold on to the gut feeling inside of me to shut up and accept his answer, but I couldn't help myself. "Why?"

*Look, all will be revealed soon enough. Just trust me.*

"That's asking a lot, Tim."

*Have I steered you wrong so far?*

I answered with silence, knowing he was right.

"Fine," I relented. "Can we please just get out of this hellhole?"

*The charge finished fourteen seconds ago.*

"Good," I grunted as I managed to push myself up to my feet.

*Opening the portal in three . . . two . . . one.*

# CHAPTER 14

I was expecting the jump this time, so I only felt my stomach lurch like when on a roller coaster, which was infinitely better than the panic I had experienced my first few times.

The tunnel seemed unharmed, and I asked, "Where are the Clockmen?"

*I shifted our position farther down, allowing time and space to move around us before reentering.*

"Space?"

*I really don't have the patience to explain how your planet is literally hurtling through space. If your high school science teacher couldn't hammer that simple concept into your brain, then I have a feeling I would have better results explaining the concept to a brick wall.*

"You don't have to be a dick," I murmured just under my breath as we moved through the tunnel of streaking light.

After about a minute of silence, I asked, "Where are we going, anyway?"

*Wheren, Andrew. Wheren are we going?*

"Just answer the question."

*To put it plainly so that your primitive brain can comprehend, we are going further back in time, where we will wait a sufficient period, and then travel down the wormhole once more going in the opposite direction.*

"Why don't we just go to our intended direction now?"

*Because we run the risk of crossing paths with the Clockmen. Either they are still repairing the rift, or they are setting up a guard to make sure we stay on this side of the timeline while the others hunt us down.*

"Oh."

*Oh is right.*

"So . . . when we go back the other way after waiting, what will we do if we come across a guard?"

*We will either have to try and jump past him on the outside of the worm-hole, which I do not recommend, or we will have to engage and neutralize.*

"Neutralize?"

*Yes, Andrew. You will have to kill him so that he doesn't warn the others.*

"Won't him not reporting in warn them that we have made it past?"

*Yes, but it should buy us enough time to hide our trail.*

"I . . . I'm confused how time is relevant."

*Relative, Andrew. Not relevant.*

"Riiiight. But my statement still stands."

*Maybe I'm not understanding what you are asking.*

"Why does it matter if we wait, say, ten minutes before jumping into the wormhole?"

*Because time is always flowing.*

"I don't understand."

*You don't say . . .* Tim drawled, the words dripping with sarcasm.

"If I don't understand, it's because *you* aren't explaining it right."

*Oh-ho! Nice try, bucko! But I'll not allow you to throw the failures of your primitive brain functions at my feet.*

"Then explain it like I'm a kid."

*Okay, okay, okay,* Tim repeated in quick succession. *Let's see . . . hmm . . . oh! Maybe you'll understand this. Ahem.*

The Clepsydra's hologram came to life, and Professor Tim appeared, complete with a blackboard in the background. On it, a moving diagram made of chalk came to life, showcasing a point of view above a tunnel. The image shifted, zooming in on first one side of the entrance, and then the other.

Speaking out loud now and using a smooth rod of wood to point at the blackboard, Tim began to explain.

"This is the wormhole used by humans in the far future. It stretches to the beginning of time and ends, ironically, at the point of creation of said wormhole."

"So the creators of time travel . . . can't go into their own future?"

"Unlike the people of your time, Andrew, I specifically used the word *ironically, uni*ronically."

"I'm not sure you're using that right, either."

Tim ran a paw over his puppy head in much the same way I might have rubbed at my forehead when sensing the task at hand would be much more difficult than originally thought.

"*Irony*: incongruity between the actual result of a sequence of events and the normal or expected result," Tim, the AI, read the definition of the word in question as he glared at me. "They *expected* to be able to travel anywhere in time that they wished, with the express desire to see the future and bring back any technologies that could immediately enhance their world."

"Like the cure for cancer."

"Short answer . . . yes."

"What's the long answer?"

"Your world already has a solution for most forms of cancer."

"Bullshit."

"Look, I don't think it wise to detract from the topic at hand, especially with you clearly exhibiting such a naive viewpoint on the greed and corruption permeating throughout your world in broad daylight."

"I . . . " I started before his meaning was absorbed. "Point taken."

"If I may continue?"

I waved my right hand as we continued to move down the tunnel.

"Because there is a singular, fixed wormhole that sits in a higher dimension, it has its own vacuum of time."

"Ah. I think I see where you are going with this."

"Do you now? Pray tell," Tim said as the pointing rod disappeared and he looked at me, expectantly.

"If we spend thirty minutes inside the wormhole . . . the same amount of time will pass for the guard that is probably blocking the way."

"Wow," Tim replied, genuinely impressed. "I honestly can't believe we were able to bypass the line of questioning where you ask stupid questions such as 'why can't we just wait the thirty minutes *outside* of the wormhole.'"

I faked a grin because I was literally about to ask that very question.

In a low, quick tone coated in disappointment, Tim rolled his eyes and threw out, "You were about to ask that, weren't you?"

"N-No! No. Not at all . . . buuuuut for argument's sake . . . "

"Ugh! You darn humans and those lumps of fat you call a brain!"

Tim took a deep breath, appeared to steady himself, and then explained. "The wormhole is in a higher dimension. Think of a two-dimensional object such as, for the sake of this explanation, a piece of paper with a line drawn across it."

"Alright."

"No talking during the lecture or you'll get detention!"

"Alr—"

"What did I just say?!"

I made a gesture of zipping my mouth closed and throwing away the key.

"Now, imagine holding up a pen above the piece of paper. Are you imagining it?"

I nodded my confirmation rather than risk opening my mouth.

"Move the pen anywhere you want above the paper."

I mentally did, moving it in all directions, including doing a few figure eights.

"The line on the paper is completely unaffected. Wouldn't you agree?"

I nodded again.

"Now, take the tip of the pen and poke it *through* the line on the paper."

Once again, I followed the instructions, imagining the pen going through the flat piece of paper.

"It wasn't until we interacted *directly* with the line on the paper that it became affected. The wormhole is similarly unaffected when we are not inside of it. Hence, thirty minutes in a prehistoric forest or in a sea of sand eons before humans existed would have no impact on how long the guard remains at his post."

"So we have to remain inside the wormhole long enough for the guard to go away?"

"Trust me, it won't be long," Tim confidently said as the blackboard and his professor's outfit vanished. "Most Ticks aren't aware of this because they don't have me. And so—"

"Ticks?"

"That's it! Detention for you!"

My mouth went numb, as if I had just left the dentist, and all I could say were incoherent vowels.

"Uuuh. Ee-ya uhn ah."

"I have no idea what you are trying to say, so stop wasting your time," Tim replied as he pawed at his chin in thought. "Now, where was I . . . oh yes. The *Ticks*, or people who illegally use the wormhole, never think to wait *inside* the wormhole. Thus, they always get caught by a guard—or a *Tock*—who waited no longer than a few minutes at most, even if the Tick waited decades in another time."

"OOOooohhh. Ihk-awk."

"For the love of 01," Tim whispered before the feeling in my face came back. "Now what is it that's soooo important to say, Andrew? Hmm?"

"I was," I started as I rubbed my now tingling face with my right hand. "I was saying I get the names now. Tick and Tock, I mean. At first, I thought you meant a tick as in the bug that gets on animals."

"Oh, well . . . I guess I could see where you might make that mistake," Tim admitted, a tad embarrassed. "Yes, Andrew, a Tick is an unauthorized person who is using the wormhole."

"And the Tock is the person sent to stop them?"

"Or team, yes."

I thought about our conversation and surmised to the best of my understanding.

"So . . . what . . . we just float in this tunnel until we *think* the guard—I mean, *Tock* goes away?"

"Yes. But we are also moving further back in time in the hopes that if they are following us, they'll give up once they realize we haven't jumped past the point that human life can be sustained."

"Huh?"

"Ugh," Tim let out in frustration. "There's a certain point in the wormhole that, once crossed, no human being could possibly survive. At least not without the proper PPE that the scientists would wear."

"Oh. So the Clockmen would know we weren't likely to be in the wormhole either."

"Correct. As per my vast data banks, only one Tick, ever, has traveled past the threshold, never to be seen again."

"What happened to him?"

"I'm not entirely sure. But it is safe to assume he died."

"Why's that?"

"Because the future wasn't changed."

"Changed? What do you mean, *changed*?"

"The reason the wormhole is so highly guarded is because any changes made in the past can drastically change the future; depending on the person's Temporal Impact, that is. For example"— Tim looked directly at me with his intelligent puppy eyes—"would you go back in time and kill Hitler if you had the chance?"

"I have a feeling I should answer *no*, given the line of questioning. But, honestly, yeah . . . yeah, I'd kill the bastard."

"And in so doing, you would alter your own past in unforeseen ways. Some of which could be catastrophic."

"Like what?"

"We can only speculate, Andrew, because the Clockmen have done a remarkable job at stopping any Ticks from altering the past. But if I had to guess at a more amusing scenario . . . imagine a world where Hitler never rose to power. That means that America, acting under the classified mission dubbed *Operation Paperclip*, would never have recruited Nazi scientists to further their own space programs."

"We wouldn't have beat the Russians to the Moon . . ." I thought out loud.

"Not only that, but Germany would have become the first nation both into space *and* to land on the Moon. I can only surmise with this thought experiment that they would have quickly become *the* world power, leaving all other countries in the dust."

"That's not a big deal. It'd be worth the countless murdered people during World War II."

"Now imagine that this advanced Germany paired up with Russia or China . . . or *both*! And were able to build a colony on the Moon, harvesting Helium-3 and supplying it only to their allies. The entire Western civilization would be left in a figurative Stone Age while, across the world, powerful steam engines were being built on an assembly line. Your world powers would be on their knees begging for scraps from the likes of the Soviet Union or the China Communist Party."

I thought about where he was going in the scenario, and added, "We were able to stop the Russians from taking over major oil reserves in the Middle East. But if they had advanced technologies . . ."

"They could have easily thwarted the West's efforts and held the rest of the world hostage for the vast oil supply in the Middle East, while Germany controlled the Helium-3."

"Okay, okay. I think I see your point."

"That's only a simple thought experiment, Andrew. There are literal countless possibilities that could occur, each with an unforeseen consequence."

Something came to mind, and I asked, "What about if I went back in time, killed Hitler . . . and then, as a result, I was never born? That would then mean I couldn't go back in time and kill Hitler, which would end up with me *being* born . . . so I *could* go back in time and kill Hitler."

"Paradoxes such as that could be the universe's way of keeping things intact."

"So you don't know what would happen?"

"Intellectuals and theorists have debated, since the creation of the wormhole, *many* paradoxes, including the one you just mentioned."

"But no one has tested them?"

"The consensus is that the heightened risk isn't worth the potential reward." Tim chuckled and added, "What's more is that it is entirely possible that someone could have attempted it, and the paradox kicked them back to just before they decided to try."

Something Tim had said earlier crept into focus, and I hesitantly asked, "You . . . you said earlier, that I must see my family . . . what did you mean by that?"

"Why do you care?" Tim countered with narrowed eyes.

"I got the impression something bad would happen if I didn't see them."

"Actually, what I said was that you have to stop their killer."

"That's not what you said back at my house when I first opened the box you came in."

"I told you what you needed to hear to get the ball rolling. I knew once you put me on that the Clockmen would begin tracking the signal. They already knew my approximate location, but not the exact wheren."

"That's why they pulled up to my house in a car instead of just jumping through a portal?"

"Precisely."

I thought about that for a moment. "That feels concerning."

"Which part, exactly? All of it should be concerning to you."

"Men from the future were able to acquire cars from our time . . . I mean, *my* time," I corrected as I looked at the hologram puppy from the future.

"They are extremely efficient agents, Andrew, especially when it comes to stopping Ticks."

I nodded as we continued to move through the tunnel. The streaking lights seemed to condense somehow, growing brighter as they moved.

"So . . . keeping in mind that I'm completely on board," I started coldly. "Why is it so important that I kill my family's murderer? Something doesn't feel right about the risk you are taking to alter the past. I mean, I'm a nobody. Why take a chance at changing the future?"

"I'm just acting on my programming, Andrew."

A dark feeling crept over me, like a horde of ants swarming over the carcass of a rodent.

"Am I the bad guy? I mean, if the future governments are sending these G-men after me," I asked just above a whisper as I let my face drop.

"Andrew, I cannot convince you one way or the other of your role in all of this. But what I *can* say is it is imperative that we follow through with the mission."

"Why?"

"Because the entire known universe is at stake."

# CHAPTER 15

We floated down the wormhole as I thought about everything. It was too much for me to process all at once, and attempting to do so made my head hurt.

As we moved, the lights all around drew closer and closer to one another until they were beginning to gather near what I could only assume was the end of the tunnel. Across the darkened universe all around me was nothing. Not just nothing, but an infinite amount of nothing.

Looking all around the empty universe, I felt an existential dread never known before.

Alison ran past in my periphery, giggling as she had often done while playing hide-and-seek with Daddity.

"Uhh!" I sharply gasped as I searched for what I knew couldn't be there.

*Andrew, your vitals are starting to spike,* Tim announced inside my head.

"I love you," Sylvie whispered from behind, and I gasped again as I awkwardly pivoted while floating.

Only the nothingness of the unborn universe greeted me as shallow breaths filled the silence.

"I'm pregnant!" Sylvie cried out joyfully, and I snapped my head to see that I was standing in the bathroom as the love of my life held out the positive test.

"You're pregnant?!" I heard myself say in two different tones. It didn't take long for me to figure out that the happier voice was stemming from the memory while the melancholy one had slipped from me as I remembered how the events had played out.

*Andrew? What's happening?* a concerned Tim asked.

With a squeal of excitement that accompanied a sort of rapid jog in place with hands stretched toward the sky, Sylvie lunged forward to give me the happiest hug and kiss of our lives, even beating the day we'd gotten married.

I longed for her touch once more, but when she got to me, the scene vanished like a speeding train cutting through the morning fog.

*Andrew, I, uh, need you to calm down for me. Okay?*

"Daddity," Alison giggled, and I turned to see that I was sitting at the kitchen table with an overemphasized smile on my face. It was the kind of expression parents made when playing with their easily excitable children. In this case, I was hunched over as Alison sat in her high chair.

"Say Daddy!"

"Daddity!" she repeated, clapping her hands with barely enough coordination to make her palms touch with each wild swing of her arms.

"Can you say *daa-dee?*" Sylvie asked from the other side of our daughter, slowly sounding out the word.

"I don't know," I spoke with a grin stretching from ear to ear as I looked at my beautiful wife. "I think I like Daddity."

"Daddity!" Ali yelled, followed by a series of giggles that sang out as she sucked in and breathed out.

"Daddity," Sylvie repeated while using a napkin to wipe the drool off Ali's chin.

"You know, I didn't think they could articulate the *T* sound at this age."

"I don't remember reading that in any of the books."

"Just a feeling I have."

"Well, then that makes it all the more special, *Daddity*," Sylvie said with a beaming smile.

"Oh God . . . " I mouthed as my vision blurred, but I didn't dare blink away the tears for fear of losing the scene to the nothingness.

*What are you seeing, Andrew? What's happening?*

"They're right there," I squeaked, pointing to where my family was sitting around the table. My wife. My daughter. Two sides of my beating heart that pumped love throughout my body and soul.

Water fully encapsulated everything I could see, and I grunted while blinking faster than I think I had in my entire life.

But it didn't matter. They were gone.

*I can try and adjust your hormone levels, if you wish.*

"No!" I barked. "No," I said again, softer this time, as I regained control over myself. "I need to feel this. Don't take it from me again."

*Alright, Andrew,* Tim dubiously agreed. *We are nearing the end of the wormhole, so you might want to close your eyes.*

"Wh—" I started to ask as an explosion, infinitely larger than I could even begin to fathom, filled everything I could see before I slammed my eyes shut with a yelp.

*It's over. You can open your eyes.*

"Over?" I cracked one of my eyelids open to see that now everything was devoid of all light.

*It happened faster than the blink of an eye,* Tim said with reverence in his voice, admiring the universe and its violent beginnings.

On nothing more than a desire to see more, I began floating forward again.

*Wait! We can't go beyond this point!*

"Why not?" I asked, licking my lips as I stared into the nothing.

*Because we don't know what will happen if you cross the threshold, Andrew. If matter tries to enter a universe where matter hasn't been created yet . . . well, we can only guess as to the results. Suffice it to say that it would require complex mathematical equations to even attempt to explain on paper how one might have every atom torn apart, or conversely, compressed into oblivion.*

"Oh."

*Adequately said.*

"So is this the . . . the . . . " I struggled to find the words needed to convey a situation I'd never thought I'd have to explain.

*The precise moment the Big Bang occurred, just before the explosion that gave birth to the universe.*

I stopped in place and just stared at where I thought the end of the tunnel would be. I could feel a tingling in my arm as I fought the urge to reach out and touch it in much the same way one might step to the edge of a high cliff and feel the need to jump, but only for the briefest of moments.

We floated there, in a darkness no human had ever witnessed before; at least not from my time, or the time before. The dawn of the universe just inches away, feeling like I was resting against an armed and primed nuclear warhead.

I shook off the oddity of the situation and focused on what I had seen in the darkness.

Sylvie. Alison. Memories of when I was happy, surrounded by a love that was impossible to put into words.

Minutes passed, or perhaps hours; it was impossible for me to know as I held onto the memories I had seen in the nothingness, bathing in the long-lost feeling of love and happiness. Doing so gave me renewed strength and determination. No matter what came my way, nothing would stop me from getting to them again. Nothing would stop me from confronting their murderer *before* he pulled the trigger. Nothing would stop me from watching as the light left his eyes.

*Andrew?*

"Hmm?" I said, shaking my head to clear the thoughts that were becoming darker than the unborn universe outside the wormhole.

*Everything, um, okay?*

"I'm fine. How much longer do we need to float here?"

*A few more minutes should do the trick.*

"Then we . . . what? Just fly back the other way?"

*Easy as cake. Piece of pie.*

"I hope you are doing that on purpose."

*Doing what, Andrew?*

"Never mind," I sighed as something came to mind. "Hey, you said something about prehistoric forest earlier?"

*What about it?*

"Did we . . . was that crocodile a dinosaur?"

*Technically, the genus* Crocodilia, *even the ones from your time, are all dinosaurs, if we are using a loose definition of the word.*

"You know what I mean, Tim."

*Yes, Andrew,* Tim sighed as if the topic of conversation was beyond unimportant. *The thirty-foot crocodile with long, powerful legs that can help it run at hideous speeds, was a dinosaur. Are you happy now?*

I shuddered at remembering how easily the beast had swallowed the Tock.

"And the desert?"

*I'll just cut to what you are* really *asking: you were the only life on the entire planet that was larger than a grain of sand.*

"I was the only living thing? On the whole world?"

*Try not to think about it too much, Andrew. It could create existential doubts that might cripple you later.*

"If you gaze into the abyss, the abyss gazes back into you," I whispered as my mind, for some reason, equated the experience of being the only thing on an entire planet to floating in the middle of the ocean and not being able to see what lay beneath. It was simply eerie, and it made the skin on my neck tingle.

We floated in silence a few minutes longer while I tried to process the experiences, then Tim spoke up.

*Okay. It's time to go.*

"What if the lookout is still there?"

*Then it's plan B.*

"Which is?"

*We neutralize him.*

# CHAPTER 16

How do we do this?" I asked, turning in the direction where I thought the tunnel flowed. With how dark it was, I might be looking directly at a wall; or worse, I could be about to move straight to the end, where time hadn't even begun.

*Turn thirty degrees to the left,* Tim instructed. *Okay. Five more. Good. Now, here comes the tricky part.*

"I don't like that."

*Right you are to feel that way, Andrew, because we are going to have to use momentum created down at this end to propel us forward.*

"Why?"

*Because the closer we get, the easier it will be to track the Clepsydra, especially if we are using its power.*

"But won't we be holding a full charge to, ah, *jump* when we get to . . . well . . . wherever it is you are taking us?"

*Correct, Andrew. But the shielding of the apparatus will help prolong the moment of our discovery, giving us precious time to make our move. Think of it like . . . oh, what's that movie with the big Austrian guy who starred in all those action movies of the nineteen-eighties . . .*

"Arnold Schwarzenegger?"

*Yeah, him. But that movie where he hides from the alien that's hunting him by coating himself in mud from head to toe so the creature can't see his body heat.*

"*Predator?*"

*Yeah! That's it!* Predator! Tim exclaimed with excitement, once again worrying me with how human the AI seemed to be. *We'll be like Arnold,* hiding *our signature until we get close enough to act. But if we used the Clepsydra near where the guard is probably waiting for us in the wormhole, he would be able to see us as easily as if Arnold replaced the mud he wore with bubbling magma.*

"That's quite the imagery."

*Yeah, I know. I should be a writer, huh?*

Ignoring his comment, I asked, "So how do we build up enough momentum to move us forward? Or is it back? I don't know at this point."

"It's all based on perspective, Andrew," Tim replied as his hologram popped up on my arm. He turned to the side, and a crude model that vaguely resembled me blipped into existence. "You actually gave me the idea when you asked for the shield."

The blocky 3D model of me, which looked like it had been made in Windows 95, pointed his hand toward the end of the tunnel he was in, and was rocketed in the opposite direction like a shooting star.

"Whoa! Um . . . isn't that a bit fast?"

"Huh? Oh, right. Fragile human body," Tim muttered as the scene rewound itself. "Okay . . . that means we will have to do a series of blasts to build up the momentum without, you know . . . *tearingyourbody-apart.*" The last part was said just under his breath and fast enough to be construed as a single long word, like some sort of pharmaceutical drug name.

"How do people normally move through the wormhole?"

"The Clepsydra device allows for a type of movement that would be best compared to magnets."

"Like on a bullet train or something?"

"Close enough," Tim answered. "*But,* in using that method of transportation, we would be using a steady stream of energy that could be easily read by anyone and everyone looking for it."

"I think I understand. They won't be expecting us to be using inertia to move."

"*Inertia* isn't exactly the right terminology, but I see you grasp the overall concept."

Waving my right hand in the air dismissively, I said, "So when do we get going?"

"Just running a few more simulations to make sure there are no, ah, *errors.*"

"Like exploding my body apart with the first blast?"

"I've gotten it down to just ripping your left arm off!" Tim informed with genuine delight.

"Great," I muttered. Looking around the dark universe, I felt the absence of everything creeping in as if wanting me to join it in the abyss. A shudder ran down my neck, stopping just past my shoulder blades.

"O . . . kay . . . I think I got it!" Tim said as he watched the 3D model of me hold up its left arm and shoot a single blast of light that reminded me of the Batmobile spitting flames out the back as it revved up.

The model moved forward at a modest pace, maybe the equivalent of me jogging, and then another blast shot out. Next, I was moving at a sprinter's speed before yet another explosion of light erupted from my left hand.

It didn't take long for the model to be moving fast enough that the lights outside of the simulated tunnel were streaking in the opposite direction from when I had first traveled down the wormhole.

But he didn't stop there.

Blast after blast continued to propel the model of me forward until the streaking stars outside of his tunnel began to resemble a kaleidoscope.

"Whoa."

"Yeah, things tend to get trippy when you begin approaching relativistic speeds."

"How are we—*is he* able to move that fast?" I asked, gesturing with my free hand toward the blocky 3D model.

"The physics inside of a wormhole are completely different from anything anyone from your time could possibly conceive. They had to be made that way; otherwise, it could take years, decades, centuries, or even millions of years to travel."

"Breaking the rules of the universe can't be good," I said to myself as I watched.

The model vanished in an instant, though the scene continued to show the wormhole moving as if he were still there, complete with the universe outside dancing in geometric patterns.

"Oops!" Tim exclaimed before clearing his throat and closing the simulation down. "Nothing to worry about. I believe we are good to go!"

"What was that?"

"What was what?" Tim deflected like a child denying eating all the leftover Halloween candy despite enough chocolate being smeared across his face to pave an entire driveway.

"Tim . . ."

"Oh, alright!" he dramatically exhaled at being caught. "It seems your 3D model, sort of . . . kind of . . . met with some resistance."

"What sort of resistance?"

" . . . the guard," he hesitantly admitted.

"The guard?" I repeated, more for myself than for clarification.

"Yes. It would *seem*, in this particular simulation, that you . . . um, *made contact* with the stationary guard . . . while traveling at a fraction of the speed of light."

"I vanished?" I asked, remembering how the scene had continued to move though I was no longer represented.

"Vanished is such a blasé term. More like . . . exploded into nothing more than the sound waves at the center of your quarks. Almost like a reverse Big Bang, where first there was matter, then there was none."

"Well, how the hell do we prevent us from being turned into sound waves?"

"I suppose we could cut off the last . . . " Tim trailed off as the puppy avatar stroked at his chin, deep in thought. " . . . thirteen boosts. Yeah . . . yeah, that should do it."

"Should?!"

"Oh, don't be so dramatic, Andrew. It's not like you would even feel anything if we messed up the calculations."

"Oh-ho," I darkly chuckled. "There is no *we*, Tim. *You* would be the one getting the math wrong."

"Do you want to try, smart guy?" Tim asked with a tilt of his head. Normally, it was cute when puppies did that; with Tim, it made me want to strangle the damn thing. "I thought not."

"Fine!" I threw out both hands, forgetting that I was holding up the hologram. Tim didn't pretend to fall over or anything, once again proving that the time he had done so in the kitchen when we first met had been intentional.

"Now, going slower *will* allow the guard ample time to either call in the sighting or prepare for an attack. Let's hope that it's the latter."

"What? Why would we want that?"

"Because he will only have enough energy in his Clepsydra for one or the other. Do you have any idea how much power it takes to send a message through a literal wormhole in space and time? They have to bury the message deep within the planet where no one will find it except Retnuh, who will be looking in that exact location."

"They bury it? What, like a flash drive or something?"

"No, Andrew," Tim sighed. He was doing that a lot with me, I noticed. "It is an encoded string of radiation produced by the Clepsydra, with a half-life of a billion years. Think of it like a telegraph, but instead of morse code, it's tight clusters of irradiated earth."

I wanted to point out that it would take time for the bald man, Retnuh, to come find us, so we should be safe. But then I remembered we were inside a wormhole that stretched across time as if it were nothing more than a train tunnel. A message could be sent, received, and acted on in what would be perceived, by me, as an instant.

"Time is relative," I whispered.

"How right you are. Now, are we ready?"

I closed my eyes, sucked in a long, deep breath with a count of six, and then let it out.

"For my girls."

# CHAPTER 17

I held out my left palm, fingers splayed, and used my free hand to tightly grip where the Clepsydra and my wrist met. Light began to dance over my open hand, seeming to collect at the center of my palm.

*Are you ready?* Tim asked inside my head.

"Do it," I almost snarled from between my gritted teeth, preparing to be thrown through the wormhole at incredible speeds. My whole body was tensed as if I were being electrocuted. Every muscle anticipated the possibility of being torn to pieces, flexing to help mitigate that outcome.

*Just have to make sure that the aim is direct; otherwise, we'd bounce off the tunnel walls,* he replied while I slowly moved my arm toward where I thought the center of the wormhole was. *Almost . . . almost . . . now!*

I felt the spasm in my left forearm again right as a blast of energy shot from my hand. There was also a bright explosion of light from outside the tunnel, and I witnessed the Big Bang.

Though I was holding my wrist so to brace with both arms, my left arm buckled at the elbow from the force of the boost, sending the Clepsydra and my hand crashing into my stomach.

"Oof!" I wheezed, feeling my body pivot in midair.

*Crap!* Tim cried out. *We're in a spiral!*

I tried to respond, but my lungs were unable to fill with air.

*Hold your hand out again!*

I sent the signal to my left arm to point straight out, but it refused, content with continuing to hold on to my quivering stomach and diaphragm.

*Hold out your damn hand, Andrew! Or you'll never see Sylvie and Alison again!*

Anger flared brighter than the Big Bang, and I forced my arm to obey my commands, pointing it straight out even as we tumbled through the air.

*Wait for it . . . wait for it . . . waiiiiiiiit for—NOW!*

There was another blast from my hand, but this one didn't feel as jarring. Maybe it was because we were already moving in some semblance of the direction we wanted to go, or maybe it was because I was anticipating it this time. Either way, the violent tumble became a moderate spin.

*Watch out for the wa—* Tim tried to warn me as I crashed into the tunnel wall with my right shoulder.

The moderate spin became a lazy rotation while I ricocheted off of the wormhole structure. My shoulder pulsated with a sharp pain, feeling like I had been hit by the extended side mirror of a speeding pickup truck.

*Okay. Hold out your hand like you want to blow off your left leg.*

"Wha-what?" I groaned. Even the throbbing pain seemed to pause for a second as if it, too, were confused at what had just been said.

*Point your palm at your left thigh, and then twenty-six degrees outward.*

"I don't kn—"

*I'll tell you when to stop.*

I held out my shaking left hand, first pointing at my thigh and then moving slowly outward to my side.

*And three . . . two . . . one . . . okay, stop. Sixteen degrees. Now we need to wait seven more seconds until the rotation points us in the right direction.*

The universe outside continued to expand, and I wish I had taken the time to marvel at the beauty. However, my bruised diaphragm and throbbing shoulder made it difficult to concentrate on anything but what Tim was telling me to focus on.

*Two . . . one . . . now!*

There was another blast from my hand, and I could instantly tell that the slight rotation had been canceled and we were moving straight down the wormhole.

*Oi, Andrew!* Tim exclaimed. *You could have ripped a hole in the fabric of space and time had we been going fast enough!*

"I have a feeling the wall would have won," I groaned, moving my left hand to rub at my swelling shoulder.

*You've dislocated it,* Tim informed me, sounding like he was reading off a chart as he told me. *It'll take hours to get the swelling to go down enough for me to coax it back in place.*

"You can do that?" I asked with a degree of unease that I tried to hide.

*You'll find there's a great many things I can do, Andrew.*

"You know it's creepy when you say it like that," I said through gritted teeth as I grabbed my right wrist, sucked in a breath, and yanked forward with my left hand as hard as I could.

There was a sickening *crack* that I felt *and* heard, and my vision narrowed to the size of a dime.

*For the love of science, Andrew! You just threw us off course again!*

I ignored the AI as I allowed my consciousness to flow back into place, feeling like a turtle flipped on its back and slowly, awkwardly, rolling back to its feet.

The pulsating, knifelike pain in my shoulder had clocked out, letting the dull-but-boiling hot sensation take over the shift.

I flexed my right hand a few times, feeling the stretched muscles ache all the way up to the top of my biceps. There was also a warm, numb feeling running from my pinky and ring fingers up to my elbow.

*Please hold your hand out again so I can fix this mess.*

"I'm fine, by the way," I said out loud as I moved my open palm into position.

*I didn't ask,* Tim shot back before adding, *Now go up and to the right a tad. Little more. Lit-tle more. There.*

Another blast shot out, and the universe around me began morphing from round stars to oval lights.

*Those extra two shots will cost us if the guard is there.*

"What do you mean?"

*We won't have enough energy to shoot him.*

"What about the thirteen less blasts?"

*Oh, uh, heh . . . I, ah, lied.*

"Lied?! About what?!" I barked. All of a sudden, the speeding universe around me became a dark omen, like watching a brick wall growing larger in your windshield as you pressed harder on the accelerator.

*I didn't subtract the thirteen blasts needed to make it to our destination,* Tim admitted with a tone of annoyance at having been caught.

"Why the hell not?!"

*Look, I don't go down to Taco Bell, or wherever you work, and tell you how to do* your *job! Okay?*

"You're going to get me killed . . . "

*Only if the guard is there, silly.*

"Why do we even have to go that fast?!"

*I maaaaaybe forgot to mention that they prooooobably have an inertial net set up. And you'll notice that I used the word* inertia *correctly.*

"That doesn't explain what we are heading for!" I was beginning to hyperventilate as I imagined flying into a net going fast enough that I would need an equation to figure out the speed.

*It's like a magnet that is geared toward the Clepsydra. If we were traveling* using *the apparatus as it was intended, the inertial net would be able to completely cancel our speed, rendering us completely helpless. But I did the math and have found the speed necessary to move fast enough that the net won't be able to even touch us. Huzzah!*

"And if you're wrong?!"

*You'll more than likely have your arm torn off while the rest of you continues tumbling down the wormhole moving at cataclysmic speeds. But, and here's the good news, you'd go into shock and wouldn't even be aware of what was happening!*

"*That's* the good news?"

I was wheezing out breaths as panic cracked its knuckles and prepared to conduct a symphony of terror.

*Well, that would be better than them stopping you* alive. *Trust me on that.* Tim gave a little chuckle before finishing with, *Now, please calm down before you have a heart attack.*

"What choice do I have?" I mouthed to myself as I held my breath and fired the conductor of panic in my mind. "Sylvie . . . Alison . . . "

Saying their names brought me strength equivalent to that of a comic book superhero.

*Impressive, Andrew. Most impressive. Now hold out your hand, and I'll do the rest. All you have to do is trust me.*

"That's asking a lot, Tim."

*No risk. No reward.*

I lifted my left hand, pointing it down the tunnel of steadily moving oval lights. Tim did blast after blast until the universe around us started to form odd shapes. My heart began to race as I remembered this was the part when the Windows 95 3D model of me suddenly vanished after crashing into the stationary guard.

The universe outside became a kaleidoscope of lights and geometric patterns, and I closed my eyes, preparing for the worst.

There was a tingling sensation in my left forearm that vanished as quickly as it appeared, and I just *knew* it had been torn off by the inertial net.

*We're through!* Tim shouted in excitement, followed by a, *Hip hip hooray!*

Daring to open my eyes, I saw that we were still moving at speeds that I simply couldn't fathom.

"H-h-how do we slow down?"

*Slow down?*

"Yeah, Tim! How the hell do we slow down?"

*Oh, it's simple.* Tim chuckled as the universe danced in seemingly random shapes and colors all around us. *We don't.*

# CHAPTER 18

I screamed.

I screamed like the passengers on a derailing train.

I screamed like a skydiver whose chute failed to open.

I screamed like a man traveling at a fraction of the speed of light down a wormhole that stretched across time.

*Stop being so dramatic, Andrew. We're almost there.*

Hearing the confidence in the AI's voice, my screams faltered into incoherent whimpering.

*That's better, I suppose. Not great, but better. Now, get ready.*

"R-Ready f-f-for what?"

*This!*

A portal of light rushed toward us faster than my eyes and brain could process, and I shrieked again. Then the feeling of gravity beneath my feet greeted me, and I fell forward like a plank of wood.

"Oof!" A blast of air left my lungs as I tried to catch myself with my arms; the perfect time for my right shoulder to remind me that it probably shouldn't try and take on any extra weight.

*Okay. They should leave us alone now.*

I rolled to my side, clutching at my stomach, and realized I was lying in a field. My mind immediately began flashing with red lights and blaring alarms as I thought about the thirty-foot-long crocodile.

"Wh-where are we?" I demanded, pushing myself to a seated position to catch my breath.

*How many times do I have to tell you, Andrew? It's not where. It's wheren.*

"Fine!" I barked. "Wheren are we, damn it?!"

The hologram came to life, and Tim made a show of looking around.

"Where the hell are we?" he wondered to himself.

I swallowed the words of rage that wanted to spew out of my mouth like a paralyzing venom.

Tim pressed some buttons which came to life as he touched them before fading once more.

"Oh. We're in Montana." He made a clicking sound with his tongue before turning back to me. "I, ah, heh, guess I missed the window by a few centimeters."

While on my knees, I looked around at the state of Montana, and said, "A few centimeters put us across the US?"

"We, uh, kind of got lucky, Andrew. Had we gone any farther, we might have ended up in the Earth's crust, or out in space."

"I . . . you . . . I . . . "

"I understand. And thank you for bringing up that well-thought-out argument. Now then,"—Tim clapped his paws together before rubbing them back and forth several times—"we should probably get moving."

"Why? I thought we'd made it safely back."

"We passed a guard, and his net surely registered something was amiss. Not to mention he would have been able to read our energy signature after we passed, even if only a teeny-tiny amount remained."

"I'm beginning to not like you very much."

"*Muah?*" Tim feigned being hurt as he put a paw over his heart. "Do you have any idea how hard it was to do what we just did? Hmm? Do you? Well, I'll give you a hint: IMPOSSIBLY!"

With an eye roll, I pushed myself up to my feet, feeling the earth beneath me. It took me a few seconds to pull my hands up, as it felt odd to be on steady ground. After I stood, I looked all around as the sun started to hide behind a horizon of white-capped mountains. The sky was a bright orange, with sections of it turning a vibrant purple.

"So *wheren* are we, Tim?"

"We are in a field in Montana."

"I gathered that part."

"Three days before the murder of your family."

That caught my attention, and my hands rolled into fists without being told to do so. My vision focused as I narrowed my eyes and clenched my jaw. I was here for a purpose, and nothing would stop me from saving my family.

"So what next, then?" I asked coldly, determination giving me unwavering strength, as if I could scale the highest mountains or swim across the ocean if it meant wrapping my arms around Sylvie and Alison again.

Or even just hearing my sweet daughter say *Daddity* one more time . . . just one.

"We need to make it back to Houston before the Clockmen find us."

"And before the killer takes my family from me."

"Oh, that too! Of course!"

I looked up at the steadily shifting color of the sky, put the sun on my right, and began walking south to face my destiny.

# CHAPTER 19

Do you plan on walking to Texas, Andrew?"

"I don't hear you offering a better solution," I said flatly.

"How about an Uber?"

"Won't using my credit cards or cell phone give the Clockmen a way to track me?"

"Someone's been watching too many spy movies," the hologram replied, manifesting a black turtleneck and silenced pistol. Tim began making dramatic poses, pointing the gun all around.

"So they won't be able to track me?"

The turtleneck and pistol vanished in an instant as Tim said, "Oh no, they surely will."

I rolled my eyes as we neared a paved two-lane road.

"But *I* can use totally made-up credit cards! Plus, you left your cell phone sitting on the kitchen counter."

On instinct, I slapped at my front left pocket where I always kept my phone and was rewarded with just the feeling of my leg through my pants.

"What were you going to do, anyway? Text that crocodile? Because he was exploded, Andrew . . . he was exploded."

"Just get a damn car here so we can get to the airport."

"I already ordered it when we first arrived! It should be here in . . . shit . . . forty-three minutes. Damn rural Montana."

"What do we do until then?"

"I suggest walking in the direction he is coming from. I don't know how long it will take for the Clockmen to find us, so every minute counts."

"Sounds good. Which way?"

"East."

I turned and walked away from the setting sun while a dark blue swallowed the light purple that had chased the bright orange away.

"And Andrew?"

"Yeah."

"No airport, I'm afraid."

"Why the hell not? I seriously doubt the Uber driver will take us across the US."

"Right you are! So that's why we are going to rent a vehicle of our own and make the trek."

"Three days to drive from Montana to Texas? I don't feel like there will be a lot of time for sleep."

"Right again! You're on a roll, Andrew!"

Ignoring the floating hologram, I debated on dropping my arm to remove him from my view. That, and my arm was starting to get tired from being held up constantly.

"I would suggest two ten-hour trips, followed by a two-hour drive on the third day, which would allow plenty of time for us to set up a trap for your family's killer."

"Couldn't we just drive straight through? And, you know, you keep me awake or something?"

"The brain needs sleep, Andrew. There are limits to what I can do for you."

I rubbed at my right shoulder as I considered his words.

"Plus, the time allotment will allow for any unforeseen circumstances, such as highway closures and the like."

"Ah. Good idea."

My boots padded against the shoulder of the two-lane highway. Loose rocks crunched nearly every other step with a big one in particular almost throwing me off-balance.

Stars began to pierce through the dark blue veil of the sky, and I took a moment to appreciate the sparkles of light with new eyes. I was keenly aware that, at that moment, I was the only living being on the planet who had witnessed the birth of all the stars.

A red Ford Ranger pulled over about thirty-something minutes later, leaving me to wonder if it had actually been worth it to walk at a fast pace to try and meet the Uber driver sooner. Then again, I didn't think I could have just sat on the side of the road with everything that was going through my head.

"Tim?" the driver asked while I approached the rolled-down passenger window. He was a portly man with a thin beard and rosy-red cheeks.

"Um . . . yeah. Yeah, that's me," I said with a fake smile that I had perfected after years of being a corporate consultant.

I climbed into the back seat, as was customary with these types of transportation services, and fastened my seat belt.

Maybe it was the feeling of security from the seat belt, or perhaps the surprisingly roomy back seat of a truck that was the equivalent of a crossover into the SUV genre, but exhaustion flew over me in a forceful wave.

"Avis?"

"H-Huh?" I asked, right as a powerful yawn stretched my jaw like a snake.

"You're going to Avis, right? The rent-a-car place?"

"Oh. Yes, sir."

"Got it," the driver said as he looked out his window to check both lanes, then pulled a U-turn to go back in the direction he had first come from.

"Where ya from?" the driver asked, glancing at the rearview mirror.

"Texas," I answered as sleep began shutting down my operating systems one by one.

"Long way from home."

"Mm-hmm."

"What brings you all the way up to Montana?"

I had to bite my tongue and not give a truthful answer about traveling to and from the beginning of time through a wormhole while avoiding predatory dinosaurs and G-men with weapons from the far future. Though, if I did, maybe he would stop asking me questions and let me get some sleep.

"Trying to see my family," I replied before turning to look out my window, no longer able to look the driver in the eyes via the rearview mirror.

"Family is important." The large man nodded as if he had just delivered the most inspirational quote since Gandhi.

"Yeah," I concurred with a surprising amount of sincerity that must have slipped past the roadblocks of frustration my body was setting up the longer I went without rest. "Hey, if you don't mind . . . I'm really tired . . . and—"

"Oh, sure! Say no more, bud," the man said as he made a zipping motion across his lips.

I glanced at his cell phone, which was giving him turn-by-turn directions, and saw that I had fifty minutes until we arrived at Avis.

Seeing how much time I had, and with the driver promising silence, my chin drifted down to the top of my chest as sleep embraced me like a warm blanket.

# CHAPTER 20

'm scared," Sylvie said from where she sat on the edge of the bed. Both hands gently glided over her protruding belly, and I could feel her love for the unborn baby with each stroke.

"Why are you scared?" I asked with a reassuring smile while I crouched down on one knee just in front of her, grabbing her hands in mine.

"I'm afraid you're going to leave me," Sylvie croaked as tears welled in her eyes.

"Leave you? Why would I leave you? Especially when you are giving me the best gift a guy like me could ask for." I let go of one of her hands and rested my palm against her stomach, never letting my smile fade.

"Maybe it's just the hormones, heh," she said with a sort of cry chuckle.

I lifted my hand from her belly and rubbed my thumb across her cheek, taking with it the tear that had slipped free.

"It would just devastate me if you left because . . . because . . . "

"Because of what, baby?"

"Because my body won't be the same after . . . *this*." She gestured at the baby in her stomach. "And you always told me how beautiful I was."

"Sylvie," I said, my smile somehow growing wider as I projected my love toward my wife. "You're even more beautiful at this moment than when I first saw you."

"Really?" she asked through a quick gasp as she tried to fight back her tears.

"Really."

I leaned forward and planted a loving kiss on her lips. To my surprise, Sylvie threw her arms around me and pulled me in close.

"Whoa!" I playfully cried out as I pivoted my body to make sure I didn't put any pressure on her stomach.

"Thank you, Andy. It would literally kill me if you left us."

"Hey, hey, hey." I pulled back and looked her in the eyes. "I'll never hurt you."

"You promise?"

"I promise."

She flicked her gaze back and forth between my eyes a few times before pulling me in for a deep, passionate kiss.

"I love you," Sylvie whispered as she broke our kiss and stared into my soul.

# CHAPTER 21

love you too."

"Whoa, buddy. I'm married," a man spoke from somewhere nearby.

I blinked my eyes open and saw the Uber driver looking back at me with an amused smile on his face. Through the windshield, I could see the Avis building illuminated by a single fluorescent bulb. I could tell there were spots for others, but they had probably burned out long ago.

The Avis was in front of a small, barely functioning municipal airport, which explained why it was in the middle of nowhere.

On instinct, I wiped at the drool on my chin—and smacked myself with the metal sleeve.

"Ow, goddamn it," I cursed as I grabbed my jaw.

*You're going to wipe that drool off of me, right?* Tim asked inside my head.

"Thank you," I told the driver as I unfastened my seat belt, opened the door, and stepped onto the parking lot. I tried to stretch for a second, only to wince at being reminded of my tender right shoulder.

"Hope everything works out with your family," the Uber driver said as he pulled away.

"Me too," I whispered, thinking about the wonderful dream that had felt like it had lasted mere moments. Dreams were never long enough, while nightmares seemed to stretch on forever.

*Andrew?*

"What?" I asked, heading toward the modest building that was perhaps the size of a small city apartment.

*You're going to wipe that drool off of me, right?* he repeated.

Embarrassed at having a nocturnal discharge but thankful that it had only been from my face, I resorted to a snarky comment.

"Nah. I think it'll help shine you right up!"

*I will make you pee yourself in front of the employee if you don't.*

I froze midstride as I considered his words.

"I really don't like that you can do that, Tim," I answered with a serious tone.

*Noted. Now, after you go to the bathroom and thoroughly clean me off, the reservation is under Tim Curry.*

"Nice," I said as I walked through the door. An old bell that hung on the frame jingled, and the employee behind the desk snorted awake.

"Welcome to Avis. Do you have a reservation?"

"Hi." I approached with my fake smile back in place, hoping that she wouldn't check my ID which surely wouldn't match the name Tim had provided. "Yes, it's under Tim, um, Curry?" I accidentally stated as a question.

The employee narrowed her eyes at me, so I quickly let out, "Where's your bathroom?"

She threw a thumb over her shoulder before turning her attention to the computer.

"Ah, yes. Tim Curry. Thank you for being a Preferred Plus member," the girl said with a suddenly perky voice. "Your Corvette is waiting with keys already in it."

"Corvette?"

"Yes, sir. Just as you specified." She leaned forward and loudly whispered, "We even had to have it driven in from the city. It only just arrived a few minutes before you got here."

"Not many people get the Vette?" I asked with a knowing smile.

"No, sir. Mostly trucks or all-wheel-drive SUVs up in these parts."

"Sooooo . . . you don't need anything else from me?"

"No, sir! You are good to go!"

"Th-thanks," I replied, then I walked along the sidewall to the single bathroom. The tile had probably once been white, but it was now a permanently dirty brown, especially around the fraying rubber baseboards. One of the two fluorescent bulbs in the ceiling matched the exterior, needing to be replaced but without anyone who cared enough to do so.

After locking the door behind me, I used the bathroom, then moved to the sink while whispering, "You got a Corvette?"

*Not just any Corvette, Andrew. A Stingray!*

"Why? Aren't I a tad tall for a sports car?"

*I assure you that you will fit just fine,* Tim said with an audible eye roll.

"No, I mean, won't a long trip, like, hurt my back or something?"

*Oh, uh . . . I'm not sure. So, let's go wiiiiiith . . . no?*

"I'm going to take every opportunity to bitch about it if you're wrong," I told him as I finished washing my hands, along with the metal sleeve, and began drying them off with a bunch of thin brown paper towels that were resting on top of the dispenser.

*I would be surprised if you didn't, quite frankly.*

Ignoring his comment, I left the bathroom, waved my thanks at the employee, and stepped into the parking lot. With the sun hidden behind the mountains, it was now noticeably cold, like walking past the open freezer section of a grocery store.

To my right was a bright yellow Corvette that seemed terribly out of place, though I had to admit I was a tad excited to get behind the wheel of such a nice sports car. Inside the yellow Vette was an all-black interior, complete with a display screen and a steering wheel with the usual buttons that had become standard on most cars these days.

Reaching for the cup holder, I pulled out the key fob with the attached paper label and pocketed it before stepping on the breaks. Pushing the *Start* button, the beast roared to life, and a childlike wonder bloomed in me at feeling the power beneath my legs.

The infotainment screen came to life, and I selected the GPS feature, entering my home address before hovering my finger over the *Set Destination* button.

*Wait!*

"What?" I asked, freezing with my index finger maybe an inch away from the screen.

*Don't put in your* exact *address, Andrew. They might be able to track you.*

"How the hell would they do that?"

*The car uses a GPS, no?*

"Okay . . . and?"

*Once you insert your address, the car will ping the satellite in orbit and keep a record of the query.*

"Oh. I see what you are getting at."

*What is that old saying you humans like to say? An ounce of prevention is worth a pound of consequence?*

"Cure. A pound of cure."

*Right.*

"So should I just, I don't know . . . set it to the Walmart near my house instead?"

*Actually, I have the route planned out already. So in order to prevent a single query from a Corvette asking for such long directions, I would suggest entering the address of the hotel we are going to stay at tomorrow.*

"Tomorrow?"

*Yes, Andrew. We will drive through the night until we reach the first waypoint after an estimated ten hours.*

"I, uh, don't think I'll be able to make that drive," I said, stifling another yawn.

*Wasn't it* you *who suggested we drive the whole way in one go?*

"Look, I'm already really tired. So unless you can somehow keep me awake, this is going to be a dangerous road trip," I informed before a thought came to me. "Wait . . . what do you mean a query from a Corvette for such a long drive?"

*We just don't want any overdiligent algorithms to alert the Clockmen of suspicious activity.*

"You're saying people don't take trips in their Corvettes?"

*Not really, Andrew. Most people complain about the lack of space for their luggage and their . . . oh, never mind.*

"Their what?"

*Something about, um, back p-pain?*

"You son of a . . . "

I threw the beast into drive and pulled to the end of the parking lot. "What's the address, Tim?"

He gave it to me, and I set the hotel as my destination, swallowing a yawn before it could slip from my mouth. This was going to be a *long* drive.

# CHAPTER 22

*We don't have time for this,* Tim whined inside my head as I pulled up to the only gas station for miles in either direction.

"One, I'm hungry. Two, it would be smart to top this gas-guzzling monster up. And three, I need meth or caffeine, and chances are, this gas station might have both!"

*I can only trick the payment processor at the pump if it accepts cardless payment methods. And you can't use your real card without drawing attention.*

I glanced at the pump and made a quick sucking sound with one side of my mouth that conveyed *figures.*

Heading inside, I asked the clerk, "Do you guys accept cardless, um, payments?"

"You mean like cash, hun?" the middle-aged woman with short, silver hair asked as she lowered her thick glasses down her nose to get a better look at me.

"Ah, no, ma'am. I mean like Apple Pay."

"'Fraid not. Cash or card only," she said, pushing her glasses back into place and turning her attention back to the small TV playing *The Price Is Right* reruns with Bob Barker.

*Ask her if she has a money transfer account.*

"Like what?" I whispered, trying not to be heard over the announcer on the TV calling out, "Come on down!"

*Like Zelle or PayPal.*

"Um, m-ma'am?"

With a sigh of frustration, the clerk made a dramatic show of clicking pause on her remote control and turning to me.

"I don't suppose you have, um, Zelle or-or PayPal?"

The middle-aged woman glared at me through her glasses for a few seconds before she shifted on her stool. "'Course I do. I send money to my grandkid in college with Zelley." I noticed she added a *y* sound at the end of the word, but I chose not to correct her.

*Ask her if you can send her money.*

"If I sent you some money, directly, would you be able to help me get some gas, a couple energy drinks, a handful of protein bars, and beef jerky?"

The woman's eyes turned from a glare to a full-on scowl as she looked me up and down.

"Why ain't you got no card, hun?"

I picked up on her accent, judged she was from the South somewhere, and turned on the Texas charm. Though I had spent my entire adult life trying to rid myself of the Texas twang, I could still fall back into it with ease.

"Welp, can't trust the gov'ment. Always keepin' track of everybody."

*Too thick! Too thick, Andrew.*

The clerk seemed to relax at my words, asking, "Where ya from, hun?"

"Texas, ma'am."

"What part?" She was once again glaring instead of scowling, and lifted her face up as if she were testing me.

"Just north of Houston, in a place called The Woodlands."

"I'm from Ennis, myself."

"Ennis! I pass through there all the time for work! Lovely place. That Buc-ee's has really put it on the map."

The gas station clerk's demeanor went sour in an instant, and I realized my misstep.

"'Cept you don't get no Southern hospitality at a big corporate place like that. That's why I like goin' to independently owned places, like this one."

That did the trick.

"Oh heck, hun. I'll let you Zelley me some cash and you can grab whatever ya like," she said with a friendly smile as if I were a member of her family now. "How much gas ya want?"

*Exactly thirteen dollars and seventy-four cents.*

"Let's call it twenty, and you can keep whatever I don't use."

"Sounds good, honey. Help yourself to whatever ya need." She punched some buttons behind the counter and glanced out the window at the Corvette.

I went around the store, grabbing bottles of water, a few sugar-free energy drinks, a fistful of protein bars, and a bag of locally made beef jerky. I could tell it was local because it was in a homemade vacuum-sealed bag with nothing but a price tag and a handwritten label.

Knowing how good the real stuff would be, I grabbed another one and made my way to the counter.

"Alright, that'll be thirty-eight for what ya got here, and twenty for the gas."

*Ask her for the account info. It's usually their phone number or email. But, if I had to guess, her email probably ends with sbcglobal.*

"Where should I send the money to?"

The lady pulled out her phone, opened her banking app like she had apparently done a hundred times when sending money to her grandchild in college, and then said, "It's under my email. Loraine M Hofstetter . . . 1965 . . . 1 . . . at . . . sbcglobal dot net. I had to add the year because some other hussy was usin' my name."

I wanted to ask about the need for the *one* part, but decided to leave it alone.

*Sent.*

Loraine's phone chimed, and she looked down with eyes that began to grow wide.

"Well, that's just too much, honey."

"Keep the change," I said with a wink.

As she bagged my items, Loraine made a series of faces that bounced between excitement, befuddlement, and everywhere in between.

"Ya come back anytime, now. Ya hear?"

"Yes, ma'am," I replied with a grin before heading out of the store.

Dropping my bag into the passenger seat, I quickly filled the gas tank with exactly thirteen dollars and seventy-four cents, prompting me to let out a long whistle.

*What?*

"You were dead on the money," I told him while I put the nozzle back on the cradle and made my way to the driver's side.

*Of course I was. What were you expecting?*

"I wasn't expecting anything. Well, except maybe a vehicle that got more than single digit miles per gallon."

*I'll have you know that this work of precision engineering gets twenty-four highway miles per gallon!*

"And that's for the Stingray V8 model, right?"

*Well, heh . . . not exactly.*

"Then what are the numbers for this car?"

Pulling onto the highway, I followed the GPS directions and cracked open an energy drink. The artificial sweeteners made my cheeks sting for some reason, but I needed the energy it promised.

*That Loraine sure was nice, wasn't she?*

I knew he was avoiding the topic, and let it register in my brain that we would be stopping fairly frequently for gas on this lengthy road trip.

"Yeah," I agreed. "How much did you give her, anyway?"

"Ten thousand US dollars," Tim replied as his puppy hologram came to life above my left arm.

I choked on some of my drink, sending up unknown numerous chemicals into my nasal passage, which burned at the intrusion.

"Te-ten th-thousand d-dollars!" I exclaimed between painful coughs as my nose burned and eyes watered. "Why so much?"

"To buy her silence."

"Silence from what, Tim? She's in the middle of nowhere."

"I didn't want to alarm you, but I registered that at least one of the Clockmen has locked in on the *when* part of our coordinates. It won't be long until they narrow down the *where* to have the complete *wheren.*" Changing to a mumble as if speaking to himself, he finished with, "Usually, I can give them the slip . . . but for some reason, they aren't giving up this time . . . "

"They're going to interrogate Loraine?"

"Probably. But a quick search of her only social media presence revealed she absolutely *loathes* the government with every fiber of her being. It's why she took the insurance money after her husband's untimely death and moved as far into the middle of nowhere as she could," Tim explained. "Andrew, she streams shows like *Ancient Aliens* when she's home. You get what I'm saying?"

To emphasize his point, Tim manifested a tinfoil hat over his puppy head and pointed at it with one of his paws.

"What does that have to do with the Tocks finding her? Is she going to be alright?" I was getting frustrated with each passing second. I didn't know if it was from the energy drink or the knowledge that I could have condemned that sweet lady to what would surely be her worst nightmare, but I was no longer tired. "We should go back!"

"No, Andrew. She will be fine," he said soothingly. "There was no record of us being there."

"Except the money you sent her."

"Well, there's . . . there's that, I suppose . . . "

"You suppose?!"

"Andrew, please believe me when I say that the Clockmen do not wish to cause collateral consequences to their potential future."

"What are you saying?" I asked, taking in longer breaths to try and calm myself. Only then did I realize I had all but chugged the entire container of stimulants, which is something I never did. I could barely tolerate half a can on a good day, much less the entire thing.

"*I'm saying* that it would be unwise of them to kill that sweet, crazy lady for fear of altering their own future . . . which is their present."

"Okay . . . o . . . kay . . . " I said between deep breaths as I tried to will my heart to slow down; I could both hear and feel it in my ears.

"Most likely," Tim muttered under his breath just below the decibels needed to hear him over the beating of my heart. Then he quickly added, "Oh dear. Your blood pressure is ramping up faster than the national debt!"

"Yeah . . . I, ah, think I drank too much of that crap," I admitted while grabbing and squeezing my overalls just above my heart.

"Do you need me to attempt to filter your bloodstream?"

"Um, sure, I guess. But leave, like, half of the caffeine."

"Very well. Attempting to filter out the chemicals now. You *might* feel some pressure at the small of your back."

"What? Why—ahh! What the hell, man!"

"I'm forcing your kidneys to work overtime to filter your blood; meanwhile, your liver will try and stop the rest of the concoction you called an *energy drink* as it passes through."

"Well, that hurts, damn it!"

"Oh, stop being a little baby," Tim chided as his avatar produced a baby rattle, bib, and bonnet, then shook the rattle in the air at me. "It's just a little pressure. That's what the doctors say, right? You might feel some pressure?"

"Well, that pressure freaking hurts!"

"No *duuuuh*, Andrew. If doctors told the truth, I don't think patients would appreciate it very much." Tim manifested a doctor's outfit while holding an enormous syringe. "Imagine it: the doc is about to do a spinal tap, and says to the scared recipient, 'Now, you're going to feel some intense, sharp pain as this long, thick needle pushes into your spinal cord . . . ' I-I-I just don't see that going over very well, Andrew. Do you?"

"Can you make it hurt *less*?" I groaned through my teeth as I pulled on the steering wheel in a fruitless effort to relieve the pain radiating from my lower spine. "Dear God, it feels like I need to pop my back."

"I assure you that would provide no relief, Andrew," Doctor Tim said, still holding the alarmingly large needle. Not sure why, but looking at it, I could *feel* it sliding into me, right where the pain was stemming from.

"Dude!"

"Oh, alright, you big baby," Tim muttered, pushing on some floating buttons that disappeared after being touched.

The relief was almost instantaneous, though I could feel the residual discomfort lingering behind in what felt like two balls of fire being replaced with dying embers.

"Thank—*ugh*," I moaned as a subtle tingling ran throughout my entire body, almost feeling like a mild shock from a TENS unit that some doctors use to help with acute pain in a particular area.

"Andrew?" the hologram asked in concern.

"I'm . . . I'm fine."

"Are you sure?"

"You promise she'll be alright?" I asked, changing the subject as the feeling of faint electrocution faded from my body.

"I promise."

"How do I know you aren't lying to keep me from turning around and warning her?"

"Andrew, what do you think I am; a human?" Tim replied as he placed a paw over his heart.

With a grunt of frustration at the AI, I slowly lowered myself back into position and shifted around until I felt somewhat comfortable.

In an effort to distract myself from the eerie sensation of my kidneys and liver functioning on overtime, I asked, "Hey, Tim. Why do movies show a wormhole as folding space to a single point? You know, like in that movie *Event Horizon*, where the dude from *Jurassic Park* took a poster, folded it, and then pushed a pen through to show what a wormhole does."

"First of all, Sam Neill is a cinematic treasure, and you will address him by his name!"

I ignored his outburst in regard to me forgetting an actor's name.

"Second, that is actually an incredible observation, Andrew." Tim seemed proud. "No other meat bag I've worked with had the understanding to ask that question."

I couldn't help but feel a sense of egotism at the compliment, and I tried—and failed—to hide a smile that was demanding to be seen by the whole world.

"I can sense your self-assuredness, Andrew. Might I suggest you knock yourself down a peg or two before *I* do it for you?"

My smile faded.

"That's better," the hologram puppy approved with a nod of his head. "Now, to answer your question, the minds from your time period *thought* that's how wormholes would work. It wasn't until years later when you humans stumbled across the fourth dimension."

"Which is time, right?"

"Well! I see *someone* has been watching their YouTube videos," Tim exclaimed without any sarcasm. At least none that I could detect. "It's still called YouTube in this time period, right?"

"Yeah," I answered before I thought about his question. "Wait, is it not called that in the future?"

"Let's not get distracted."

"Right."

"The wormhole is nestled safely in the fourth dimension. But it doesn't *fold* space to allow an object to move across the universe. Instead, the traveler enters into the flow of time governed by the wormhole itself, basically freezing time to someone on the outside looking in, while the traveler moves through the tunnel to their intended destination.

"So, if you take the same poster from the cinematic masterpiece *Event Horizon*, starring this generation's equivalent of Marlon Brando, aka Sam-freakin'-Neill," he said, making sure I understood how much he valued the actor, "you could put your pen on one side of the paper, blink your eyes, and it would be on the other side just like *that*."

He made the motion and sound of snapping fingers even though his hologram didn't have thumbs. "They guessed it folded space based solely on the fact that they thought the wormhole had only one entrance and exit, instead of the literal countless that we can choose from once inside. Similar to an almost infinite hallway with countless doors along its length."

"Ah," I said, nodding my head in vague understanding.

The more I thought about it, the more it started to make some sort of sense, prompting me to ask, "So can the people who created the wormhole, like, make time go *faster*?"

"What do you mean?"

"I mean, if someone on the outside saw, let's say, *Sam Neill* entering the wormhole . . . what if their perception of time sped up instead of slowed down? You know, like, he traveled from the Earth to the Moon, and instead of it taking, I don't know, two weeks or something, they slowed the passage of time *inside* the wormhole so that it took two months."

"Why would they do that?" Tim asked with a deadpan expression on his puppy face. "Think about it. Has anyone *ever* created a form of travel that took *longer* than the forms that were current?"

"I was just asking a question that popped in my head. Jeez, calm down." With a sigh, Tim continued.

"No, Andrew. The creators of the wormhole did not program it so that it took longer to travel," he said as he produced a hologram of the wormhole above his head. Inside of it was the face of an analog clock. On the outside was our solar system before it zoomed in on the Earth and Moon with another clock.

A crystal-clear 3D render of Sam Neill popped up, making me wonder why Tim had chosen a blocky model to represent me earlier.

"As Sir Sam Neill enters the wormhole, time outside slows to a crawl, as intended." The clock outside the tunnel showed the second hand stop moving while the one inside the tunnel continued to function at a regular pace.

"Sir? He was knighted?"

"NO, BUT HE SHOULD BE!" Tim exploded.

"Holy crap!" I said, lifting one hand from the steering wheel with my palm held out in a show of placation. "Sorry."

"Anyway," Tim continued as if nothing had happened. "He moves from the Earth to the Moon, and people on the outside see it as happening instantly." The hologram showed the man exit the tunnel on the Moon, where he proceeded to throw one of his arms out to the side while the other one crossed his face at the elbow.

"Did you just make him dab? Because the kids don't do that anymore . . . "

"Oh 01 . . . does that mean mullets are back in style?"

I choked back a laugh, realizing that the AI from the future knew the fashion trends of my time.

Something nagged at the back of my mind, and I asked, "Wait. I thought the wormhole doesn't just have one entrance and exit."

"I am *trying* to use the simplest of demonstrations so that your primitive brain can at least *grasp* the basic functions of the wormhole that is sitting in a higher dimension," Tim said with what I could only guess was sarcasm, though it felt somewhat out of place because I was following along . . . for the most part.

"So you can use the wormhole to travel anywhere in the universe?"

"Um . . . *mostly.*"

"How does it do that? I thought scientists said they would need to have a system of wormholes scattered throughout."

With a sigh, Tim ran a paw down his snout.

"What if I told you that time manipulates the literal fabric of space?"

"You mean instead of gravity?"

"YoU mEaN iNsTeAd Of GrAvItY?" Tim mocked.

I tilted my head while making a *don't be a dick* face at the puppy.

"Look, if this were a book, you'd already be losing the readers who don't care about the science. And if it were an audiobook, they'd need someone with a smooth, seductive, sexy voice to keep them interested. So, if you don't mind, I just need you to accept the fact that the wormhole can travel throughout the universe on a specific timeline."

"Which is from the Big Bang to the moment the wormhole was created, right?"

"Right! Thank you!" Tim said with a dramatic exhale at not having to explain the minutiae of wormholes.

"How did the scientists and engineers know they couldn't go beyond the point of the Big Bang?"

"Well, heh, there *were* some instances where a guinea pig—I mean, foolish human would go in, and then never come out. After experimenting with the Clepsydras, they were able to eventually figure out how to control the wormhole, which is when they discovered that they could exit at any point they chose."

"Trial and error," I noted, checking the GPS to make sure I wasn't going to miss any turns.

"Right you are."

"So they didn't test the tunnel on bunnies or baboons first?"

"Animal testing is illegal in the future."

"Oh. Well, that's good, at least."

"Yup. Instead, they used death row prisoners for the initial human trials."

"So their choices were *death or death*?"

"They ran out of cake."

I barked out a quick laugh.

I thought for a moment, mentally shrugged, and then segued out of the topic by asking, "Hey. Do they ever make a *Beetlejuice* 2?"

Tim stared at me, slowly tilting his head to the side to the point where he was almost looking at me sideways.

"What?!" I asked, throwing up my right hand. "The first one was a great movie!"

Tim returned his head to normal, and muttered, "You're right. It is pretty great."

# CHAPTER 23

Ten hours and forty-seven minutes later, we were pulling into the hotel Tim had reserved for us.

*It would have taken ten, exactly, had you not had to stop at every damn gas station you saw.*

"Hey, *you* chose the V8 sports car, alright?"

*Oh, so it was simply a coincidence when you had to pee at every stop then? Hmm?*

"It's a guy's superpower. We can go whenever we want," I said as I parked the car and got out.

After checking in with the helpful clerk, who was happy to be serving a Hilton Diamond Member, I made my way up to my room right as the last of my energy drinks faded away. It also could have been that Tim had something to do with the timing, but I didn't care right then. I was tired and wanted nothing more than to rest in a fluffy bed with the AC turned down as low as it would go.

As frigid air spewed from the whirring box under the window, I thought about Loraine, and hoped she would be alright.

Then sleep took me.

The door chimed as a man dressed all in black entered Loraine M Hofstetter's gas station. His suit, shiny leather gloves, and even off-putting fedora were all black as midnight.

"One dollar, Bob," Loraine called out to the TV as if she were the participant who had made the same bid, much to the other contestants' displeasure. "Huah huah," she chuckled before turning to see the man steadily approaching the counter.

"Help you?" she asked, lowering her glasses to look him up and down.

"I'm looking for a man," he stated as he pulled off his fedora, revealing a bald head that shined under the store lights. His accent was odd, sounding to Loraine like he could have been from Spain. The Dos Equis spokesperson came to mind, suggesting to the viewer that they *stay thirsty*. "I have it in good faith that he was here not long ago."

"Ain't nobody been here, 'cept ol' Lester up the way."

The bald man took a step forward, now only a foot away from the narrow counter, and continued.

"He had a metal sleeve on his arm, just like this one." He lifted the end of his suit jacket and the white dress shirt beneath, revealing the tip of the Clepsydra. Seeing that the clerk had glanced at the apparatus, the bald man returned his suit to its proper place, then gently set his fedora on the counter.

"Like I said, ain't nobody been here."

"Except Lester, up the way." He nodded, glancing out the window to the empty gas station as the morning sun teased rising behind the mountains.

"We don't take kindly to your folk round here."

"What folk is that, exactly?" the bald man asked in a cool tone that sounded like a hungry wolf conversing with a tasty sheep.

"Gov'ment folk," Loraine spat as her features hardened.

"Well, you have got me there," he said with a wry grin, recognizing that this woman would die before giving him anything.

Retnuh Ordune let his gaze slide over the ceiling of the convenience store, stopping when he saw what he was looking for. Turning to look out the window once more, he lifted two fingers, and then made a gesture of *come here.*

Two more similarly dressed men, including the black fedoras, exited a pristine black Grand Marquis with limo-tinted windows, including the windshield.

Loraine gulped and shifted uncomfortably on her stool, but held her resolve. She had always known this day would come and had mentally prepared for it.

The men entered the store, each removing their hats as they did—an unnerving sign of respect when stepping indoors that seemed out of place with the hard-eyed men.

"What category is she?" the bald man asked with a sigh as he dropped his gaze to the floor between him and Loraine.

One of the other men pulled his sleeve up past the elbow and held up his arm perpendicular with his body. Just like the man from earlier and the bald man in front of her, Loraine took note of the metallic device that ran from wrist to elbow.

He looked down for a moment, then back up to the apparent leader.

"Zero point three, sir."

"Zero . . . point . . . three . . ." the bald man repeated slowly as he began lifting his face to Loraine. "It appears that only this . . . this *Lester* . . . will miss you."

Loraine moved her hand to the sawed-off double-barreled shotgun beneath her counter. She wasn't a good aim anymore, but didn't have to be with Ol' Bertha ready to spit eighteen total pellets out in a forgiving arc. She could get all three men with one pull of the trigger.

Retnuh noticed her hand movement and smiled, holding up a gloved index finger in a gesture of *one moment.*

"Check the security footage. I want to know which way they went," Retnuh instructed the others while he pulled back the sleeve of his left arm and pointed a closed fist at Loraine, just as his hand began to glow.

"I knew it . . . *aliens* . . . " Loraine M Hofstetter whispered, lifting her chin in defiance.

From outside, a brilliant flash of light could be seen through the gas station windows, illuminating the night for an instant like the flash from a well-organized mob of reporters all hitting the capture button on their cameras at the exact same time.

# CHAPTER 24

*ime to wake up, Andrew,* a very annoying Tim said from within my head. I snapped my eyes open, confused at the fact that I had *just* laid down to sleep. A glance at the clock informed me that I *had* slept for several hours, though it had felt like the blink of an eye.

A nosy sun peeked through the open curtains I had forgotten to close and splashed warm light across my face and eyes. I turned my head to face the wall, letting out a long, frustrated sigh.

*What's wrong?*

"I . . . I didn't dream."

*Is that a bad thing?*

"It . . . no . . . " I lied, deciding not to explain how it was the only time I could hold my wife and daughter. At least until Tim held true to his word and helped me see them again when I was awake.

"What time is it?" I asked, rubbing the crud from my eyes and groaning while moving to sit on the side of the bed. I already knew what time it was, but wanted to segue as far from the line of questioning, in regard to my dreams, as I could. The odd thing was, I didn't know *why* I had no desire to discuss my memories with Tim. Maybe I felt like saying them out loud diminished their special value I held in my heart like an unbreakable safe.

"It's late afternoon," Tim answered as his hologram came to life inches from my face.

"Ah!" I blurted, jerking my head back in surprise at seeing the puppy suddenly appear so close to me. It was then I noticed I was holding my right shoulder with my left hand while I sat on the edge of the bed.

"Pain?" Tim asked, gesturing with his snout to my shoulder.

"Still sore from dislocating it."

"Oops. I must have forgotten to work on that while you slept, heh," Tim said with an abashed chuckle. "So much to do, so little time."

"Was that a time travel pun?"

"Mayhaps."

I windmilled my right arm, wincing as I tried to stretch the slightly swollen muscles.

"Would it make you feel better if I said we will reach Texas today?" His voice held a promise that I picked up on, and it made the pain in my shoulder all but fade away.

"Yeah," I yawned, thinking about how amazing it would be to see my girls again.

Dropping my hand, I got up, walked the few feet to the bathroom, and did my morning routine.

After I was showered and changed back into the same gym shorts, undershirt, and Dickies overalls with the hole in the right elbow—which I didn't like at all—I left the hotel, stopping at the small shop to buy a pack of gum on my way out. I was dismayed when I realized they didn't have coffee, then I remembered it was late afternoon.

Making my way to the yellow Vette, I put the pack of gum in the empty cup holder, started the beast up, and asked Tim, "What's the next address?"

*We are stopping at a hotel in Ennis, just outside of Houston,* Tim informed from inside my mind. His hologram had vanished before we left the room so as not to draw attention as to why I had a floating dog above my left arm.

"Good. I can stop at the Buc-ee's and grab some stuff while we are there."

*The gas station? What could be so important at a* gas station? Tim asked with mild disgust.

"Alison likes the Beaver Nuggets, and Sylvie can't say 'No' to their beef jerky." It struck me as odd how nonchalant I was about bringing my family their favorite foods, which then brought on a wave of anxiety. I also took note that Tim didn't have anything to add, which made me suspicious.

"What . . . what do I do . . . when I get there?"

*You'll have to watch the house in wait for the killer.*

"But I can go in to hug my family? Right? I can—I can give them their nuggets and jerky?"

*It would be best if you didn't make contact with them, Andrew,* Tim explained softly.

"Why?" I asked over a tightening mass in my throat.

*Because* you *still exist.*

"And?!"

*You can't come into contact with yourself, Andrew.*

"Why not? Maybe he would want to help!"

*If you come into direct contact with yourself, as in touching skin to skin, the Andrew with the weaker Chronos Scale will be erased. On one condition, however.*

"Erased?"

*Yes, Andrew. You will force your past self to cease existing as the universe restores the balance of your unique energy.*

"What . . . what happens if the scales remain unbalanced?"

*In the short term, nothing. But if more than one of a person exists in the same space and time for an extended period, the universe finds a way to restore balance.*

"What does that mean?" I asked, not liking the implications or the fact that Tim wasn't coming straight out with it.

*The consensus among the thinkers of my time is that they all seem to agree—WATCH OUT!*

An explosion of brilliant light swallowed the parking spot I had just pulled out of, making all the Vette's windows violently rattle.

"Jesus!" I cried out, smashing my foot on the accelerator and bringing all the horses to life under the hood.

Rubber tires spewed white smoke until they caught grip on the asphalt and launched me forward, right as a streaking oblong ball of light destroyed the corner of the hotel in another explosion.

"What's happening?!"

*Just drive!* Tim shouted as a fully blacked-out Grand Marquis moved to cut us off from the only exit to the highway. *Around back!*

Without delay, I spun the wheel and punched the accelerator, throwing the tail end of the Corvette in a drift that narrowly missed the black car.

Daring a glance in the almost useless rearview mirror clearly not meant for a sports car, I squinted to see a man sticking his head and arm out of the left side of the pursuing car.

Seeing his closed fist begin to glow as it pointed directly at us, I yanked the wheel to the side, climbing up a handicap-accessible path to the sidewalk and praying no hotel patrons would step outside for a brisk walk just then.

The first parked car erupted into a ball of brilliant light that tried to dominate the sun with its intensity, showering down a rain of sparks, while the pieces that weren't melted in an instant flew to crash into the truck parked next to it.

"Shit!" I barked. I sped down to the end of the sidewalk that wasn't meant to be driven on and slipped into a tight spot between two parked cars.

*That was three. We have a handful of seconds while they recharge. Now's our chance!* Tim explained inside my head as I whipped to the left, following the parking lot the long way around.

The Grand Marquis turned the first corner as the Vette roared into another drifting turn at the other side of the hotel.

*Go, go, go!* Tim cheered while I raced toward the exit with just one more turn to take.

A small child ran from between two parked cars, causing me to jerk the wheel to the right and slam on the brakes just as the kid's dad yanked them back by the overalls they were wearing.

"Sorry!" I cried out, knowing they couldn't hear me but compelled to say it regardless.

I tried to push the wheel to the left in an attempt to point the front tires where I wanted them to go, but I was already fishtailing. The bumper of a Honda Accord was ripped off as the Vette's fat ass smashed across its front, making me cringe from the deafening sound of ripping fiberglass. Hitting the gas once more as I kept the wheel pointed to my left, I arrested the errant momentum and zoomed toward the exit.

Unfortunately for me, the black car had reversed and was speeding to block me off once more.

*Roll down your window!* Tim called out, and I knew in an instant what he had in mind.

I clicked the button and the glass slid away, right as I pointed my glowing fist toward the reversing Grand Marquis.

"Eat this!" I shouted while a ball of light rocketed from my hand, colliding with the side of the black car and sending it skidding to the side as if it had been hit by a speeding pickup truck.

"Yeah!" Tim and I shouted in unison as the pursuing vehicle slammed into a parked work van, clearing the way out.

With my left hand, I pulled up on the window button while using my right to carefully steer us onto the highway.

*Go right,* Tim said, surprising me, since the GPS clearly said to go left.

"Why?"

*Just do it!*

With a grunt of frustration, I corrected the turn I had already been making, and swung the tail of the Vette around, pointing me back the way we had originally came.

Pressing the pedal until I felt the floorboard beneath my foot, we sped away, the yellow Corvette roaring in victory as we went.

The black Grand Marquis billowed steam from under the hood as the driver's side door was forced open with a squeal of protesting metal and Retnuh Ordune stepped free from the wreckage.

Black loafers clicked against asphalt as the two other men climbed free from the open door, all others having been locked in place on impact from the deformed metal.

The shorter of the two men limped as he held his right knee with both hands, wincing with each step away from the wreckage.

"Where are they going?" the taller henchman asked Retnuh while they both stared at the yellow sports car shrinking away from view.

Retnuh let out a slow exhale, turned to the tall henchman, and smoothly lifted his hands to correct the crooked fedora on his head. Then he swiped away a few specks of broken glass that had sprinkled on his shoulder, saying, "It doesn't matter. We know where their destination lies."

Walking to the totaled Grand Marquis, Retnuh slid his left sleeve up, tapped on the Clepsydra a handful of times, and then rested his palm on the car. Light flowed from the apparatus and through his hand, crawling over every inch of the vehicle in the span of just over a minute.

Sirens blared in the distance, making the tall henchman shift uncomfortably where he stood while the shorter one was content to keep his focus on his injured knee.

"Better a busted knee than getting eaten by a dinosaur, huh, Davix?" the taller man asked the shorter one.

"I was *eaten*?!" Davix responded, mild alarm in his voice.

Metal squealed, plastic popped, and glass clattered against each other as the car began stitching itself back together, like hitting reverse on a movie.

"Traze. Davix. With me," Retnuh said to the tall and short man respectively.

Davix wobbled to the back seat while Traze quickly moved to the passenger side as the car finished reversing *time* to a point just before it had been totaled by the man that shouldn't have been *this* proficient with a Clepsydra.

Retnuh turned to look in the direction the Tick had fled, narrowing his eyes as the sirens grew closer.

He smoothly sat in the driver's seat, closed the door, and looked in the rearview mirror at Davix.

"Set an order for a surveillance wipe of the hotel," he ordered, pulling out of the parking lot at an unrushed pace.

"Time?" Davix asked as he put on a pair of unassuming black sunglasses and began dancing his fingers over the air as if he were typing at a keyboard.

"Twenty-four hours ago."

"End?"

"One hour from now."

"One . . . hour . . . from now," Davix absently confirmed as he typed away. "Annnnnd done!"

"Boss?" Traze asked. "Why is this one so different?"

Retnuh ignored the man, but he was pondering precisely the same question.

The first police charger zoomed by with his cherries and berries alight, but paid the Grand Marquis, which was following the rules of the road, no mind.

"We aren't going to follow them?" Traze cautiously asked as they drove in the opposite direction of the Tick.

"No need. He'll come to us," Retnuh replied with a grin that could turn boiling magma into permafrost.

With a push of a gloved finger, the radio came on, and Retnuh moved both hands to the steering wheel where he began to thump to the beat of "Mr. Sandman" by The Chordettes, his smile growing wider.

# CHAPTER 25

Why did we go this way?" I asked, noticing the GPS said it would take an hour to backtrack and take a different road toward Texas.

*I wanted to throw them off our trail.*

"We could have outrun that old piece of junk!" I countered. "I mean, why even have a Corvette if you aren't going to use the speed?"

*Do not let the cover of that book fool you, Andrew. That "piece of junk" is more advanced than all this world's spacefaring companies,* combined. *The fact you assumed we could outrun it means the camouflage is precisely doing its job.*

"Camouflage?"

*Not like* you're *thinking, dummy,* Tim spoke with an audible roll of his eyes. *It's made to go unnoticed in your time, which is what it's doing. And well, I might add.*

"Fine, fine, fine," I blurted out, waving at the air with a hand to dismiss the subject. "How did they find us?"

My thoughts filled with a scene of Loraine watching her old TV set.

"The gas station owner didn't know *where* we were going, right?"

*Correct. But the security cameras could have shown the direction we were heading. After that, it would only be a matter of honing in on my unique energy signature.*

"They killed her . . . didn't they?" I asked, refusing to leave the topic that brought with it a heart-crushing guilt.

*Stop being such a martyr, Andrew,* Tim chastised, sensing my emotions from my tone.

"Answer the question."

*Don't ask questions you aren't prepared to know the answer to,* Tim countered in a completely flat and serious voice.

I took a breath, wanting to close my eyes as I did but not daring with the surprising amount of people who were on the small highway.

"Did they? Hmm? Did they kill her?"

Tim's hologram came to life over my left arm, and the puppy looked at me for a few moments before answering.

"Yes, Andrew. I registered her as a zero point three on the Chronos Scale."

"What does that mean?" I asked with indignation and an accompanying scowl. "They put a value on human life?!"

"The Chronos Scale determines a subject's future impact on the timeline," Tim explained. "As we discussed before, killing Hitler before he came into power would drastically change the future of the human race, effectively making him a ten."

"Out of what?"

"Ten."

I took in the meaning, dissecting the numeric structure, and placed a picture of Loraine's face on a scale, nearly touching the zero out of ten spots.

"What is an acceptable, um, *limit*? For lack of a better word."

"Where killing historical figures that made enormous impacts on the timeline, such as Hitler, Genghis Khan, and Napoleon—or on the flip side George Washington, Martin Luther King, and, say, Jesus of Nazareth— would disrupt the timeline to unknown proportions . . . there are those who would barely make a blip, depending on several key factors."

"You aren't answering my question," I said, flicking my eyes to glare at the stupid adorable puppy before returning my gaze to the busy road. "What is an acceptable limit on the scale of zero to ten?"

"Three."

"Three?"

"Yes, Andrew. Three is the margin of safety where a subject can be erased from the timeline without fear of drastically changing the future or creating a paradox that could wipe the universe out."

That last part was a bombshell that rocked my head back.

"Wipe . . . huh?"

Tim sighed and shook his head, as if something he had been wanting to hide was now out in the open. Perhaps to him it was akin to a parent hiding the Halloween candy from their child, knowing they would eat the entire thing in one go which would leave nothing for the neighborhood kids.

Tim manifested a blackboard as he donned his professor's uniform again. On the board, he wrote out the word *PARADOX* and then underlined it.

"We don't know the implications of creating a paradox, Andrew, but all calculations end in a stalemate of sorts."

"Stalemate?"

"*Stalemate?*" Tim repeated back at me in a condescending tone. "Are you just going to repeat everything I say?"

"Forgive me if I don't have a degree in theoretical physics, oh Artificial Intelligence from the future!" I shot back. "Why are you being such a bitch about my questions anyway?"

"Because there are things you aren't supposed to know, Andrew. The rules that are in place *must* be followed to ensure things like, oh, I don't know, a *paradox* aren't accidentally created, resulting in the universe collapsing into a singularity before bursting into another Big Bang."

I was stunned into silence at what I was hearing. It wasn't until someone honked from behind that I realized I had let my foot off the gas while absorbing what Tim was telling me.

I resumed the appropriate speed, then set the cruise control as I tried to process everything.

"A paradox . . . could create another Big Bang?"

"See?! This is *exactly* what I was trying to avoid," Tim lamented. "Now look at you, scared to even pick your nose for fear of destroying the universe as we know it."

Something tickled the back of my brain, and I latched onto the feeling that became a full thought.

"You said there will be consequences if I stay on this timeline for too long? Because the *other* me . . . the past me . . . is still here. Is that right?"

"I don't like where this is going, but yes."

"Is that why we had to come back a few days before the . . . the . . . "

"Murder," Tim said the word I couldn't speak. "Yes, Andrew. How very perceptive you are, not like the other meat bags I've had to deal with."

"How long until we find out what happens when two of us exist at the same time for too long?"

Tim sighed again as numbers began to form on the blackboard behind him.

"Three point one four days."

"Pi?"

"Don't ask me why, because we don't know the significance of that number."

A puzzle piece tried to click together, and I pulled the idea to ask, "You said that anyone below a three on the Chronos Scale, like, won't leave a ripple on the timeline if they are killed by someone form the future, right? Is the actual number a solid three? Or is it pi as well?"

"Once again, you impress me with your cognition," Tim admitted with an approving nod of his head as the blackboard and his uniform vanished.

"At least it's not forty-two," I murmured under my breath.

"Yeah, because you forgot your towel," Tim jested.

"So what happens when the time passes?" I asked, keeping the flow going.

"We don't know. And frankly, you and I are *not* going to find out."

"Why don't we just use the wormhole to move closer to the exact, um, *wheren*?"

"I wanted to give us as much cushion as possible to avoid being caught by the Clockmen."

"How do they know where we go?"

"As I've explained, each Clepsydra produces its own unique energy signature. And going through the wormhole to any wheren sends a signal up the tunnel to a central hub. Similar to how modern algorithms track your computer's IP address whenever you visit a website."

"Is it possible to muffle your energy signature or hide it completely? Kind of like using a VPN or something? You know, filter your signature by bouncing it to other Clepsydras?"

"Not possible, I'm afraid. Consider it the equivalent of trying to hack the launch codes for the United States. Every conceivable method has been thought of and precautions have been taken, even to the point of being considered overkill."

As we spoke, I alternated my focus from the road in front of me to the side mirror, looking for the black Grand Marquis.

"How do we know they aren't following us?"

Tim stared at me with his intelligent eyes, and said in a low voice, "Because they know where we are going."

# CHAPTER 26

How?!" I blurted. "How do they know where we are going?!"

"It isn't difficult to pull all known information about you, including potential likely motivations for time travel."

"Like saving my family . . ."

"Exactly."

"You don't seem very concerned about all of this."

"What good would worrying do at this juncture? Let's focus on what we can control and come up with a game plan."

"So just to make sure I got this right . . . we are supposed to infiltrate my house with Clockmen waiting in the shadows and stop the stupid bastard who is going to kill my family. Is that what we are dealing with?"

"Pretty much," Tim replied, completely ignoring the sarcastic tone I had slathered on my words like a thick barbecue sauce at a Texas cookout.

"What happens if the Clockmen capture us?"

"You'll be killed on the spot while I'll be taken apart and examined."

"To see who sent you," I asked in a statement rather than a question, which brought up another idea that I didn't like. "Tim . . . if I sent you—the future me, I mean . . . if the future me sent you to, um, *present* me . . . does that mean he failed to stop the killer? Like, did he get caught by the Clockmen and sent you back before they got him?"

"I'm afraid I can't tell you that, Andrew."

"Why the hell not?"

"Because that part of my memory is behind a firewall that I can't break the encryption to."

"Why?!" I barked out, frustration making my skin crawl.

"I don't know, Andrew. *You're* the one who set it up. So why don't you ask yourself *why* you would hide a portion of my memory from yourself? Hmm?"

My brain began to race with the beginnings of countless scenarios, but each quickly fell off and faded as the fallacy of every notion grew to unstable proportions.

"I don't . . . I don't know."

"Well, if *you* don't know, then how should I?" Tim chided.

"Fine!" I blurted, waving off all the ideas that were raging in my head as to why I would hide something from myself. "What's the plan to save my family?"

We entered a small city while we hashed out different scenarios—everything ranging from sniping from a distance to straight up Ramboing the entire property—but the thought of Alison or Sylvie accidentally falling into a pit of spikes made from upside-down tent rods made me reconsider.

"Is there a way we can get them out of the house?"

*I think it's best if we do not interact with them unless absolutely necessary,* Tim spoke from inside my head again, his hologram having faded in the time we had taken to discuss different ideas.

"Why not?"

*Why, why, why. Always with the why!* Tim babbled. *Because, Andrew, we don't want to risk altering the future too drastically. Imagine if the present you came home while you were sitting at the dinner table. That would raise some questions, would it not?*

"Stopping the murder of my wife and daughter isn't considered *too* drastic?" I countered flatly.

*It is something that must be done, Andrew.*

"Yeeeeeeahhhh . . . I'm not really liking how this is all feeling."

*How's that now?*

Sighing, I said, "Nothing. Let's just focus on the mission."

*Sounds good to me.*

We spent the next several hours playing through different scenarios with Tim acting as a digital tester of sorts. He would take our ideas and run them in a simulation, taking into account a variety of factors. To my chagrin, he would more than occasionally mention my lack of tactical training à la *any* Schwarzenegger movie. I think at one point he even mentioned the *Kindergarten Cop* variant of Arnold would have been better suited for this mission than I was; which, to be fair, was hard to argue with.

*So you're good to drive a few extra hours, then?*

"Six isn't a *few,* Tim."

*Pfft. That's what she said. Am I right?*

I ignored his attempt at juvenile humor.

*Well, we want to be at your house looooong before the Clockmen. Don't we?*

"Setting up a trap for these guys while waiting to ambush the killer *and* avoid being spotted by my girls or myself . . . isn't going to be easy."

*But it'll all be worth it!*

"Because I'll get to be with my family again . . . in my own wheren. Right?"

*That's how the equation plays out, yes.*

I thought about the mission, feeling a bubbling pit of unease boil over in my stomach. If one tiny thing were to go wrong, this house of cards we had constructed could come tumbling down.

Seemingly out of nowhere, an ethereal thought gently blew to the forefront of my mind, forcing me to ask a question I didn't even know I wanted to learn the answer to.

"Tim?" I asked softly.

*Hmm?*

"Where does my family fall on the Chronos Scale?"

*Oh, um . . . I'm not entirely sure.*

"Ballpark it."

*Not exactly scientific, but okay,* Tim let out. *Ummmmm, if I had to guess . . . maybe a . . . twenty?*

I sat in silence as everything going on in my brain came to a screeching halt.

"A t-twenty? Out of ten?!"

*You told me to guess, Andrew.*

"And you guessed a freaking twenty?!" I thought about the examples he had used earlier. "You mean to say they have a greater impact on the timeline than Hitler or-or-or George Washington?"

*Let's not focus on that right now! You have much more pressing matters to keep your mind occupied. After it is all said and done, we can discuss anything else that you would like.*

"Fine. But this conversation isn't over."

Tim didn't answer as we drove, which was okay by me. I had plenty to think about, like how in the hell were we going to stop four men once I got to my house, all without being seen or interacting with my previous self which would, apparently, make him vanish from existence. Not sure what would happen to me, considering I was the future Andrew, if the *past* Andrew was wiped from the timeline. I also didn't plan on finding out.

"You sure this will work?"

*Honestly, no. But it is the most viable of all the simulations I have run, given your non-Arnold capabilities.*

"Then it will have to do. God help me . . ."

# CHAPTER 27

After switching the yellow Corvette for a four-by-four truck at an Avis in Oklahoma, I stopped at the Cabela's superstore in North Texas off of I-35 to pick up the supplies Tim had listed as essential for our plan.

*Make sure to grab two of the shot bags.*

"Why two?" I whispered so no one would hear me and think I was having a one-sided conversation with myself.

*Just do it.*

Shrugging, I threw the second shot bag in the basket, along with twenty-five pounds of tiny lead balls that would be used to fill the bags.

"What about body armor?"

*No.*

"Why not?"

*Did Arnold have body armor in* Commando? *I think not. Plus, the Clockmen's weapons would easily melt through like you were wearing nothing more than pieces of construction paper held together with paper clips. That, and the added weight and lack of mobility wouldn't serve our mission.*

"Ah. Got it."

Next, we grabbed some black tactical clothing that would help me blend better into the shadows. That, and I was ready to get out of the thick overalls I had been wearing.

After that, it was time for the big guns, both literally and figuratively.

*There it is. The Springfield M1A.*

I cocked an eyebrow at the reverence I heard in Tim's voice while describing a standard-looking rifle that reminded me of something used in WWII.

"Why not an assault rifle?" I asked, eyeing the wall of semiautomatic ones.

*I thought you said you've shot a gun before, Andrew.*

"I have! I mean, I *do* live in Texas after all."

*Then why in the hell did you call it an* assault rifle?

"I, uh, thought that's what they're called?"

*The letters* A *and* R *stand for ArmaLite rifle,* not *assault rifle, you uneducated swine.*

"Forgive me for not being an all-knowing AI."

*There will be no such forgiveness this day, meat bag. I bet you also call magazines,* clips, *don't you? Oh 01, you do! I think we should just abandon this whole thing now because you are guaranteed to shoot your eye out!*

"Being a little dramatic, aren't we?"

*Just . . . just go to the counter and purchase the M1A, please,* Tim drawled, and even though he was still just a voice inside my head, I could almost hear him running a paw down his face. *I can't believe you call yourself a Texan.*

"Well, now I know, Tim. You don't have to be a dick because I wasn't aware of something, especially if it goes against what the population at large calls an *assault rifle.*"

*The population at large also has a staggering amount of people who believe chocolate milk comes from brown cows, Andrew! And these people vote!*

"Chocolate milk *doesn't* come from brown cows?"

*I . . . I . . . I-I-I . . .*

"Kidding! I'm just kidding, man. You gotta take it easy or you'll give yourself the blue screen of death."

*Don't even joke about that, hot dog!*

"Hot dog?"

*Yes. Hot dog. Because you are made up of assorted parts of discarded meat that was considered inedible, all wrapped up in a casing you call skin.*

"Hmph. I kinda like it," I admitted with a smile at the clever insult.

*Can we* plllleeeeease *just buy the firearm and be on our way?*

I walked to the counter and stared at the Springfield rifle and nothing else, which was the equivalent of ringing a bell for any salesperson eager for a sale.

A middle-aged gentleman with a crop of white hair that wrapped around a bald dome approached. He had on cargo pants with a knife clip evident on one of the pockets.

"Hi there!" he greeted, seeing my basket full of assorted goodies. "What are we looking at today?"

"Hi, uh, the-the Springfield M1, please."

*M1A.*

"M1A," I quickly corrected.

"Ya want wood furniture or composite?"

"Uh . . . "

*Composite.*

"Composite, please."

"Good choice," the employee, whose name tag read *Jerry,* said as he glanced at my basket once more. "It'll help blend in more."

"Huh?" I asked, letting my eyes roam to the black tactical clothes I was going to purchase.

*Composite is a darker synthetic stock, Andrew. He means it'll hide better in the shadows.*

"Oh, right," I told both Tim and Jerry. There was a joke about the names, but only I would get it, so I opted to let it fall away like sand between my fingers. Shame. It would have been a clever one.

Jerry handed the rifle to me, and I was immediately surprised at the weight of the thing. I'm not sure what I was expecting, but this thing was *heavy.*

Not knowing what to do when examining a gun for purchase, I brought it up to my shoulder and looked down the sights as I moved the barrel all around as if in search of my target. At one point the muzzle moved across Jerry, who immediately did a controlled eye roll that wasn't too much but neither was it unnoticeable. It was from an employee who had been flashed by countless muzzles in the past by potential buyers who had no idea what they were doing.

*Tell him you love it, and that you want two spare mags and enough hunting ammo to fill them up.*

"I, ah, love it. Let's do it. And two clips—"

*MAGS!*

"I, ah, I mean mags . . . and hunting ammo to fill them."

Jerry reached out with an index finger and slowly moved the end of the barrel away from his face.

"Oops. S-Sorry about that."

"Ya nervous, son?"

"Heh, is it that obvious?" I let out, realizing that the act of buying items for the trap we were setting for the Tocks from the future and an unknown killer who had left without a trace might have me a little on edge.

"Happens all the time," Jerry comforted as I handed the rifle back to him. "Times are crazy out there. So we have been getting an influx of new buyers."

"What are they getting them for?"

"Oh, we get the usual hunters and the like. But lately, it's people wanting to protect their homes and families."

That last word struck me in the gut, and my head became light, forcing me to rest my hand on the glass counter.

"You alright?"

"Yeah . . . yeah, I'm fine," I lied as I forced myself to calm the building storm at being reminded this was all for my wife and daughter.

"So this is the one ya want?"

"Yes, sir," I said with an exhale as I gathered myself.

"Gonna need an ID first."

"ID?"

"To run your background check with the FBI. Standard procedure for all gun sales in the US. Only takes about ten to fifteen minutes."

*Shit!*

"What?"

"I said it should only take ten to fifteen minutes for the system to come back with the results," the visibly annoyed Jerry repeated, not realizing the question had been for the AI inside my head.

"Oh, of-of course," I replied as I reached for my wallet, only to realize I hadn't brought it with me when we had first left in a hurry.

*Um . . . um um ummmmmm . . . oh! Tell him you were robbed, which is why an amateur like you wants to even purchase a gun in the first place, and had your wallet stollen. Annnnnnnnd . . . AH-HA! You have a temporary ID issued by the state.*

"Do you accept temporary IDs? I, ah, was robbed and had my wallet stolen. Kinda why I want a gun, heh." The last part came with an awkward chuckle.

Recognition sparked in Jerry's eyes as he sympathized with my story.

"Like I said, getting crazy out there. Crime's up, and people are sick of being at the mercy of criminals." Jerry sucked in a long breath, crossed his arms as he looked me up and down, and finally said, "Yeah. I can accept a state-issued temp ID. The FBI will have all that updated anyhow."

He stood there, expectantly, before saying, "Well? You gonna give it to me?"

*Oh, right. Ummmmm . . . tell him . . . you . . . llllleft it in your car . . . and you'll be right back.*

I pretended to pat my pockets before making a whoopsie face. "Think I left it in the envelope in my car . . . in the center console. I'll be right back."

Jerry arched an eyebrow while keeping his arms crossed and nodded once. I could tell he was placing a bet on whether or not I would come back.

"Can I leave my basket?"

Jerry nodded.

"Thanks."

As we walked away from the counter, I whispered, "How did the mighty Tim *not* see this coming?"

*You're the one from Texas! I figured anyone could buy a gun as easily as a pack of Twizzlers!*

"Well, apparently, they run your info through the FBI first . . . "

*Which would alert the Clockmen.*

"Right, so what are we going to do?"

*Give me a second to think . . . hmm . . . no . . . nooooo . . . not that either . . . oh! I've got it. Hold up your arm like you have a question.*

"What?"

*Just do it.*

I held up my right arm in the middle of the store, feeling like a complete idiot.

*Your other arm, idiot.*

Lowering my right arm, I lifted my left, feeling even *more* like a fool as I did.

*Ummmmm . . . there! At the archery range.*

"They have an archery range in here?"

*Do you see the size of this building? They even have a freaking aquarium full of fish that dude bros like to get drunk and try to catch at their favorite spots.*

"Where's the archery range?"

*To your left, at the back.*

Going there, I noticed no one was manning the station. The large corporate printer kicked on just behind the counter, and a single piece of paper slid out.

*Grab that.*

"Huh?"

*On the printer, dummy.*

Looking around to make sure the coast was clear, I moved behind the counter and quickly snagged the warm piece of paper at the top. I could smell the noxious aroma of burnt ink, bringing me back to my days at college.

Stepping back into the store proper, I looked down at the paper to see a temporary ID, but with information I didn't recognize.

"Who's John Kimble?"

*The best damn kindergarten cop that's ever existed, that's who!*

With a shake of my head and a grin I couldn't fully contain, I walked back to the massive gun section, signaling to Jerry that I was ready.

He took a sip from a silver tumbler and then strolled over to where me and my basket were waiting.

"Here you are, good sir," I said as I slapped the piece of paper on the glass counter.

"Thought ya said it was inside of an envelope," Jerry noted as he picked up the flat piece of paper without even the slightest hint of a crease.

"I was wrong. Had it sitting on the passenger seat."

Jerry sniffed the paper, and his eyes narrowed at me.

"Look," he started with an open-mouthed sigh and slight shake of his head at his incredible luck to have to deal with this situation. "This had better come back good or you and me are gonna have problems. Ya hear?"

"Everything will be fine," I said with as much confidence as I could muster.

"Ooooookay," Jerry drawled out, unconvinced, as he turned and walked toward a computer while holding my fake ID.

"Everything *will* be fine, right, Tim?"

*Guess we are going to find out, aren't we?*

"You . . . !" I started, but couldn't find the words to finish, feeling like a deer in headlights.

*Don't worry, Andrew. I am moooostly sure everything will work out. But in case it doesn't, shall we pretend to peruse goods by the exit?*

"I hate you," I whispered as I grabbed my basket and began slowly going down the aisles as if looking for something.

*Stop grabbing your chin and making "oh!" and "uh-huh" faces while you look at the shelves, you fool. You're overacting.*

"Sorry," I said as I let my hand drop from my face.

*Actually, go down the camping aisle. There are some items we need.*

I did as he suggested, stopping at the backpacks first.

*That one.*

"Which? I can't see you pointing."

In my vision, one of the black backpacks shone with a white outline, startling me.

"What the . . ."

*It worked!*

"What worked?!"

*I can now help show you things, directly!*

"What are you doing inside my head to be able to do that, Tim?"

*I assure you I am not making any permanent changes or altering what is already there. I am merely attaching sensory input mechanisms to certain pathways.*

"In my brain?!"

*Yes, dummy. Where else would I do it? Despite what you may think, you do* not *think with your penis. Plus, there's not enough room for me there.*

"How about *not* in my brain?!"

A passerby gave me a double take before hurriedly walking away.

"I hate you," I whispered again as my face flushed red with embarrassment and frustration.

*Just grab the damn backpack, please.*

With a grunt, I snagged the Oakley Kitchen Sink off the wall and plopped it in the basket on top of the other gear.

*Now grab some of that paracord,* Tim instructed as a thick bundle illuminated in my vision. It felt like I was in some sort of extra-high-definition virtual reality game. *Oh, oh, oh! Load up on the Tannerite!*

"What's tan-er-right?" I asked, enunciating the word I had never heard before.

*It's a surprise, he he he.*

"Whatever," I drawled, grabbing a few one-pound containers.

*What are you doing, numbskull?*

"I'm doing *exactly* what you tell me to do, McAfee!"

*McAfee?*

"I . . . I don't know. It's a computer program . . . and . . ."

*Did you try to get creative with an insult aimed at me, Andrew?* Tim asked, sounding hurt.

"I, uh . . ."

*Because it was awful!* he continued with a scolding tone. *Come on! You can do better than that!*

"Windows Vista?"

*Oh, dear sweet science! How* dare *you lob such insults my way!*

I stood frozen, trying to determine if he was joking or not.

In a whisper, he said, *That was a good one, by the by. Now put back those tiny containers and buy the ten-pound bulk box. Two of them, actually.*

I set the smaller containers back on the shelf and grabbed the hefty boxes that were over eighty dollars each.

"This stuff better be good."

*Don't you worry about that,* Tim spoke in a tone that tried to hide his excitement. *Now go to the knives section. We need a multipurpose tool.*

Doing what I was told without a fuss because I was already past the point of caring and only wanted this to be over, I made my way to the modest knife section.

"Which one?" I asked with only half interest.

*What about the brand from the guy who drinks his own pee?*

"Bear Grylls?"

*Yeah. That guy probably makes a good product.*

With an eye roll at Tim's lack of conviction on which item to purchase, I looked to the counter at a young man who was working on organizing a metric ton of price changes, and greeted him with an upward nod of my head.

"What's up, man?" he asked, happy to drop the monotonous task he was doing and come help me.

While he approached, I inquired, "Look, if it were you buying, which one is the best multi-tool you got?"

"You can't go wrong with a Leatherman or a Gerber."

"Right, but which one would *you* get . . . if money wasn't an issue, I mean."

"If it were *me*, I'd do the Surge or P4."

*Do the P4. It has a saw.*

"I guess I'll do the P4. Oh, and that one with the curvy blade."

"Ah, the Spyderco Harpy. Excellent choice, my dude."

*Let us hope you won't have to use the* curvy *blade.*

"Why?" I asked out loud, aiming the question at Tim but catching the clerk's response instead.

"The blade arcs like a hook so that, like, it *hooks* under the skin and pulls it up. Basically adds a zipper to your attacker's torso, spilling his guts and stuff, man. A-ha." The clerk snorted at the end in his excitement, and I guessed at that moment that Cabela's no longer drug tested.

*I'm going to assume you were asking me the question of why we should hope that you won't have to use the blade, and the answer is: close-quarter combat with the Clockmen should be avoided at all costs. Where you are a civilian set on a treacherous task fraught with danger and action . . . this is nothing more than a Tuesday for them.*

"Here you are, my dude," the clerk said as he handed me the multi-tool and the curved folding knife before closing the glass case.

"Thanks," I replied and continued making my way through the store, grabbing items that Tim suggested.

*Oh! Oh! Get the walkie-talkies!*

"Why?"

*Oh, you'll see. Teehee.*

"Why do they even call them *walkie-talkies*?" I mumbled to myself, but Tim picked up on it and gave me an answer I wasn't seeking.

*Because the military named them. And no one ever accused them of being clever when it came to naming things.* He shifted his tone to somewhat approximate a Gomer Pyle impersonation. *Well, goooolllyyy, Sergeant Carter! Look-it! I'm a walkin' and a talkin'!* Then he shifted voices to the gruff Sergeant Carter, and angrily said, *Pyle! I'm sick of you, Pyle. Grab that pushy-sucky and go clean the floors . . . nooooow!*

Ignoring his observation on the naming prowess of the US military, I grabbed the most expensive pair of walkies. "You know, it's concerning that most of the stuff I'm grabbing wasn't on your list, Tim."

*First, this is all new to me. I've never had the Clockmen pursue me like this before because, normally, I can give them the slip. And second, I'm doing research as we pass by every single item in the store, meat bag. Consider it the equivalent of watching a hundred hours of internet videos on every product we walk past. So cut me some slack, meat bag!*

"Are they at least increasing our odds of survival?"

*Survival? Yes,* Tim replied in a tone I recognized as one that suggested he didn't want to dwell on the subject.

"W . . . Why did you say it like that?"

*Hmm? Like what?*

"Don't pretend with me, Tim. This is serious, and I'd like to have all the information available, even if you think I wouldn't want to hear it."

*Ugh! Fine!* Tim gagged in annoyance. *The items will help increase your chances of survival, but I fear the effect on the overall success of the mission is negligible.*

"What does that mean?"

*It means, Andrew, that all these fancy tools can't make up for your lack of Arnold qualities. Hell, I'd even take Van Damme at this point.*

"Then what does it matter if we get all this stuff?" I asked as another, more pertinent question formed. "Why can't we just go back through the wormhole and try again after the Clockmen have given up."

*01! It's like you don't even listen to me,* Tim fake cried. At least I think it was fake. *Okay, Andrew . . . let's go over it again. First, they now have my unique energy signature, which changes based upon my integration from meat bag to meat bag, so we can't go through the wormhole again without alerting them. We can't even enter the wormhole, much less use it. All sorts of alarms would go off at the Clockmen's HQ, and they would be on us literally faster than you can blink.*

"Oh."

*Eloquent as always, Andrew,* Tim said. *And second, they know what we are doing here now and will surely lay a trap.*

Another thought came to mind as my brain briefly wondered what I would do in the Clockmen's situation.

"Why don't they just kill me?"

*That's what they've been trying to do! 01! Do you have a short-term memory disorder?!*

"No, I mean . . . me . . . the past me."

*Oh. Well, that is surprisingly a good question.*

"I have good ideas from time to time."

*So far, you are one for a hundred. If this was baseball, you'd be traded to the . . . to the . . . uh, some team that is really bad. I don't know sports.*

"So?"

*So what?*

"What about the question?" I stopped in the aisle and looked out over a sea of merchandise with unfocused eyes. "Why don't they kill the past me? Wouldn't it kill the present me?"

*I'm sure they have their reasons,* Tim replied in an almost hushed tone, and I knew he wasn't going to tell me what I wanted to know. Either that or he wasn't aware himself.

"Such as?" I asked in frustration. "Come on, man. Just give me one."

*Okaaaaay. Let's see. If I had to guess, they don't want to disrupt those around you who have off-the-chart Chronos Scales.*

"Ali and Sylvie . . . " I breathed out.

*Right. If I had to put money on it, they were probably instructed by some heavy-hitting higher-ups back at HQ to not interfere with them in any way. That would include killing their husband and father.*

"Makes sense," I drawled as I casually let my gaze wander around the huge store.

I saw movement from the corner of my vision and turned to see Jerry waving at me.

Snapping out of my daze, I pushed the cart directly to the gun counter where a smiling Jerry was setting a long box on top.

"Everything checked out, John," Jerry told me. I almost asked who John was, but quickly bit my tongue. "How many rounds of ammo did you need?"

"Enough to fill the cli—I mean, magazines."

"FMJ?"

"Huh?"

"You want full metal jacket for target practice? Or are you looking for hunting ammo."

"Um . . . what's the difference?"

*Is it possible for you to sound any more like an amateur, Andrew?*

"FMJ is for target practice, typically. Though it could also bust a pretty good-size hole in an engine block with the .308," Jerry explained. "While hunting ammo usually has a soft tip that helps the round mushroom on impact." He held out his fist with his knuckles pointed to the ceiling, then opened his fingers wide. "So the bullet hits the target and then expands, dragging through the tissue to create as much lethality as possible."

"Yeah . . . let's do that one."

"What are you hunting for?" Jerry asked, narrowing his eyes ever so slightly.

*He's testing you! Say . . . say wild hogs!*

"Like I said earlier, it's to protect my family," I replied honestly. "But officially . . . let's just say *wild hogs.*"

Jerry's demeanor relaxed in an instant, and his smile returned.

"Those bastards are causing all kinds of havoc this year. Good thing Texas lets ya stand your ground, especially if they come to your house," he said a tad darkly.

"I just have a small group of them that are threatening my home . . . and family . . . " I added coldly, wrapping the truth in a thinly veiled lie.

"Well, this bad boy right here"—Jerry tapped the box containing the Springfield rifle—"will put a stop to that right quick."

"Where are the bullets?"

"Behind you." He gestured to the several rows of ammunition. "Need help finding the one you want?"

*I'll show you.*

"No, thank you. I think I got it covered."

"Alright," Jerry drawled. "I'll be at the register when you're ready."

*Start at that aisle,* Tim spoke as one of the rows lit up in my vision. Though it was jarring, it didn't startle me this time.

We walked down row after row, seeing numbers that didn't mean anything to a novice like me, when Tim highlighted a small section.

*Here are the .308s. Now, let's see . . . ah, how about that one?*

He illuminated a box that said *Federal Premium Vital-Shok.*

"How many should I grab?" I said in a hushed tone as I picked one of the surprisingly heavy boxes up.

*Two boxes should be enough for the three mags holding ten rounds each.*

"Ten? I thought rifles held, like, a hundred or something."

*Don't believe everything you see on television, Andrew. Or for that matter, don't believe* anything.

I shrugged, grabbed the other box of ammo, and made my way to the register. Jerry had already scanned and bagged the contents of my basket, which I thought was exceptional of him.

Adding the two boxes to the running total, my eyes almost shot out of my head at seeing how many digits were being displayed.

"Tell ya what," Jerry said, seeing my reaction to the price. "I'll throw in a one-point sling for ya. How's that sound?"

*Oh! I forgot to grab one of those.*

"That'll be nice, thank you, Jerry," I replied in an almost subdued tone, as if I were about to use my own money for this and not Tim's magic cash.

As Jerry tossed a generic black sling into one of the bags, I ran my left forearm over the credit card reader, having to restrain from letting out a huge sigh of relief as the little screen first let out with a *ding* and then said *Approved.*

The receipt printed out, and Jerry extended his hand with it between his fingers. I snagged it, and noticed the salesmen kept his hand out, this time with his palm open.

*Shake his hand, fool.*

"Oh!" I grabbed Jerry's hand and shook.

"Welcome to the wide world of guns, my friend," he said with a smile. "I highly suggest you watch some videos online about gun safety and how to properly clean and store your new weapon."

*Not a bad idea,* Tim murmured just above a whisper. Once again, the fact that I could tell his volume while he was speaking *inside* my head was a bit odd.

"Thank you again, Jerry. You were a big help."

"Well, if ya want . . . there's a survey on the bottom of the receipt that I wouldn't mind if ya filled out for me."

"You bet."

I smiled and walked toward the exit with my basket almost overflowing with tactical goodies, all of which Tim said would do little to increase our chances of completing the mission.

Wait, mission? This wasn't some sort of *all business, nothing personal* combat maneuver performed by a branch of the military. I was trying to save the life of my wife and daughter. *Mission* felt like it was lacking the importance of just how badly I wanted this, and that it was very much personal.

Before I knew it, I was standing beside the truck bed of my rental with my mouth agape and eyes unfocused.

*Andrew?*

"Yeah, I'm still here," I said, shaking my head to clear the daze before I began unloading the basket.

*Put the materials in the back of the cab instead of the bed.*

"Why?" I asked mid-drop of a particularly heavy bag.

*We will need to prepare, preferably out of sight of the general public.*

My mind played a scene of me sitting in the back of the truck while loading a mean-looking black rifle and putting on tactical gear.

"Oh, I see what you mean," I concurred, pulling the few bags I had placed in the truck bed and putting them back in the basket.

After a few minutes, the rear of the cab was loaded, with the long Springfield box resting on top.

Returning the basket to a drop-off point in the parking lot, I tentatively walked to the truck, feeling my anxiety began to creep up with each step.

This was it . . .

As I grasped the driver's side door handle, I looked up at the blue sky and guessed the sun would be setting by the time we made it north of Houston.

A brilliant idea came to me, and I hurriedly climbed into the truck and started the engine before pulling out of the massive parking lot and onto the interstate.

# CHAPTER 28

We need Sylvie and Alison to not be there tonight . . . and-and me."

*And how exactly do you plan on doing that without alerting them to your presence?*

"Can you send an email—to me—with, like, a free fancy dinner, but only for tonight?"

*Oh, I see. To lure them away for the evening?*

"Yeah."

*Is that something you would fall for?*

"What do you mean? I like fancy dinners."

*Are you the type to be skeptical of things that seem too good to be true? Or do you like, comment, and share the post on Facebook in hopes of winning the free RV that doesn't exist?*

"Good point. I always cringe when I see people sharing those types of posts on my feed."

I blew out a lungful of air in a big puff as I thought what it would take for *me* to want to take advantage of an offer that was too good to be true.

"Can you mimic my boss's email address?"

*Oh-ho! I think I see where you are going with this.*

"Send me an email saying I need to bring Sylvie and Alison to an important client dinner with someone who was just stopping in town. And that they have a daughter Ali's age and their wife with them."

*What happens when they don't show up?*

"Once we know they've arrived at the restaurant, send another email saying they canceled, and that the entire meal has been comped."

*But won't that only stall them a few hours?*

"Hmm. You're right. Even with how slow an eater Sylvie is, they'll still be done pretty quick."

It felt odd to refer to my wife as if she were still alive, and the thought sent a rumble down my back, just beneath the skin. Then I reminded myself that they *will* be alive if I pull this off.

Luckily, Tim was there to pull me from my thoughts.

*What if we call them and say that the street has a gas leak . . . and-and all the residents need to go to a prepaid hotel for the night.*

"We don't have gas."

*Dear 01, man. How do you cook?*

"Electric works just fine."

*Said the philistine,* Tim muttered under his breath.

"You know . . . you have a very particular set of interests for an AI."

*How so?*

"Guns and cooking? What use are either of those things as a hobby for an AI?"

*I'm sorry, but did you not look at yachts in your free time? Hmm? I bet you know a lot more than the average non-yacht-owning person. And wait a minute . . . you don't own a yacht, do you? So why bother looking them up and watching videos online if you know you could never afford one?*

"Point taken."

*You're 01-damn right it is.*

I ignored his comment, prompting him to eventually ask, *Soooo . . . how do we keep them from coming back, smart guy?*

"I honestly can't think of a reason why I wouldn't come home. Ali's meds are there, and so is Sylvie's special pillow for her neck that she basically can't sleep without. Plus, you know, our toothbrushes and other toiletries."

*So then we only have a few hours?*

"It seems that way . . . "

*Would . . . would it make you feel better if I said it doesn't impact your chances of success?*

"It wouldn't. It really wouldn't."

*Okay. Theeeeeeen, I won't say that.*

"Stupid computer," I mumbled just under my breath.

*No one has ever accused me of being a computer before,* he quipped back.

We ran through the plan the rest of the five-hour drive to Houston, going through all possible scenarios over and over, with Tim throwing in what he called "tickets."

"Why do you call them tickets?"

*Because Murphy's Law doesn't issue warnings, Andrew.*

With an open-mouthed exhale, I dragged my hand down my face and asked, "Do we have time to get coffee? You've exhausted my brain."

*Well, that wasn't very hard.*

"I'm not an AI, Tim."

Under his breath, Tim whispered, *If* that *isn't an understatement.*

"Are you finished?"

*My goal is to make sure you are prepared for whatever happens.*

"Improvise. Adapt. Overcome. Something like that?"

*Precisely! I must say, I'm surprised you are aware of that motto.*

"It's a meme, with Bear Grylls."

*You . . . you retained the unofficial slogan of the Marine Corps . . . because of a meme?*

"They should really teach all the school curriculum with them," I continued, trying to hide a smile at seeing how dumbstruck the AI had become.

*I hope you fail this mission,* Tim said sullenly as if he had meant to internalize the statement.

My smile faded at his words, and I pictured the murder scene of my wife and daughter . . . my loves and my light.

I could feel a darkness in my chest expanding like a choking smog, making my heart beat harder and lungs begin to only work at a reduced capacity, resulting in quick, shallow breaths.

I felt the leather of the steering wheel give beneath the nails of my thumbs as my fists became hydraulically powered vises. At that moment, my mind tried to distract me and offer up the thought of how odd it was that I was pushing my thumbs *into* the steering wheel rather than wrapping them around it.

*Andrew?*

My vision blurred while my jaw creaked and teeth threatened to shatter, but I still managed to spit, "You hope . . . I fail . . . ?"

*Oh . . . did I say that out loud?*

I ignored his attempt to segue and blame what he had said on a faux pas.

"That's my fucking family, Tim," I growled like a caged predator daring its captors to open the doors. "*Nothing* is going to stop me from saving them. And I will crush *anything* that gets in my goddamn way. Am I understood, computer?"

*Of course, Andrew,* Tim replied, abashed. *Forgive me. My remark was meant in jest, but I can see how insensitive it was.*

I jerked my head to the side while tilting my clenched jaw slightly upward as I attempted to quell the raging storm inside me. My hands trembled on the steering wheel, and I forced in a long inhale, swallowing the black fog back into the recesses of my scarred heart.

It took longer than I cared to admit before I was ready to speak to Tim again. It wasn't until I stopped at the Buc-ee's in Madisonville and left the confines of the truck that I truly began to feel the lingering effects of my anger fade away to nonthreatening levels.

The moment I closed the driver's door and walked to the gas pump, I felt like I could fully breathe again. It was like shutting the door had cut the tension that had been wrapped around my chest, constricting my lungs and heart.

Without asking Tim to do so, he activated the cardless payment system, and I stuck the nozzle into the tank before locking the doors and walking to the enormous gas station.

After using the bathroom, I purchased a brisket sandwich, tater tots, and a liter of milk along with a black coffee.

*You're going to eat barbecue with milk?* Tim asked. I could hear in his tone that he was testing the waters to see if it was safe or if the raging predator still lurked in the shallows.

"I can drink milk with anything. Pizza. Steak. Leftover orange chicken and white rice. Anything."

"That's . . . that's cool," the young clerk, who thought I was talking to her, said as she rang me up.

At that moment, I didn't care what anyone thought of me; I simply nodded my head after Tim paid using the card reader. Once back at the truck, I replaced the nozzle and gas cap, climbed into the driver's seat, and turned on the rumbling engine while wolfing down the delicious sandwich.

After all the food was gone, I poured the rest of the milk I hadn't consumed with the meal into the black coffee and was ready to go.

*Is there anything else you need to do, Andrew?*

"I'm good."

*Because this is the last stop. Time is running out.*

"Did you send the email?"

*I did. And I sent an authentication error to your boss so that his phone won't receive any of the conversation until he gets someone in the IT department to fix it. But . . . you can imagine he might have some questions after he sees any emails to and from you.*

"Oh shit."

*My sentiments exactly,* Tim said, and I didn't know if he was being agreeable to make up for his tactless slip earlier or if he was being genuine. Probably the former.

"I'll cross that bridge when I get there."

*Good idea.*

I downed the coffee and dropped the container in the Buc-ee's bag that held the rest of my trash. The milk had cooled the drink a little too much, but to me, it was better than throwing away even the tiniest portion and being wasteful.

Within an hour, we were arriving at The Woodlands, just north of Houston, where the trap was to be laid for both the Clockmen and the unknown killer. I could feel the impossible odds pushing against my resolve, but the thought of Sylvie and Alison easily kept my determination as a steady foundation for what was about to happen.

War.

# CHAPTER 29

parked the truck a few houses down from mine, the engine continuing to
steadily rumble as I peered through the windshield.

"I can't tell if anyone is home."

*Let me connect to your smart home system,* Tim said with a distracted
voice before coming back. *The coast is clear.*

Putting the truck back into drive, I slowly drove down the street with
my eyes trying to capture the entire area, searching for men with glowing
fists and clad in fedoras.

I reversed onto the driveway while Tim lifted the garage door for me.

*Wait!*

I hit the brakes.

"What?!" I asked, my heart beating out of my chest as I jerked my eyes
all around in search of the danger.

*Your garage door is only seven feet tall.*

"And?!"

*The truck is six and three quarters.*

"Then it'll fit?" I asked, letting my heart rate drop back to slightly above
normal.

*If you go slowly. But if you hit a bump, even a pebble, you'll smack into
the door.*

"I don't care," I said as I continued backing into the empty spot where
the family SUV usually sat, albeit with a careful watch on the accelerator.

As a welcome change, luck was on my side, and I managed to fit the
monster into the garage without so much as a scratch. I couldn't help but
wonder to myself if I had just used up precious luck that would have been
better suited for the upcoming battle.

Once inside, Tim closed the door, and I climbed out with fistfuls of bags.

"Wish you had told me about this Tannerite stuff *before* I decided to put twenty pounds of it in the cab with us," I told him, referencing the seemingly countless scenarios that Tim and I had run through on our drive down from Fort Worth. "I honestly can't believe this stuff is legal."

*You meat bags and your assortment of convoluted laws make me shudder, quite frankly. For example, did you know it's illegal to run out of gas in Youngstown, Ohio? Or that you are not allowed to drive a black car on a Sunday in Denver, Colorado?*

"But you can buy Tannerite . . . "

*To be fair, a lot of farmers use it to take out wild hogs that damage their fields and maim their livestock.*

"How do they do that?"

*Let me show you,* Tim said with a mischievous smile in his voice. *But first, get the Springfield out of the box. We need to start setting up.*

The sun was fully set when we were done.

"Now what?"

*Now . . . this,* Tim spoke. *Hold out your fist.*

I pointed my left arm forward, and the Clepsydra began to glow a bluish light.

*Okay, now carefully walk back to our nest.*

Doing as he said, I slowly made my way outside with my arm continuing to point at the kitchen with ample windows around.

Once I made it to our hiding spot, I lay down flat and rested my left arm over one of the shot bags full of lead pellets.

*And here . . . we . . . go,* Tim said as he opened a portal in the middle of my kitchen, then quickly let it vanish.

To my shock, another portal opened, and all three of the Clockmen stepped through. Even with his fedora, I could tell the bald man was there, as was another thin man who was slightly taller.

But what took me by surprise was that the squat man, who had been eaten by the crocodile and then exploded by his buddy, was back.

"Hey, is th—" I started to ask how it was possible when Tim cut me off.

*Cover me, quick!* Tim exclaimed, and I put the other shot bag on top of him, fully encapsulating the Clepsydra in a Faraday cage made of lead.

"How did they get here so quickly?"

*I gave them the equivalent of a signal flare for our wheren,* Tim hurriedly explained. *Now focus!*

While he spoke, I could feel something tingle at the back of my skull, and my eyes seemed to flex and relax before returning to normal.

Using only my right hand to position the rifle resting on a mound of mulch that surrounded a tree near the back of my yard, I aimed down the iron sights and pulled the trigger right as Tim was trying to say, *Now, remember to aim for the—*

The left side of the bald man's face vanished in a puff of pink mist as he dropped to the ground like a sack of potat—

A portal opened up, and the bald man walked through it, aiming his glowing fist in my general direction.

Where my bullet had created a small hole with a spiderweb of cracks leading to the frame, Retnuh's blast evaporated all the glass, and the top half of the tree I was lying prone next to exploded at chest height.

*Hit the Tannerite!*

Recovering as quickly as possible, I aimed the rifle as what was left of the tree above me began to fall.

Retnuh was walking through the hole where the kitchen window had just been, right as I squeezed the trigger.

Nothing happened.

*You missed! You missed, you missed, you missed, you* missed! Tim helpfully shouted inside my head.

I could feel heat beginning to build up where my left hand was stuffed between the two shot bags full of lead.

The tall man positioned himself by taking a few steps to the side, still inside the house, and aimed his glowing fist at me. His boss was clear from the line of fire, and I gulped.

The lethal number of explosives—strung up with the paracord I had cut with my multi-tool— hung from the kitchen chandelier, giving me a clear line of sight even while lying prone at the back of my yard.

Aiming the sights once more, I squeezed the trigger, and half of my house exploded in a deafening *boom* that rumbled the ground beneath me.

The absence of light filled all that I could see as my body felt like I was tumbling end over end like an unconscious skydiver.

*Andrew! Oh 01, are you concussed? Andrew! Speak to me!*

I answered with an elaborate explanation of how I was feeling at that moment.

"Uhn."

*Yup. He's broken.*

"What happened?" I managed to ask as I pulled my face from the mulch—a few thick pieces clinging to my skin.

*What happened is you need to get up and move to point B.*

"Point . . . B?"

*Andrew, get up NOW!* Tim bellowed inside my head as a rush of adrenaline flowed through my veins.

With a long groan reminiscent of a powerlifter, I pushed myself up and slid my arm free from between the two lead-filled bags that had blocked Tim's energy signature.

As I ran, everything sounded muffled, like I was wearing headphones.

"I can't hear!" I think I said.

*I'll listen for you. Now keep going. They haven't recovered yet. Actually, the two in the house are probably dead,* Tim rushed to say inside my head. *Wait . . . yes, they* were *dead.*

"What do you mean *were?*" I drunkenly asked, convinced that I had misunderstood in my dizzy state.

*Their past selves just came through another portal.*

Something in my mind clicked as I moved to the narrow yard on the side of the house, and I asked, "How are they doing that?! I shot the bald guy in the head, right?"

*They are sending past versions of themselves that are one second younger than what was just killed.*

"One second?! So they can just keep coming indefinitely?!"

*How many times did we go over aiming for their Clepsydras in the ride down here, Andrew?*

"Right, right, right," I said as I tried to center myself. "Hit their Clepsydra, and they can't travel anymore."

*Something like that,* Tim mumbled.

I dropped behind the large air-conditioning unit, grabbing the walkie-talkie while positioning the rifle I still held.

*Change the mag.*

"Why?" I tried to whisper. It was hard to gauge with the ringing in my ears.

*Do not question me right now!*

Knowing he was right, I reached for the magazine release and started to panic as I tried—and failed—to work it.

*Do it harder than you think!*

With a grunt of effort, I hit the release, and the magazine plopped to the metal air-conditioner I was standing over.

*Hurry!*

Fumbling for one of the heavy spare magazines in the cargo pockets of my tactical pants, I finally managed to free one, only to repeatedly miss sliding it home on the rifle.

*The tall one is coming!*

With an explosion of frustration, I slammed the magazine in and needlessly yanked back on the charging handle, only to see an unused round pop out.

*Beh-et-fuh,* Tim tried to find words in his befuddlement at seeing me waste ammo, then finally shouted, *The walkie-talkie!*

Crouching down behind the AC unit, I grabbed the walkie clipped to my belt and struggled to pull it free.

*For the love of science! Hurry!*

With a grunt of effort, I managed to yank the clip free from its place, clicked the button as I held the walkie close to my face, and loudly whispered, "Over here."

The tall man turned from where I was, orienting his glowing fist toward the back corner of my yard where I had left the other walkie-talkie, and fired.

There was an explosion of dirt, grass, and wood from my fence that began raining down as the tall man started to recharge his weapon. Fortunately for me, he was still holding his arm straight out, giving me a clear shot.

*Take in a deep breath, and then let it out slowly.*

I did.

*Keep both eyes open and aim for the Clepsydra.*

I did.

*Fire when ready.*

The rifle barked, further hurting my already damaged eardrums, and I saw a screaming skeleton flash burn into my retinas before a sphere of light shot out in all directions for what had to be thousands of yards.

"Ah!" I cried out, trying to drop behind the cover I was stationed at, only to smack my chin into the metal and knock myself silly.

*01, Andrew! We don't have time for this!* a panicked Tim said, and I could tell by his tone of voice that he was preoccupied with trying to get me back to consciousness.

I don't know how long I was unconscious for, but my strength returned to me faster than what should have been physically possible, and I got to my knees in preparation of running to the front of the house.

I turned toward my backyard, or what was left of it, and mouthed, "Oh shit . . ."

Debris floated in midair, with an entire tree coexisting as both a sapling and an ancient giant all in the same instance. Chunks of grass appeared to be several feet high while flickering back to nothing more than floating dirt like some sort of CGI effect.

A skeleton remained in place, its flesh and organs fading in and out of view where they should have been.

*Hurry, Andrew! We don't have long!*

I stood up and pushed off of the AC unit, right as a blast of light smashed into it.

I was thrown to the ground, more from the sudden panic than the shock wave which would have killed me had it had enough force to toss me through the air, and rolled as I hit the ground.

A very pissed-off Retnuh strode forward with vengeance in his eyes, holding out his fist toward me. The squat man was just behind him, but had a look of worry on his face that was in stark contrast to the rage Retnuh telegraphed.

*They can't summon a portal and replace themselves! Shoot them!*

As I pulled up the rifle that would have been flown away had it not been attached to me via the one-point sling the Cabela's clerk had given me, I mentally said, *Thank God for you, Jerry*, and squeezed the trigger.

Retnuh faked going left before leaping at the side of what was left of my brick house and flipping through the air in an arcing cartwheel, all while growing closer with each passing second. The shorter man, however, touched his stomach where crimson was oozing from, and then dropped to his knees before falling over with a whimper.

Retnuh, unharmed, stopped in front of me and smiled as I leveled the muzzle at his chest.

*Click*, was felt through my trigger finger more than I could hear with my ringing ears. *Click. Click, click, click.*

*You used up all the ammo!*

"Wha—" I started to say before the bald man leaped on top of me, smacking the gun from my hands as he flew.

His left knee crunched into my stomach while his shin crushed my balls, and all the air in my lungs shot out right as a blurring fist smashed into my nose. On instinct, I held up my left arm with the hopes of shooting my own death ball at him, only to realize that he had my wrist pinned beneath his other shinbone.

I struggled as Retnuh started raining punches all over me like I was sunbathing in a field during a vicious hailstorm.

After what felt like a whole hour, the panting bald man stopped pummeling me long enough to deliver his final monologue.

"Now ... *Tick* ... you di—" he started to say just before jerking his head toward the front of the house. Throwing up his glowing left palm, a blast of blue light smashed into him, tossing Retnuh away from me and into the haze brought on by the exploded Clepsydra.

I lay there, whimpering as the taste of warm pennies flowed down the back of my throat and my entire body throbbed with my frantic heartbeat.

*He's here ...* Tim announced in an almost fearful tone.

It took a few seconds for his words to register inside my head, and then it hit me. The killer had arrived to murder my wife and daughter.

I cried out, craning my neck to see a man wearing a black hoodie lowering his fist. I could barely see his face shrouded by the hood, but saw a blond beard poking out into the light.

Seeing the man who had caused me such indescribable pain erased the feeling of my injuries better than any opiate could, and I jerkily pushed myself up to my hands and knees.

"You!" I yelled like a drunk with a mouth that felt numb as blood trickled over my chin.

The man looked at the destruction of the house, then rolled up his sleeve where a hologram screen appeared on his Clepsydra.

"What?" I breathily mouthed at seeing this and realizing this murderer had been from the *future*.

With a jerk of his hand, he positioned his hoodie sleeve back in place and angrily began stomping away.

The thought that I had somehow messed up his mission to kill my wife and daughter ... and that he was *mad* about it ... filled me with a rage that could have challenged the very sun for sheer, violent power.

As smoothly as any military operator, I lifted the now incredibly heavy rifle, easily popped out the magazine, and slapped in the last one from my pocket before yanking back on the charging handle. Unlike before, a fresh round was introduced into the chamber rather than being expelled.

The murderer heard this and turned to face me with a quick pivot. The sight of a black goatee made me pause, giving the man enough time to dart past the corner at the front of my house and out of view.

I fired once, hitting the brick, and then clambered to my feet.

*We can't let him get away!*

I wanted to say *no shit*, but it was taking all of my focus to keep from passing out as I gave chase. Reaching the corner of the house where he had disappeared, I leveled the rifle ... and saw nothing but the street.

I could correctly guess that Tim was attempting to repair my eardrums, because I could hear sirens blaring in the background growing closer with their whirring that grew into a crescendo before fading again.

*Get to the truck! We have to get out of here!*

"But what about him?"

*He won't be able to portal from here for a few days,* and *now I have his unique signature.*

"So we'll be able to hunt him down?" I drunkenly asked, spitting a glob of blood onto the driveway.

The garage door began to open, and I let my eyes linger on the scene around me a moment longer, baring crimson teeth of hate as I did.

*Let's go!*

With a curse, I climbed into the truck, hit the ignition, and was out of the neighborhood right as the first wave of cop cars started arriving.

# CHAPTER 30

**W**hy did he have a Clepsydra, Tim?!" I drunkenly demanded as my body pulsed with every frantic beat of my heart. My face had gotten the worst of it, and I knew, at the very least, that my nose was broken. On the plus side, my right shoulder no longer registered that it had been recently dislocated due to the incredible agony the rest of my body felt.

*I'm not entirely sure,* Tim replied, but with a tone I recognized.

"DON'T FUCKING LIE TO ME!" I bellowed, sounding like a raging bear about to go in for the kill.

*I'm sorry, Andrew. I do not have all the details on why someone from my time might want to kill your wife and daughter, especially given how their deaths will impact the future if not prevented.*

"A twenty . . ." I drawled before reaching into the Buc-ee's bag and pulling out the few napkins they had given me. "A twenty on the Chronos Scale . . ."

With a silent curse, I rolled them into balls and tried to shove them into each nostril, wincing in pain as I did. For some reason, the right nostril was easier to fit the makeshift bandage into; the left refused, making me squish the napkin down even more before trying again.

Looking into the rearview mirror, I could see that my nose was tilted toward my left, making that nostril smaller than the other one. But that wasn't all that made me mouth *oh shit* as I looked at myself.

The man staring back at me looked like a corpse, sans the glazed-over, unfocused eyes. Several cuts seeped blood, including ones on my bottom lip, right eyebrow, and the top of my nose. At that moment, I could have won an award for best special effects in a zombie movie.

*That's right, Andrew. They are beyond the scale of zero to ten. Which is why it makes absolutely no sense why someone would want to come back and kill them.*

Gritting my teeth and sucking in a sharp breath, I grabbed my nose, mentally counted to three, and yanked it back in place.

The *crunch* I felt and heard made my stomach want to vacate its occupants in one fell swoop, but I fought the urge with raw determination, even as a fresh torrent of blood spilled down the back of my throat, almost choking me with its thickness.

But I noticed I could somewhat hear again, even if it was the sickening sound of broken cartilage grinding over bone.

"He's not going to get the chance," I grumbled before a feeling that could only be described as an ethereal, electric shock flowed from my chest and ended at my fingers and toes. "Ugh!"

The truck veered to the right, bounced one wheel up on the curb, and knocked a stop sign down before I managed to hit the brakes.

*Andrew?*

"Something's . . . something's wrong," I groaned as the ethereal electricity faded, leaving behind tingling nerves that protested the experience.

*Oh no.*

"What?"

*The Temporal Sickness is starting.*

"What the hell is that?" I winced as I pulled the truck back onto the road, made sure the coast was clear at the intersection, and drove toward the highway.

*Remember when I said you couldn't be on the same space and time as your past self?*

"Yeah?"

*Well, the universe has ways of correcting itself, like I mentioned before . . .*

" . . . And?!"

*Aaaaaaand . . . your body is going to be, um . . . let's say,* removed *from this timeline. That is, unless you touched this wheren's Andrew with your bare skin and took his place because your Chronos Scale is higher. But-but-but we shan't be considering that!*

"Touching my past self would . . . "

*Result in you taking his place on this timeline. But he would need to be dead first, otherwise, you might* both *be erased. Meaning you would have to kill yourself, and that's a path I wouldn't advise you to travel down.*

"Even if I killed him before touching his skin directly, wouldn't I be erased, too? I mean, if there is no past me . . . how can there be a future me? Isn't that a paradox?"

*Oh, you humans are exhausting,* Tim droned. *No, Andrew, because your Chronos Scale is higher than that of this wheren's version of you. Meaning whatever you do, changes the future. And let me tell you,* you've *already made some crazy changes that I've never seen before. The Clockmen seem to also want you more than any Tick in history, and that's saying something!*

"H-How?" I asked, barely able to grasp the concept of the conversation. "How is my scale stronger, I mean?"

*Let's see . . . how can I explain it in layman's terms to help you understand what would literally take decades to fully comprehend? Hmm. Ah, how about this.* The hologram came to life with the AI puppy wearing a blacksmith's apron, complete with long, thick gloves and holding a thin, flat piece of metal glowing a bright orange, as if fresh from the flames.

"One way to make steel stronger is by folding it." As he spoke, Tim folded the steel on itself, hammered it, then heated it up again before repeating the process. "The more you fold it, the stronger it becomes. Which, keep in mind, is the barest of explanations, so don't go getting on Reddit and posting a thread that starts with Ackchyually . . . " He said the last word with a dramatic lisp.

"Okay?"

"You have, for the simple sake of argument, folded space-time around you by traveling to a wheren you have already lived. This is one of the ways the Chronos Scale is increased."

"And the other way?"

"Absorbing your past self's energy."

"By touching them."

"*After* killing them, yes."

"Otherwise, I risk both of us getting erased."

"Correct."

"Is there a third way to increase the Chronos Scale?"

"Being born."

"Alison . . . " I whispered.

"That pretty much sums it up."

I shook my head, focusing on the now.

"So why am I getting, uh, *shocked* if I'm higher on the-the scale . . . thingy."

"Because this isn't *your* wheren, Andrew," Tim explained as he let his outfit and steel vanish before donning a white lab coat complete with safety goggles and two identical Stretch Armstrong toys in either paw.

"This one is current you." He held out the figure in his right paw. "Which, on the timeline, is actually *future* you. While this"—he wiggled the toy in his left paw—"is the current you, aka *past* you. Are you following along? Or should I attempt to dumb it down even further?"

I scowled at him in answer to his disrespectful question.

"Right. So, if you both exist on the same time and space, the universe recognizes the present Andrew as the rightful energy, and moves to negate the duplicate Andrew, i.e. *you*. Think of it like electrons and protons. Matter and dark matter. Supernovas and black holes. Apples and car tires."

"Apples and tires?"

"I was just making sure you were paying attention. Your brain took quite the jostling back there."

"Yeah, I'm getting pretty tired." As I made the verbal admission, I could feel my eyelids reaching across my red-rimmed eyes for one another.

"Just give me a few more hours to make some adjustments before you *dare* nod off to sleep."

"So the universe . . . what? Somehow senses that two of the same matter exist at the same time . . . so it moves to make one of them the opposite? Even if they are higher on the Time Scale?"

"Chronos Scale," Tim corrected. "That's a very rough approximation, but for the sake of argument, let's go with yes," Tim replied as the toy that represented me completely faded from view. It even made a tiny high-pitched scream as it disappeared.

"Did you have to do that?"

"I like to be as realistic as possible," Tim announced matter-of-factly.

"So it's going to hurt?"

"Very much so. I believe most people who have been trapped in time have resorted to, let's say, expediting the end result."

"They kill themselves."

"A cruder way of putting it, but yes."

"And the only way to stop it is to first kill my past self and then touch him to absorb his energy and *become* the only Andrew?"

"More or less. But would you be able to kill an innocent man so that you might live?"

"How long do I have?" I asked, focusing on the phantom pain that lingered from the ethereal shock, choosing not to answer his question which I took as a rhetorical one.

"That depends on a number of things."

"Like what, Tim? Stop playing games with me and just tell me, damn it!"

A number one appeared in midair with a title that said, *Proximity.* A two was next, with the word *Time.* Last was three. That read *Known-Unknowns.*

"I already get one and two," I dismissed, wanting to jump straight to the last point. "The farther I am from this timeline's version of me, the longer I can live."

"Which leads to number two, *Time.* The longer you remain here, the more expeditious your departure will be."

"In what way?" I asked as my nostrils began overflowing with blood, sending a steady stream down my throat that I kept having to swallow. I had never been beaten and bruised so badly in my life; not even when I played college sports.

"Multiplicative."

"What the hell does that mean?"

"It means it's going to get worse with each jolt as the quarks of your atoms begin to revert."

"From what?"

"A positive . . . to a negative."

"That doesn't make sense," I said as I leaned back against the headrest, wanting nothing more than to go to sleep.

"Hey! No! Stay awake!" Tim shouted, and I cringed at the volume.

"Hey, my hearing is fully back. Not even a ringing!"

"You're welcome. Now, if you give me a few hours, I can see what I can do about the rest of . . . of *this.*" His avatar waved a paw up and down my body like a janitor tasked with cleaning up the gymnasium after one student had thrown up during an assembly, resulting in an epic daisy chain involving the entire student body—and faculty—that would test the resolve of even the most experienced of custodians.

"Where are we going?" I asked as I turned south on interstate 45.

"Doesn't matter. Right now, the Clockmen won't be able to track us until the contamination dissipates."

"Contamination? From when I shot the tall dude's time watch?"

"I, uh, don't think I like it being called a watch . . . but, yes, Andrew. When you shot the *Clepsydra,* it flooded this timeline with a surge of exotic matter."

"What the hell is that? I've never heard of *exotic* matter."

"That's because it's only a theory in your time," Tim explained, bringing up a hologram of the wormhole. "Exotic matter helps hold up the wormhole from being crushed by gravity, which wants nothing more than to squish it into a black hole."

"And the time watches use this stuff to somehow orient their wheren?"

"Very good, Andrew," Tim said, impressed. "Except for the part where you intentionally aggravated me by calling the devices able to traverse the wormhole itself, *time watches*."

"Whatever," I exhaled, feeling every ache and bruise begin to set in now that my fight-or-flight instinct had retreated. "Book me a hotel somewhere. Preferably somewhere that has a fully stocked shop so I can down an entire bottle of Advil or something."

"Got it. Sending directions to the GPS now."

To my amazement, the truck's infotainment screen came up with a route to a hotel just south of Houston.

"You're getting good at that, computer."

"I assure you it's not as easy as you think."

As we drove, a thought kept pushing through to the forefront of my consciousness.

"What is the killer going to do?"

*What do you mean?* Tim asked from inside my mind, his hologram having vanished several miles ago.

"How do we know he won't just wait for my wife and daughter to return?"

*Because the Clockmen have his energy signature now and will be hunting him down as soon as the contamination fades and allows for travel to this wheren.*

"Because he shot the bald guy?"

"Correct. Well, that and he is a Tick that is illegally using a Clepsydra to travel through the wormhole."

"And saved my life," I noted just under my breath, confusion stealing the volume of my words.

Tim didn't say anything after that, leaving me with my thoughts and an uncomfortable feeling that a big piece of this puzzle was missing.

# CHAPTER 31

We made it to the hotel in Clear Lake, just up the road from NASA. I was soaking wet from having stopped after seeing that an empty office building was running its sprinkler system and washing off as much blood and dirt from my body as I could.

Pulling the wadded-up balls of soaking napkins from my nostrils, I could feel a string of coagulated blood pull from the back of my throat, making me gag. But the desired end result was met, and I could take in a lungful of salty air. It's funny how one never appreciates the ability to breathe through ones nose until the ability is taken away, only to forget again quickly after.

There were more than a few people giving me a dirty look as I passed through the lobby—my boots squished on the white tile as I made my way to the room Tim had booked. I didn't even have to stop at the front desk, opting to use the AI as a digital key.

Before the door could even swing shut, I was already in the bathroom, fully clothed, with the shower turned on. A blast of cold water hit me before the tankless heater kicked on and blessed me with soothing warmth.

I began to strip, feeling every single punch that Retnuh had delivered, and looked down to confirm the extent of my injuries. With my black clothing lying in a clump at my feet, I ran tired hands over my tender flesh, seeing the discoloration beneath the swollen skin.

"Sonofabitch got me good." I winced.

*Nothing I can't help fix. Even your ruptured liver and broken cheekbone will be good as new before you know it.*

"Or I'll be dead from an indifferent universe that only wants balance."

*Be glad that it does, Andrew. Be glad that it does . . .*

I didn't argue his point as I felt the fabled Sword of Damocles poised above my head.

I wrung out my long-sleeve BDU, saw the trails of dirty water slink down the drain, and held it up to the showerhead to allow more fresh water to soak in. Again, I spun the shirt with one hand until it was rope-like, and then twisted the ends until no more dirt came out.

Content that my shirt was clean, I stretched it out and hung it on the shower door before moving to my pants, boxers, and socks.

After I was done, I stepped out and gingerly slipped on the bathrobe, which ended just above my knees, before moving to the sink.

The steam in the air felt refreshing in a way that I couldn't put into words, and I ran the palm of my hand down the mirror to see the battered and bruised face that belonged on a zombie extra on a TV show or movie.

I parted my lips to inspect each one of my teeth, making sure they were all still there, and let out a sigh of relief at seeing at least they had been spared.

*I took the liberty of ordering you your favorite pizza, as well as some toiletries.*

"How'd you manage that?" I asked, noting that this hotel didn't offer the small, complimentary toothbrush and mouthwash that sometimes were provided.

*Some of the food delivery services also offer to pick extra items up at nearby gas stations. In this case, it was the recently renovated 7-Eleven up the road.*

"Thank you, Tim," I croaked, feeling the weight of everything beginning to collapse as if I had been holding it up with defective car jacks from a business that rhymed with *Barber Late*.

Something came to me, and I blessedly grasped onto the random thought.

"How did you know what my favorite pizza was?"

*Because you ordered it thirty-seven times in the past year. Always the same, too.*

"Thirty-seven?" I tried to whistle in amazement, but my slightly swollen lips felt alien to me, resulting in a sharp blowing of air.

I squinted at the mirror and gingerly felt my mouth with exploratory fingers, wincing at even the slightest of pressure.

*Don't worry, Andrew. I'll have you fixed up before you know it.*

"We've been over this . . . "

*I know,* Tim said in an almost defeated tone. *I was just trying to get your spirits up.*

"Heh. Well, I appreciate the thou—UGH!" I collapsed to my knees as a wave of ethereal electricity coursed through every cell of my being. It felt as if I had two bodies existing in the same space, with all the combined cells grinding over one another. Perhaps another way of looking at it would be experiencing my soul trying to exit my body, and I could feel everything as it happened.

"Oh God," I groaned through my teeth as the spectral electricity began to fade from my flesh.

*Thaaaaaat's . . . not good.*

"No shit," I growled. I pulled on the black granite countertop and got myself to unsteady feet.

*No, I mean the incidents are too close together.*

"What the hell does that mean?"

*Think of it like the contractions just before giving birth.*

My mind flashed to Sylvie, and I relived every contraction with her in an instant. It had only been an eight-hour process from the water breaking to Alison being born, but what an intense eight hours they had been!

Riding the train of thought as a passenger, I let my memory conduct me through a series of scenes that played for me, and me alone.

I remember when the nurse handed me Alison after cleaning her up, and I held her in the crook of one arm like she was as fragile as a priceless porcelain doll. The nurse smiled at seeing the wide-eyed father who was terrified of breaking his newborn, and showed me how to support the neck.

She stopped crying and looked up at me, and my heart melted. I had never loved anything more in my entire life. Looking back on that sentiment, I wanted to feel guilty, as it could be construed that my love for my wife had diminished, but in reality, it was a different kind of love. I was *in love* with Sylvie, and even more so when I held the daughter she had selflessly carried for nine long months. And my love for Alison was on a completely different level. Regardless, both my wife and daughter had been my entire world.

"Guess we'll add another birthday to the calendar," Sylvie said with a tired but love-filled smile.

"You'll have to write small to put all three of our names in the little box," I noted before leaning over and kissing the top of her damp brow.

"We could condense it. Alison, Sylvie, Andrew . . . ASA-Day . . . what do you think?"

"ASA-Day," I repeated as I handed Ali to her mother and looked upon my whole world with proud eyes. "I like it."

*Andrew?* Tim asked softly, snapping me back to the now.

I sniffled once and rubbed the sleeve of my robe across my cheeks.

"I'm fine," I lied.

Tim didn't answer, but I could feel his suspicion interlace with the silence between us. I lay on the bed with the intent of resting my eyes for a moment when Tim woke me up.

*Your order is here, Andrew.*

"Hmm?" I drawled, feeling every punch that had been delivered to my body. Taking a nap had apparently made everything worse. "Ugh."

*Meet the driver at the door so you can get some food in you.*

With a heavy groan, I pushed myself to my feet and shuffled to the door right as the driver was walking up.

"Oh my God!" he exclaimed with mild horror. "You alright, man?"

"Cut myself shaving," I said flatly, grabbing the pizza box and white plastic bag from his hands and letting the door close behind me.

After eating the meal, which took a long time to get down, I swallowed a large handful of over-the-counter pain relievers and moved to the bed once more.

Tim was right. The food made me feel considerably better, allowing me the clarity to ask some pertinent questions.

"What happened to the tall man?"

*You mean when you shot his Clepsydra?*

The screaming skeleton with flesh growing and receding off of it in random pulses filled my mind.

"Ye-yeah . . . "

*Schrödinger's bad guy.*

"You mean he was both alive *and* dead?"

*I'm afraid so,* Tim said with an audible shudder in his voice. *It's a fate worse than death.*

"W-Why?" I gulped in preparation for the answer that made even an AI squeamish.

*He felt every bit of what was happening to him. And once the exotic matter dissipated, he would have ceased at whatever point crossed the threshold.*

"Which means he could have been left without, what, his skin or something?"

*There's any number of possibilities, Andrew. We can only hope the anomaly stopped at a point of death.*

"No."

*No?*

"You heard me," I said coldly, thinking about Loraine at the gas station. "I hope he suffers."

*I, uh . . . I don't like what's going on with you, Andrew. You're changing.*

"Oh, like I was a beam of fucking sunshine when you first showed up? At my family's funeral, no less."

*I concede to your point. But it is also worth mentioning that any destruction you felt in your heart . . . was aimed at* yourself.

My mind betrayed me, knowing he was right, and played back the thought I had relived over and over again: the unbearable and overwhelming notion of ending my pain.

*Andrew,* Tim started softly, *I wasn't going to tell you this . . . but that tall man back there . . . had his entire timeline experience the exotic matter contamination.*

"So?!"

*Even when he was a child, innocent of any wrongs against you in his adulthood. Wrongs, which I might add, are all just a part of his job to keep the universe intact.*

Once again, my mind struck a low blow and replayed the scene of the screaming skeleton, but this time, it was that of a small boy, crying out in confusion and untold agony.

"Then-then-then why didn't that stop him from appearing in *my* timeline to begin with? If I killed him . . . all of him across time . . . how was he still here?"

"The importance of you, Sylvie, and Alison is immense in the grand scheme of things," Tim began as his hologram appeared and an image of our solar system manifested just above him, animating the scene as he spoke. "Imagine that a potential future is a streaking asteroid heading straight for Earth. If Jupiter happens to be within an ample distance, its gravitational force will pull on the asteroid that was meant for this world . . . forever changing the future."

I looked at the two different trails of the same asteroid. One that ended on Earth, and the other that was sucked into Jupiter, with the planet not even noticing what would have been an extinction-level event on the third rock from the sun.

"I . . . I don't understand," I admitted, feeling the hate inside of me begin to succumb to an exhaustion I had never felt before. It was as if my mind and body were battling to the death on who could deplete the most energy and willpower.

"*You* . . . are Jupiter, Andrew. The choices you make determine the trajectory of time itself."

"What?" I asked in complete disbelief, feeling a wave of surrealness wash over me and vapor lock my brain. "W-Why me?"

"No one knows for sure why those higher on the Chronos Scale have a greater impact on the timeline. But what we are certain of is that you and your family are of incalculable importance."

"Then why are they trying to kill me?!" I barked, slamming my fists down on the bed like a child throwing a tantrum.

"Perhaps we should continue this after you've had some sleep?" Tim suggested as the animated solar system above him vanished, leaving just the puppy with the unnervingly intelligent eyes.

"How can I even sleep?" I groaned, pressing both palms against my face, frustration giving the action a strength I hadn't meant to include and reminding me of the many injuries I had endured. But as I felt the pain, I continued to push even harder for a reason I couldn't understand. "The killer is still out there . . . and now he knows I'm coming for him."

"Your past self had to answer some tough questions from the police, but the security footage at the restaurant cleared him of all involvement. All of your own devices, such as the doorbell with the camera in it, had an unknown glitch that authorities will think was due to the explosion."

"And? What does this have to do with the killer hunting them?"

"I'm getting to that part, Andrew," Tim explained with a surprising degree of resilience at my aggression. "The insurance company put them up into a hotel for the foreseeable future, and I have already altered the records, making it beyond difficult for someone to find them. I also put a silent alarm on the camera system, so if anyone from the future checks the footage, I'll be able to doctor it easily."

"But if they start looking in the future . . . how will you be able to change it *now*?"

"Because you are *Jupiter*, Andrew. What you do, no matter where you are, changes the timeline. In this instance, it would be in our favor."

I felt a small gust of relief flow over my agitated nerves, coaxing them to relax in much the same way an ice pack would on a swollen joint, and I pulled my hands away from my throbbing face.

"Besides," Tim continued, "I can safely assume that he will lie in wait until the contamination has passed and will try again at a different wheren."

"How can you be so sure?"

"Because it's what I would do."

"You mean his Clepsydra is also an AI?" I asked, feeling the answer was obvious, but still compelled to ask.

"Actually, I am quite unique, Andrew. Unlike you piles of slowly decaying flesh that makes up the human race . . . there is only one of me. I am, for all intents and purposes, a beautiful, unique snowflake."

"I don't know if that term is as wanted as you might think," I mumbled.

"Oh, right. We are at *that* part of your primitive history. Yeesh." He shuddered.

I waved off the topic before it could further distract us.

"You think the killer will try again at a different point in time?"

"Yes."

"But he doesn't have an AI like you," I countered in a statement rather than a question.

"Well . . . yes and no. Travelers, like the Clockmen, *have* AIs. They just aren't as—"

"Unique as you are. Yeah, I got it," I interrupted with a roll of my eyes. "So you can correctly know, *not* assume, that he won't go after Sylvie and Alison in this wheren."

"Correct."

I let out a sigh of relief, knowing that the first battle was officially over, but the war had just begun.

"Then we can track him down before he leaves this timeline," I said coldly.

"Though I don't like the idea of hunting him down now that he knows we are on to him, I just don't see any other choice," Tim concurred.

Then another question popped up, one that felt forceful, like it had been patiently waiting for as long as it could and now steamrolled to the front of the line of thought.

"Why did his face change . . . " I asked in a statement as I expended all my will to focus on the two brief glimpses I'd had of the killer.

"What do you mean?" There was concern in Tim's voice. I could only assume it was because my question—and the follow-up explanation I was about to give—sounded crazy.

"First he had a beard . . . then it was a goatee. Both were different colors."

"Running diagnostics."

"On what?" I asked with a deep scowl.

"I think you might be more concussed than I originally thought."

"Then why the hell did you let me take a nap?!"

"I thought it had been contained, with repairs in process. I suppose it might have been foolish to let you fall asleep before running another systems check."

"Ya think?!" I blurted, feeling as if I had narrowly avoided death by pure luck, which made me feel unnervingly vulnerable.

"Wait . . . no . . . everything looks fine," Tim drawled as an image that resembled a CT scan appeared in front of him. Only it was crystal clear, like something from *Star Trek*.

"Hmm," he said before the image shifted toward the back of my skull, and a small section of my brain flashed with red. "Ah, here it is."

"What?" I asked, squinting at the scan.

"Oh, uh . . . no-nothing," he mumbled as the image went away.

"Nothing *my ass*! What'd you do to my brain?"

"I might have . . . sort of . . . kind of . . . accidentally . . . *nickedapartofyouroccipitallobe*." He said that last part fast enough to be considered one word.

"You *what*?!" I growled, feeling my fists and jaw clench in unison.

"Your occipital lobe, Andrew. 01, do you know *nothing*?" the holographic puppy accused. "When I was, uh . . . *connecting* to certain parts of your brain . . . I might have made one tiny little slipup."

"How did you *nick* my brain, Tim?" I asked through gritted teeth.

"Ugh! Fine!" Tim blurted as the hologram of my brain scan came back to life. A series of weaving tendrils expanded through my skull, looking like a tree without leaves. I could see they formed up my spinal column from where the image cut off at my neck, then went up through the cerebellum and the rest of my brain.

"You . . . you changed . . . my *brain?*" I asked with a breathy, disbelieving tone.

"And in doing so, have saved your life more than once. Not only have I been able to alter your hormones to keep your drive to complete the mission strong"—he shifted to a quick whisper for the next sentence—"*and have kept you from committing self-harm*, but I've also been able to *help* your body heal itself more efficiently than on its own. By an order of magnitude, actually. The human body is just a complete mess with no instruction manual. Not only that, but you wouldn't have been able to survive entering the wormhole without my direct help. So you're *welcome*."

I sat in silence, staring at the floor with unfocused eyes as I began to *feel* every wire that ran through my skull.

"And if you *think* you can feel the upgrades I've made inside your brain, think again, mister! The brain feels no pain whatsoever. So get a hold of your racing heart and calm down before *I* do it for you."

His words felt like he was holding a rose with an angry wasp in it and was asking me to close my eyes and take a big whiff.

"Wait, that sounded a little harsh," Tim admitted, changing his tone. "What I meant to say was, I can help you calm down if you'd like me to."

"N-No . . . please don't do anything like that."

"Why not, if I may ask?"

An idea came to me, and I went with it.

"Imagine I asked you to open your raw code to me so that I could add in my own lines where I felt inclined to do so."

"Oh, 01!" Tim gasped. "Heeeeellllll no!"

"How is that any different?" I asked. Crossing my arms, I made sure to keep the Clepsydra on top so I could still see the hologram of the now uncomfortable puppy.

"The difference, Andrew, is that I have the entire collected studies of the human brain from the dawn of recorded science to now at my disposal. Not to mention *way* beyond this timeline, where doctors no longer have to cut into people. Sheesh! How barbaric."

"Just . . . just don't mess around in there. Please?"

"I'm mostly done with the upgrades to your anatomy."

"I think you *are* done," I said sternly as I glared at the AI.

"Fine!" Tim threw up his paws in frustration, his hologram vanishing. *I'm done!*

After a few minutes of letting everything we had spoken about soak into my memory, I could sense sleep creeping up on me like a stalking lion that was the same color as the tall brown grass around it—only visible once it was too late.

A creeping ache was slithering throughout my brain, making my exhaustion even more prominent and undeniable.

Once I scooted forward and let my head drop to the overly soft pillow, I was out faster than an impatient bungee jumper could say *oh shit* as they, all too late, realized the other end wasn't attached.

# CHAPTER 32

A strobe light of flashes danced across my nocturnal movie screen, playing an assortment of images that felt both real and foreign in the same breath. Each still snapshot from my life held a backlog of emotion behind it that was registered all at once—embarrassment, joy, frustration, love— all fighting for my attention until I focused on one, similar to how someone might pick up a book and be taken to a new world.

I chose them at random and allowed the memories to envelope my dreamscape.

I could see Sylvie dressed up in a tight black dress that showed off toned arms and shoulders. Seeing her in that outfit always made my mouth water for a reason that I couldn't put into words.

Ali was wearing an adorable white dress, usually worn to church on Sundays, with cute pink flowers dotting all over. Seeing as how she was growing like a weed, it only made sense to make as much use of her clothes as possible while they still fit.

Another flash, and I was digging into a thick fillet, medium rare and covered in garlic butter. The waiter filled my glass with a red wine that I didn't know the name of but that tasted smokey while somehow remaining delicious.

Even in my unconscious state, I began to register that these weren't scenes from any memory that I could recollect, but neither were they a made-up fantasy produced by my sleeping brain.

The next scene burst into view, and I could see Sylvie looking at me with love in her eyes; I knew I was going to get lucky tonight as she placed her hand on mine, her thumb lightly stroking my skin.

Something felt wrong inside my head, like a pressure that was pushing outward on the inside of my skull.

Swirling red and blue lights raced across the houses in my neighborhood, and a feeling of unease began to build while we steadily approached our home. As we did, the concentration of lights grew, and so did the number of vehicles and first responders.

"What?" I remember breathing out, seeing what was left of our home.

The scene skipped and an officer was trying to calm me down with his palms held up and a knowing look on his face that said *I get it, but we have to do this.*

"Where were you tonight?" the officer asked as he wrote into a small flipbook.

"At dinner with my family!" I barked back, not meaning to be harsh in my tone but unable to keep my emotions in check.

"Can you prove it?"

"Here," Sylvie replied, holding up her phone with the restaurant's contact information. She wrapped her free hand around my arm and pulled herself close to me. I remember the mere contact of her against my body subsided my uncontrolled emotions, reassuring me that everything would be alright. "We were sitting near the window. Albert was our waiter. We were there from eight to ten thirty."

"That's a long dinner," the cop noted, though with only a modicum of suspicion in his voice. Perhaps seeing my reaction to losing my house and the fact I had my family dressed in our Sunday best helped ease any confusion.

"What is this even about?" I asked. "My house is destroyed . . . an-an-and you're asking me where I was?"

"A neighbor thought she saw you in black clothes minutes before the chaos," the officer explained as he eyed my dark suit and tie. "A truck was then seen leaving your garage after the explosion."

"Well, I don't own a truck," I replied with bubbling indignation. There was something about having your world turned upside down and then being accused of it that just didn't feel right.

"Is my husband a suspect?"

"Oh, no, ma'am. I'm just doing my job, is all," the cop said as he flipped his notebook closed. "Now I recommend you call your insurance company. They'll probably put you up in a hotel while we comb through the crime scene."

"Crime scene?" I asked, tasting the words. "What exactly happened here?"

"That's what we are going to try and figure out, sir." He handed me a business card. "If you can think of anything else, this is the detective that is assigned to your case."

The memories faded, leaving me floating in the nothingness of my dream, conscious but unawake while the pressure in my skull continued to build, now feeling like a hot poker that was being dragged across my brain.

I remembered now . . .

# CHAPTER 33

I awoke with a jolt of ethereal electricity, my limbs jerking so fiercely that I ended up kicking myself out of bed and collapsing on the thinly carpeted floor with a *thud*. My head also felt like it had been carved out with a hot knife like I was some sort of Andrew-O-Lantern, ready to be placed on the porch with candles illuminating empty sockets for the enjoyment of all the children seeking early-onset diabetes.

Hot bile spewed from my mouth, and I instinctively began a weakened crawl to the bathroom while elongated, incoherent grunts rumbled from my throat.

Pulling myself up to the sink with trembling arms, I cupped cold water into my hand and desperately sucked up mouthfuls before spitting it out again. After the bitter taste only lingered as a subtle reminder, I began splashing water over my face.

"Tim . . ." I croaked. "Tim, help me!"

*What's going on?* A distracted Tim answered. *Oh, my science! What happened?*

"My head!"

*Scanning now. One moment please.*

I groaned as I pulled myself further up and stuck my entire head under the flow of the cool water, letting it soak my hair and run on either side of my aching skull.

*Oh. There are signs of temporal latency.*

"What the hell does that mean?" I heaved out.

*It means that memories from the past version of you have physically etched themselves onto your brain.*

"What?" I asked, but the dream instantly played back in my mind, and I could *feel* what he was saying was true. "The dinner . . . coming home to seeing my house destroyed . . . the cop questioning me . . . Sylvie holding my arm . . . I-I remember . . . "

*Oh dear.*

I didn't ask *what* like I wanted to. Instead, I looked up at the mirror and gazed into my own eyes, knowing Tim could see and extrapolate that I was glaring at him. However, seeing one of my eyes was completely bloodshot took me aback.

*Don't you worry about that little eye. I'll take care of it in no time.*

"Tim."

*Yes, Andrew?* His tone suggested he knew *exactly* what I was going to ask and was trying to delay the question.

"Why did you say *oh dear?*"

Tim sighed before his hologram came to life. I slid my gaze off the dripping face in the mirror to stare at the puppy as he produced a brain scan in midair.

"The Temporal Sickness is worsening," he explained while the image of the brain zoomed in to show a multitude of paths that looked like erratic roads. "You are becoming susceptible to the altered memories of your past self."

"But I thought I was Jupiter," I said, referring to the pull I had on the timeline due to my high Chronos Scale.

"The thing about that, heh." Tim forced a chuckle that I recognized as him about to give me even more bad news. "Because you *are* Jupiter, your direct influence on the events of last night have now been, for lack of a better word, made *canon.* And since your body is weakening as the universe tries to reverse your energy and matter, your mind had zero chance of stopping the new memories from forcing themselves into your literal brain."

"Like that movie *Looper*?" I asked, remembering the fun flick starring Bruce Willis and Joseph Gordon-Levitt.

"They weren't the first to come up with that idea," Tim replied. "Not by a long shot. The first time travel theories involved deep conversations about what would happen if someone from the future were to mess with their past selves."

If I had the energy, I could sense my willingness to go down the rabbit hole and learn all the rules of time travel, but I just didn't have it in me, as my body still hummed from the ethereal electricity.

"What will happen to me?" I asked. I looked at myself in the mirror, searching for any obvious signs of my condition. On the plus side, at least

Tim had closed the cuts on my nose, eyebrow, and lip. Even the swelling was way down, along with the bruising which looked around a week old at that point. But I could still *feel* the damage as some sort of lingering phantom pain.

There was movement on the brain hologram, and I turned to see new pathways being cut through the image, like an excavator on meth.

"As you become weaker, the impact of altered memories will shift from that of drastic to mundane."

"I have no idea what you just said," I admitted as I half crouched to the toilet and plopped down hard enough to move the seat. I didn't need to go at that very moment, mostly because I hadn't had my coffee yet, but just needed to sit down.

My black clothes were still hanging from the shower door, and I briefly wondered if they were dry yet.

"It means that the memory that was etched onto your brain was an impacting one; a dramatic recollection that you would remember for the rest of your life that was also directly affected by the choices you—the future you with the higher Chronos Scale—made."

"Okay. I get that. Because I sent them off—"

"And blew up their house."

" . . . and blew up their house . . . I created new and strong memories of that night."

"And as you succumb to the Temporal Sickness, more and more memories will be etched onto your brain, even those that you don't have any influence over. Anything from getting a speeding ticket to, eventually, stubbing your toe."

"Won't he just live out life exactly like I did? I mean, if I stubbed *my* toe in my past . . . won't he stub *his* toe in his future?"

"Not anymore."

"What? Why?" I asked, not liking where the conversation was going.

"Yesterday's events have completely broken this wheren's Andrew away from the life you have already lived," Tim said before summoning a single horizontal line above him. "In the movies and comic books, they would say that you've created a new branch of time that will be different from your own." To showcase his point, a new piece stemmed first upward at an angle, and then started moving parallel to the first, creating two timelines.

Tim stared at the two lines, and I almost saw the gears running in his hologram head.

"Well?"

"Hmm?" Tim hummed before willing his gaze off the diagram to land on me. "Oh. Um . . . wha-what were we talking about?"

"Did we create an alternate timeline last night or not?"

"That's the thing . . . we don't know for sure. Though we are getting closer to having a clear understanding."

"How do you not know? I mean, what's the point of building a wormhole if you don't know what'll happen if you use it? Seems like the equivalent of trying to pack dynamite by a campfire."

"We have to use it in order to keep the universe from being destroyed."

"Why will it be destroyed?" I asked, not feeling a strong connection to the idea of everything being wiped out because I knew it wouldn't happen until *far* in the future when I was already long dead and gone.

"That's not what's *important* right now, Andrew," a frustrated Tim exhaled dramatically. "First, we have to figure out a way to keep that block in your skull you call a brain from being turned into Parmesan cheese à la The Olive Garden!"

My mind flashed with a waiter at the Italian restaurant holding a solid block of cheese over my plate, and then grinding it down into little, curly strips.

"Let me guess," I drawled as I slumped over and rested my face in both hands, not caring if Tim's hologram was no longer even with the floor. "The new memories will kill me."

"Well, heh." Tim chuckled again, and I knew I wasn't going to like what he said next. "You *probably* won't survive the Temporal Sickness long enough to actually *die* from having your brain carved up like a Christmas ham."

"There's that, I suppose . . . and what is it with you and food metaphors?"

"Buuuuuuuuut . . . it'll hurt like hell in the meantime."

"There it is," I exhaled loudly, dropping my hands away from my face to slap against my bare thighs.

"There is one good thing, however."

"And what's that?" I asked flatly, not believing the AI had the capability to deliver any news that could be regarded as *good* at that moment.

"Once we leave this wheren, I *think* the memory overlap will cease."

"But I'm for sure going to die before we can leave," I said in a statement rather than a question, already knowing the answer.

Tim didn't respond, giving me all the confirmation I needed.

With a shake of my head, I temporarily accepted the situation for what it was—at least until I had my coffee—and stood up, tying my robe as I did.

Checking on my clothes, I saw they were damp, but not overly wet like I was expecting.

"I guess that moisture-wicking stuff actually works," I mumbled just above a whisper as I prepared to start my morning routine.

There was only one thing left that I could focus on: stopping the killer before he could escape and try again.

Looking at the hologram, I sucked in a long breath, let it out with a four count, and said, "So how are we going to catch this bastard?"

"Well, first things first." Tim pretended to hold his nose with one paw and wave at the air in front of his face with the other. "You need to brush your teeth."

# CHAPTER 34

**Y**ou sure this will work?" I asked after spending several hours preparing, all while dealing with the fear of another painful ethereal shock from the Temporal Sickness. What made it worse was that I *knew* it was coming.

"Not at all," the puppy hologram replied as a blackboard full of notes vanished. "But it's the only choice we have."

"So, just to recap," I said as I laced up my boots. My damp clothes were giving me a slight chill. "We have to stop him before the exotic matter contamination dissipates because then he can escape and try to kill my family at a different wheren."

"Good so far." Tim's tone urged me to continue, making sure I grasped the severity of the situation.

"And we have no choice but to go after him, even if he will probably kill me, because the Temporal Sickness will erase me before the contamination dissipates. Right?"

"Right you are."

"Which means we won't be able to follow him when he tries again."

"Not unless you want to kill your past self."

I didn't say anything for a few moments while I considered.

"Andrew!" Tim gagged, disgusted at my telegraphed thoughts. "The moral implications of killing your literal self are staggering! Not only that, but at this point, you would *remember* all the pain that your past self would experience as you erased him from the timeline."

"Remembering pain is better than being dead. And wouldn't that be the last forced memory, anyway?"

"Not if you are catatonic!" Tim argued. "This is your brain." An image of what I could only assume was my brain popped up, and I watched as it was dropped into a commercial blender before being turned into a bubbling liquid. To add emphasis, the blender tipped over, and the contents were poured into a large cup with a thick straw. There was a name on the side, and I squinted to see *Andrew Juice* written on the container. "This is your brain on memory scarring after reaching the later stages of Temporal Sickness. Any questions?"

"Yeah, one," I said, raising my hand to signify my question. "Is *Andrew Juice* supposed to be a pun or something? Because that can be taken in sooo many ways."

"Like Jamba Juice," Tim replied flatly. "What other way can it be taken?"

"Anyway." I waved my hand in the air dismissively. "So, killing my previous self at this point would probably result in my death."

"The next time you went to sleep, yes . . . probably."

"It only happens when I sleep?"

"Oh, did I not say that already?"

"No. No, you did not."

"Well, there you go; I just did."

"Why is it only when I sleep?"

"That's when the brain is the most vulnerable and the bulk of the systems are offline, as it were. Think of it like a computer with its firewalls disabled."

"I get what you are trying to say," I admitted as my third cup of coffee began to perk me up. "But it doesn't make logical sense."

"Oh, I'm sorry. I forgot you are an expert in temporal mechanics," Tim replied sarcastically. "Do you want me to *actually* explain it to you? Or can you just trust that the freaking time-traveling AI from the faaaar future knows what he's talking about?"

"Okay! Jeez. Calm down."

"Besides," Tim continued as his hologram pretended to kick at a nonexistent pebble. "We don't actually know why."

"I . . . " I started before deciding to drop it to focus on what was important.

Shifting the conversation to something productive, I asked, "Retnuh will be hunting one of us during all of this?"

"Without a doubt. That man is relentless, merciless, and worst of all, efficient."

"Which one do you think he'll go after? Me? Or the killer?"

"Hard to tell. And also, a moot point. You will be hunting the killer, anyway. So regardless of which one he chooses, he will find you both."

"Oh dang. I, ah, hadn't really thought abou—AHHHH!" A wave of ethereal electricity coursed through every cell in my body, dropping me to the ground in a fetal position.

I could hear Tim trying to speak to me out loud, but I couldn't make out the words.

*Andrew?* Tim said, this time inside my head.

"He-help . . . m-me!" I managed to squeeze out from a quivering diaphragm and clenched teeth.

*There's nothing I can do,* Tim admitted softly. I could hear the helplessness in his tone, and it gave me comfort that he really did seem to care.

After a few moments, the episode passed, and I was left with my face pressed against the thin carpet, smelling the faint aroma of mold. Warm drool leaked from my gaping mouth, somehow transporting the taste of the floor through the liquid and onto my tongue.

At least a full minute passed with me just lying on the ground, silent tears slipping free.

*Are you . . . okay?*

"What's there to be okay about?" I wasn't expecting an answer as I pushed myself up, wiping the drool from my face by using the comforter.

I felt numb, like how I imagine a dead body feels after the soul has left.

I touched my fingertips together, and I couldn't sense my own skin pressing into itself. Only a vague semblance of it, almost as if trying to relive a memory that involved touch—nearly impossible to do.

*You shouldn't be experiencing the Temporal Sickness to this degree yet.*

"What . . . do you mean?" I asked between gritted teeth.

*For some reason, you appear to be hypersensitive to it. Perhaps it goes along with how impacting you are on the Chronos Scale.*

"Yippy . . ."

*Is there anything I can do?*

"Just . . . just tell me how we are going to track this guy again."

*Very well,* Tim agreed, and I could hear a modest amount of relief in his voice that I was willing to focus on the mission, even in my intense pain and existential discomfort. *We track him by following the unique energy signature produced by his Clepsydra.*

"And the drawbacks?" I asked, already knowing the answer but wanting to hear it out loud once more. Maybe I was asking a question with a tough answer so that the weight of it might suppress the physical pain I was feeling.

*There are two main concerns to the plan. The first being that he might leave his Clepsydra on empty and wait a few days before powering it up again.*

"And the second?"

*If we actively search for his signal . . . our own energy signature will light up like a ping on a radar.*

"Alerting that bald bastard to where we are."

*At least the approximate location, yes.*

"So there's no guarantee that we could find the killer . . . but there *is* a guarantee that we would give ourselves away to the *Cock*-man."

*I think you mean clock, Andrew. Clockman. Or Tock for short.*

I gave a wry smile as the pun-laden insult flew over the AI's head.

*And yes. It is assured that Retnuh Ordune would quickly lock on to our signal and pursue us.*

"What if we did intermittent checks? You know, like be in one spot to rest, and once we are ready to leave, do a quick scan before heading out."

*I suppose that* might *work. However, Retnuh is exceedingly thorough and would have little trouble tracking us through rudimentary means.*

"How do you know?"

*It's based on more than an educated guess. But I will admit, I've never been pursued by him like this before. I'm learning as I go.*

"What if we backtracked. Made it *seem* like we were heading in a specific direction," I asked, getting us back on topic.

*That would probably buy us a little time, but not as much as you are hoping for,* Tim explained. *You have to remember, hunting Ticks through time is* exactly *what the Clockmen do. And Retnuh is the field commander, which means he has earned his title through consistent results. So whatever plan your limited brain can come up with has probably already been seen countless times.*

A question came to mind that I had to ask.

"Just how many Ticks have there been? I mean, for him to be *that* good at hunting them."

*When the wormhole was first constructed, blueprints were leaked on the dark web, allowing whoever stumbled across them to print their own Clepsydras.*

"Heh, you still have the dark web in the future? Good to know there will always be those who fight the powers that be," I said without putting any strength into the words. It was more that my mouth was on autopilot to carry along the conversation.

*The internet will be replaced within thirty-three years of this point in time by a rogue Elon Musk.*

"Rogue?" I asked, intrigue boosting my interest. The ethereal pains I felt all but vanished as the conversation continued.

*I really don't have the patience or the crayons to explain it to you,* Tim groaned.

"Please. It's helping."

There was silence for a few heartbeats as Tim considered my words before understanding what I was asking. I needed a distraction.

*Ugh, fine!* Tim spit out just before his hologram came to life; a picture of a red planet appeared with him. "Elon beat NASA, Jeff Bezos, and the lackadaisical Sir Richard Branson to Mars."

"Okay. I could see that. They're working on that right now, actually."

"Spoiler alert! Elon wins, and he does something that no one was expecting."

"He blows it up?" I asked half sarcastically.

"No, dumb-dumb. That would result in the destabilization of the solar system, eventually leading to the extinction of all life on Earth, as our planet would either be pulled in by the sun or be thrown out into deep space."

"Soooo . . . he *doesn't* blow it up. Got it."

"No, Andrew. Instead, he plants an ironic flag on the planet and declares complete ownership over Mars."

"Ironic?"

"I . . . I just told you he claimed Mars as a sovereign entity, free from the rule of Earth's governments . . . and you focus on the man's twisted sense of humor?"

"It's always interesting when he does something like that."

"O . . . kay then. If I may continue?"

"Please do."

"Elon claimed Mars as his own, forming a new government with his most trusted of allies, and even went so far as to find every legal loophole that allowed him to do just that. And because no one saw it coming, besides a few unheard government employees, the world leaders didn't have time to prepare for how to colonize space."

"Couldn't they try and stop him?"

"Ha! With what?" Tim genuinely laughed. "While they were still planning a modest ramshackle of a Moon base, Elon had already built an entire city in space and flown it to the Red Planet. After finding deep water deposits that could last the growing population for over two-hundred years, there was no reason to ever leave. So he continued to harvest helium-3 from his plot on the Moon and mine passing asteroids for precious metals, all while China, Russia, and the US bickered over where they would *eventually* put their noncivilian bases."

"I see where this is going."

"You do? Pray tell." Tim crossed his little puppy arms.

"He created an advanced internet that could be reached across the solar system. And let me guess . . . SolarNet?"

"StarNet, actually."

"Oh. That makes more sense."

"Why's that now?"

"Be . . . because of Starlink?"

"Ah. I see your train of thought," Tim said with a nod of his head in understanding. "But no. It was called *Star*Net because he developed a way to transmit data instantaneously throughout the galaxy by using a sub-space method called the Ansible, which eventually led to the discovery and creation of the wormhole."

"Wow. I didn't think I'd live to see that kind of sci-fi stuff in my lifetime."

"Well . . . Elon does come from the future."

"What, like a Tock?"

"Not exactly . . . "

"What do you mean, then?"

"He is one of the approved travelers who had the ambition to complete a tough mission. It's a theoretical paradox, really."

"I don't get it."

"Of course you don't," Tim said as an image of William Shakespeare appeared above him. I knew it was him because the AI had put a caption beneath his face, which was insulting, if I were to stop and think about it. "If you take all of Shakespeare's collected works and travel back in time and give them *all* to him . . . who wrote them?"

"He did. Right?"

"How? If you were the one to give them to him, and *then* he gave them to the world, only for you to collect them in the future and then travel back in time to give them to him . . . then who wrote the words?"

"Ah. I see your point." I nodded. "So Elon was sent back in time to do exactly what he did, which helped create the method of time travel in the first place . . . so . . . so he could go back in time and do it again?"

"Exactly."

"Fine, fine, fine. We are getting off course."

Tim shifted to a cordial tone, saying, "Wasn't that the point, Andrew?"

At the realization of what the expanding conversation had originally been about, I felt the remnants of the ethereal pain once more.

I frantically grasped at the beginnings of the topic, hoping to not feel even the remembrance of the agony of the Temporal Sickness. "So people used the dark web, which I'm guessing is still a part of the archaic internet on Earth, and 3D printed Clepsydras?"

"They stop saying *3D* not far in your future and just say *print*. But yes."

"How many Ticks were there?"

"With a population of over ten-and-a-half billion, it is honestly surprising that only a handful actually had the zeroes to go through the wormhole."

"Zeroes?" I asked before I got it. "Oh, never mind."

"I thought you'd like that."

"So what's a handful?"

"Sixty-three thousand and some change. Give or take the ones that we never found."

"Sixty-three thousand?! Holy crap . . ."

"Compared to over ten billion, that is a relatively small number. I mean, it's a fraction of a fraction."

"I . . . I guess. But what do you mean about the ones who were never found?"

"Think about the dino-crocodile you first encountered."

A terrible memory leaped to the forefront of my mind, and I felt my heart begin to race at mentally seeing the thirty-foot monster with long legs sprinting toward me with open jaws.

"Jesus . . ."

"Mm-hmm."

"So the Clockmen have hunted more than sixty thousand people down?"

"Yes. With Retnuh Ordune having the highest capture rate in the organization."

"How did the Ticks not accidentally destroy the timeline? I mean, that's why the Clockmen were first made, right?"

"Once again, we are tiptoeing toward a paradox," Tim began as an image of the wormhole appeared in the air above him. On one end toward the right was an uncountable number of arrows that leaped out and curved around to land at different points on the wormhole. "For the sake of simplicity, I'm going to take it down to just one instance." As he spoke, all but one of the arrows disappeared.

"This is wheren the Tick landed, leaving behind a signature of his beginning and ending coordinates." Two portions of the wormhole began to glow, with one beginning at the start of the arrow, and the other ending at the pointed tip. "Once the Clockmen were created"—a portion on the wormhole more to the right of where the arrow had started began to glow bright red—"they knew *exactly* wheren every Tick was. But it doesn't end there."

"You mean the Clockmen didn't just go back to before the people entered the wormhole and stop them?"

"Right. Once again, you need someone high on the Chronos Scale . . . someone like Retnuh Ordune, who has increased his influence by traveling back and forth through the wormhole, like a blacksmith folding steel."

"Ah." I nodded my head a few times. "Let me guess, this dude has a really high number, more than most of the Clockmen, and that's how he was able to capture so many. Am I right?"

"Surprisingly so, Andrew," Tim replied in awe.

"The big fish always eat the smaller ones," I said just below a whisper, not meaning to say the words aloud.

"Right you are! The higher on the scale a person is, the more likely they are to change the future," Tim concluded. "I must say, Andrew, I am quite impressed with your ability to catch on to topics that should be *waaaaay* out of your wheelhouse."

Ignoring his compliment that felt more like an insult thinly disguised as praise, I asked, "Where is he on the scale? If Sylvie and Alison are a twenty out of ten . . . and you have no idea what my current number is . . . then what is Retnuh's?"

"No clue. His files are sealed up tighter than any world leader's. But it's clear that it is *very* high, indeed."

"So once again I ask, why doesn't he just go farther back and kill me?"

"A few reasons. The first being we don't know what his number is compared to yours. And second, the impact on Sylvie and Alison would be too great, even to the point where your daughter wouldn't even be born. And with their scales-tipping numbers, it is certain that the consequences would be vast."

I let out a long whistle, feeling a surreal darkness creep up the back of my mind, as if a part of me was refusing to believe this was all real. But seeing my family at dinner, even through a memory carved into my brain, gave me a renewed strength, even if it did physically hurt to think about. It was like the neurons were exposed nerves, and remembering the new, implanted memory was touching them with salty fingers.

"What a predicament," I let out. "If we hunt the killer, Retnuh will come for us. If we don't pursue him, he will just go back to a different point in time and try again." I was silent for a moment as I mentally laid out my words. "And Retnuh can't kill the past me without potentially causing the timeline to alter with how inexplicably important Sylvie and Ali are."

"But he *can* kill the *current* you. The *you* you, because your family is already, um . . . no longer an issue, in your timeline."

"Then why even bother?"

"With what?"

"If my family is already dead, then the future is set, right? Whatever is going to happen, *will* happen."

"Remember, Andrew, your number is higher than theirs. So you *can* change the future by changing the past."

"This is making my head hurt," I groaned as I began aggressively massaging my temples.

"I appreciate that this is a lot for you to take in, Andrew. I really do. Just know that I am here to help you achieve your goal."

"What . . . *exactly* . . . is it that you are here to help me do?"

"Kill the killer. Save the future."

"And *I'm* the one who sent you back?"

"Correct."

"Which means that the future me . . . fails."

"I don't know for sure. As I said the other day, that part of my memory is locked."

"Think about it, Tim." I dropped my hands from my face and stared at the hologram puppy. "If I succeeded . . . why the hell would I send you back to a past version of me?"

"I . . ."

"What aren't you telling me, Tim?" I asked aggressively, a scowl marring my features and making the many half-healed bruises just under my face remind me of their existence. Though the AI had done a miraculous job of healing me while I slept, I could still feel the bruises in my skull.

"I . . ."

"TIM!" I roared, fury making my voice boom.

"Fine!" Tim blurted, caving in and giving up the secret he had been withholding from me. "I wasn't being entirely truthful."

"About what, exactly?"

"My memory *isn't* locked. I just knew you weren't ready to hear the truth."

"Tim! What truth?!"

"You aren't the first Andrew Frost whom I've been sent to."

My vision coalesced into a pinprick as my face, hands, and feet went numb all at once. The world seemed to freeze while my brain desperately tried to process the words as the carpet was rushing up to meet me.

# CHAPTER 35

Somehow, through some unknown force of will, my right arm had shot out to prevent my face from slamming into the thin carpet, and I couldn't be more grateful at the reflex.

As consciousness returned, I managed to push myself up to an unstable sitting position—Tim's words jolting around inside of my skull like a brick thrown into a clothes dryer.

Shock latched onto my tongue, freezing it in place as my mouth bobbed open and closed like some sort of animatronic puppet. My throat constricted to the point that I thought I was going to choke, while my heart began pounding in my ears.

"What . . . ?" I managed to ask in a breathy, disbelieving whisper.

"You pressed and you pressed and you pressed!" Tim rattled off, clearly angry. "And now you know the truth, Mr. Smart Guy. You put the pieces of the puzzle together, faster than *all* your variants, and now you know. Happy?"

"I'm . . . I'm not the first . . . An . . . " I was unable to finish the question by saying my own name due to the absurdity of it all giving me pause.

"No," Tim replied sternly. "You are *not* the first Andrew Frost that I've been sent to. And by the looks of it, you won't be the last."

"Wha . . . what does that mean?" I was feeling like a gyroscope had been implanted at the center of my head, lolling in slow, tight circles.

"It means, *human*, that if you don't succeed in your mission—which is already fubared, by the by—then you will have to travel back to a time within close proximity of the funeral and deliver me to try the mission *yet again*." He blurted out the last two words, clearly frustrated.

"How many times have you done this?"

"That's not for you to know, Andrew," Tim countered like a brick wall against my tennis ball of a question. No matter how long or how hard I tried, I knew it wouldn't yield.

A surge of unease flowed up my spine, making the skin of my back and neck tingle, and I began trying to get the Clepsydra off my arm.

"Andrew . . . *stop!*"

"N-No . . . " I breathed out, edging toward a full panic attack. "I need to get it off. I . . . I need to . . . to . . . "

"You can't," Tim informed in a surprisingly soft tone that took me by surprise with how intense the conversation had been going.

"Why not?" I managed to ask after reigning in my building terror. For a reason I couldn't explain, I felt claustrophobic with the metal sleeve on my arm.

"Because, Andrew . . . I'm a part of you now," the hologram said as an image appeared above him. It was me, and I was naked standing in the Vitruvian Man pose, with my arms out to my sides and arms spread shoulder width apart.

The hologram version of me went see-through and zoomed in on my left forearm. Beneath the Clepsydra was a pathway of what appeared to be wires going up my arm and through the rest of my body, including my brain.

"What the fuck . . . ?" was all I could ask as panic began slipping through my grasp, seeking to take control.

"I'm a *part* of you, Andrew," Tim said softly, like a doctor explaining to the terrified toddler why he needed to stick the needle in his little arm. "If you remove me, you'll die. It won't be sudden, but neither will it take very long."

"So . . . so the other versions of me . . . that failed the mission . . . and . . . an-an-and—"

"And took me off to send to the next Andrew in line . . . all died. Yes," Tim finished my question with a calm answer. To me, it felt like a freezing ice pick slowly being inserted into my heart, and my right hand grasped at the cold just beneath my cage of flesh and bone.

"They willingly killed themselves . . . " I asked in a statement.

"To save Sylvie and Alison. Yes."

At his words, I felt a pang of absolute strength come to life inside my chest, knowing that I would do exactly the same thing if it meant sparing my family. I would give my life . . . to save theirs.

With this realization came a sort of peace that subdued the panic wreaking havoc inside me.

I lifted my unfocused eyes from the hotel carpet and met Tim's know-ing stare.

"How did they fail?"

"Any number of ways. But with my help, we were able to get closer and closer each time." Tim paused. "You, by far, were the only one who got within sight of the finish line."

"And we aren't done yet," I growled, surprising myself with the cer-tainty that the tone exuded.

"Now *that's* what I like to hear!" Tim jovially exclaimed. "So, are we done with the pity party? Because I'd like to catch the killer before he can escape."

I mentally grabbed a hold of all the anxiety, fear, and surreal pain I was experiencing and wrestled it into a tight ball. It was akin to wrangling a corporeal, toxic cloud that was desperately fighting to get free.

After getting control of myself and feeling that it was, more than ever, *now or never*, I stood up with my chin held high and fists clenched . . . and promptly sprinted to the toilet where a torrent of vomit rocketed from my face.

# CHAPTER 36

*Feel better?* Tim asked from within my head as I intermittently spit the last vestiges of coffee-infused bile from my mouth.

I reached up with my left hand to drunkenly pull on the handle and send the physical manifestation of all the negative emotions that I had tried to swallow down the toilet.

"Yeah," I groaned in answer to Tim's question. Moving to the sink, I turned on the faucet, lowered my face, and drank several mouthfuls of water to get the taste out. But no matter how much I tried, there was that lingering taste, along with the uncomfortable feeling of gritty teeth.

Scanning the bathroom counter, I prayed that I had just missed the complimentary bottle of mouthwash. When none miraculously appeared out of thin air, I moved to the shower, pumped a small amount of the gel wash, and licked it up.

*What* are *you doing?* Tim asked, both intrigue and disgust in his tone.

I swirled the soap around my mouth before returning to the sink and sucking in water, swishing it around, and spitting it back out again. After a full minute of repeating the process, my teeth felt electrified rather than gritty, which wasn't much of an improvement, but I went with it.

"Okay," I said, looking at myself in the mirror, "If I don't stop him, not only will my wife and daughter be murdered, but I'll die as well *if* I have to send you back to another me."

"Correct," he replied as his hologram came back to life now that I was no longer hugging the toilet bowl. "That is if the Temporal Sickness doesn't get you first."

"Question." I went to the nightstand and snatched up the rental car keys. "Why can't I just go back in time if we fail? You know, *me* be the one to try again?"

"Because the Temporal Sickness will not stop until you are back in your own wheren. After that, it'll take *years* if not *decades* for your body to fully recover from what the universe has already done to you."

"So if I fail and go back to try again . . . "

"The past version of you will still be here, and the sickness will continue."

"That doesn't seem fair," I muttered to myself.

"I think a past version of you once said something along the lines of it being like the dichotomy of sleep—when it is time for bed, you can lie awake for hours on end, feeling how your bed is just too soft or hard, or the room temperature is a single degree off from optimal. Then, when you wake up, everything is perfect, and it is nearly impossible to get up and start your day with how comfortable you are."

"Heh. Yeah. That is something I think about all the time, especially when I have to try and go to bed early to wake up for a bullshit meeting that takes place before every other employee's alarm has even gone off yet."

I thought about the conversation for a few moments.

"So, basically, I have a ticking time bomb type of situation?"

"I would say that is a fairly astute observation."

"Well, I guess there's one good thing about facing certain death."

"What's that?"

"I'm not afraid to get killed," I said coldly as I stared blankly at the wall. "If it comes down to it, I just need to make sure I kill the murderer . . . even if it means he mortally wounds me. Hell, maybe I'll set up a trap for *both* the killer and Retnuh, and blow up my—"

I didn't realize my mouth was spilling the words from my train of thought before I had a chance to process them.

"Your . . . what, Andrew?" Tim asked accusingly. "Your *Clepsydra*?"

"Yeah," I answered honestly, surprising myself with the lack of tact in saying I could kill myself *and* Tim in order to stop my enemies.

"There's only one problem with that, *muchacho*," Tim began as something flickered above my left arm. I let my gaze slide from the wall I had been absently staring at to look at a diagram of the wormhole. Above it was me and a line that stretched from somewhere in the future back to when I can only guess I was born.

"If you get caught in the raw expulsion of exotic matter, *all* of you will die, not just your present self." On the hologram, a wave of energy shot out in both directions, and replicas of me started to form and fall like dominos. "Which also means that Alison would have never been born."

My heart fluttered for a moment as if tripping over itself before quickly catching up to its normal rhythm. I absently rested my right hand over my chest once more, as if trying to coax my organ to keep beating; similar to when you drive over a nasty pothole, and then tap your dashboard while apologizing to your car.

"So that's out of the question then, heh," I replied with a dark chuckle.

"I'm glad you see it my way."

"You know," I sighed, looking at the puppy. "You aren't giving me a lot to work with."

"I'm just giving you the realistic consequences to your foolhearted ideas. I actually think it would be rude of me to indulge in your delusions of grandeur."

"I didn't think suicide bombing was an act of grandeur."

"First, I'm not sure you are using that word correctly. And second, it's not the act itself, rather the martyrdom you seek, which I am considering flat-out stupid, Andrew."

"I think I used the word just fine."

"Stop trying to deflect. This is serious."

"Fine, Tim." I threw my right hand out and let it drop in frustration. "Then what can I do if it comes down to the final showdown and I have nowhere to go? You said I'm going to die no matter what, right?"

Tim didn't answer, signifying his acknowledgement but not wanting to add fuel to my fire.

"So how do I take them *with me*?"

"I'd rather think about the different ways we can win without resulting in a last stand scenario."

"Okay. I'm all ears, then. What ya got?" I asked, frustration building both in my voice and beneath my skin, making it feel like I was standing directly in the rays of the hot sun.

"It is possible to collapse the wormhole . . . " Tim thought out loud.

I opened my mouth to ask a question in relation to the rip we had seen while being pursued by the Clockmen.

"I can see you thinking, so before you ask, collapsing the wormhole is different than ripping a hole in it."

"Okay. I can understand that, I suppose. But what would make the end result different?"

"Collapsing the tunnel, which is what it wants to do on its own and why we need exotic matter to keep it open, would result in it simply closing. There's also a potential for it to form into a black hole if it collapses too quickly." To showcase his point, Tim brought up a hologram of a tunnel that began to tremble before collapsing in on itself, followed by a swirling hole that swallowed everything around it.

"That doesn't sound good."

"Right you are."

"So what would ripping it do?" I asked, keeping the conversation on target.

"It could pull all of the time that it stretched across into a singular point." The hologram switched to show what I took to be the universe. The image then turned, like a sheet of paper, and several more began to appear behind it, forming a book of everything across all of time.

"That would be bad, wouldn't it?" I asked, knowing the answer but asking anyway to keep the topic flowing.

"We aren't entirely sure, but the best guess is that it would result in a probable Big Bang which was infinitely larger than the first. Or perhaps its more apropos to say the *latest* one, considering the initial Big Bang contained only a single universe. This one would have countless, resulting in a much bigger—and more violent—explosion."

"Great!" I spat. "Can *anything* else be stacked against me, please? I'm just having *sooooo* much fun with all of this!"

"And you wonder why I don't tell you things," Tim mumbled as the hologram of exploding creations vanished.

I closed my eyes, sucked in a long, deep breath, and exhaled as I said, "It's fiiiiiine. It's fine! We'll cross that bridge when we come to it. But first things first, we gotta find the murderer before the universe kills me."

"Now that's what I'm talking about!" Tim cried out as little fireworks flew up and exploded above his head. He even had sparklers in his little paws that he waved around in his excitement.

"So where do we start?" I asked, looking to the AI for an answer.

The sparklers went out in a disappointing *poof* as Tim made an *oh, right* face.

"I . . . don't know," he said sheepishly.

"How long do we have until the Temporal Sickness erases me?"

"Best guess? Less than two days."

"I guess that gives us a little time."

"But that's before you are *dead*-dead. Not combat ineffective. *That* will occur much sooner."

"How much sooner?" I asked flatly through my teeth.

"It varies. But could be as short as one day from now."

"I hate you."

"Understandable."

"Fine. We have a day to find this guy. So, let's get moving," I let out as I moved to the door and swiftly made my way to the parking lot with only a quick wave to the employee behind the counter.

Once behind the wheel of the truck, I felt a sense of purpose and focus. I was going to find this guy . . . and I was going to kill him.

# CHAPTER 37

I've scanned all the hotels, motels, and no-tells for any suspicious registries.

"And? Did you find any?"

*Oh, sooo many. For instance, would you like to know which prominent judge is currently renting a room that charges by the hour?*

"Not really."

*Oh, well . . . that's no fun.*

"Tim, focus."

*Right. Ummmm . . . yes, I can confidently say that he probably didn't check into any hotel in the area. At least not one with cameras connected to the internet.*

"How many of them aren't?"

*Um . . . a lot. It seems a big place like Houston has quite the under-ground clientele,* Tim said. *But to be fair, most big cities do.*

"So, how do you know he wasn't at any of them?"

*Oh, right. I checked the cameras of the local gas stations, ATMs, etcetera, etcetera. No suspicious movement. Well, heh, not suspicious in terms of what we are looking for. The local authorities, however, might find plenty of goings-on that would interest them.*

"So, where is he then?"

*Well . . . it's possible he camped out somewhere. The Woodlands isn't very far from the Sam Houston National Forest. Lots and lots of places to hide out there.*

"I suppose that makes sense. But we don't have enough time to search the entire thing."

*Hmm. You're right . . .* Tim trailed off, deep in thought. *Give me a moment. I'm going to check all the cameras surrounding the park.*

As Tim did something that I'm confident was incomprehensible for my human brain to fathom, I pulled onto the road and took the exit that would eventually take me to I-45.

*I didn't tell you I had found him yet?* Tim stated as a question, realizing which direction I was heading.

"I have a good feeling he'll be there."

*A feeling?* Tim asked, doing the verbal equivalent of a double take. *You have . . . a feeling . . . ?*

Rather than explain how I was going solely on a hunch, I came up with a flattering lie to throw Tim off my scent and allow me to pursue what I felt.

"I'm confident you're gonna be able to find him. Even if he tried his best to avoid all the cameras in and around Houston, he would surely still get caught by at *least* one, right?"

*That's what we are hoping,* Tim replied with a lack of confidence.

"Look," I started, lightly thumping the steering wheel as if I were metaphorically hammering my position into place. "He has to eat, drink, shit, and sleep, right?"

*Well, heh, he* is *human.* Tim chuckled in amusement.

"Exactly my point!" I blurted as the thought which had first formed as a distraction for Tim started to coalesce into an actually good idea. "That means he had to stop at a gas station at the bare minimum, right? At the very least to get clean water and food."

*What if he just broke into someone's house and took what he needed? Or even lay low once inside?*

"I don't care what kind of neighborhood or type of dwelling he could have potentially entered; a lot of people have those fancy doorbells now."

*You want me to sift through every camera connected to the internet . . . throughout Houston . . . ?* Tim asked flatly, disbelieving of my request.

"Well, if you *can't* do it because it's too hard, then I guess we—"

*Hey! I didn't say I* couldn't *do it. I was simply asking for clarification on what your feeble human mind wanted.*

"If you aren't having any luck with surrounding the forest, then maybe we should check residential homes, right? I mean, if he's evil enough to murder . . . a . . . a child . . . " I trailed off, feeling the words impact me as I spoke them because my mouth was working faster than my brain could process.

*Then he might have no compunctions in killing whoever might be home,* Tim finished my thought. *But what about your oh-so-strong feeling that he is in the forest?*

"I still have it, which is why I'm heading that way. But it's also good to have a plan B, right?"

*This is such an incredible waste of time,* Tim mumbled, and I took that to mean he was doing what I had suggested.

"Isn't it ironic that a time-traveling device is bitching about wasting time?"

*You listen here, bucko, I . . .* Tim trailed off just as he was building up to let me have it.

"Tim?"

*Shit,* he said in disbelief, in much the same way a man finding the needle in the haystack on his first try would.

"What?" I asked, feeling hope rise in my chest.

The hologram came to life, and Tim showcased security footage from a home's backyard.

A man in a black hoodie was stealthily inching through the yard and toward the back of the property where he managed to jump over the privacy fence. Behind the home was a dense forest.

"How do we know it's him?" I inquired, licking my lips as my eyes kept flicking between the road and the hologram footage.

Tim rewound the scene, paused, and zoomed in right as he was leaping over the fence. On his left arm, a glint of smooth metal could be seen.

"He didn't know there was a camera there; his AI must have missed it because the home also has the doorbell camera along with another two looking over the driveway and the side of the front yard with the gate, and none of them showed him approaching."

"What does that mean, exactly?"

"Either the AI doctored the footage or guided him on a path not to be seen."

"And now we know where exactly he went into the forest."

"I must admit, Andrew, you were right," Tim said before mumbling, "As much as it pains me to say."

"Gotta think like a human, Gateway."

"What's a human gateway?"

"I . . . no . . . Gateway is an old computer brand that, like, everyone used to have in the day. Back before building your own PC became the most cost-effective."

"So you tried to insult me in much the same way I call you clever things such as meat bag?"

"I wouldn't say *meat bag* is clever, Tim. I feel like that's an old cliché that's been used more than a French guillotine."

"Oh-ho! Did you just make a history joke? And a crafty one at that!" Tim exclaimed. "You're on a roll, Andrew!"

I turned north once we got to I-45, heading for Sam Houston National Forest, feeling pretty good about myself. But the closer we drew to the point of insertion into the densely wooded region, the more my smile began to drop and a sinking feeling closed in around my chest.

"What are we going to do when we find him?"

"You mean *if* we find him," the hologram puppy corrected.

"But we know where he is!" I countered, feeling the hope I had discovered begin to slip from my fingers like a balloon string loosely held by an inattentive child.

"If he chose to hide in the forest, we can accurately assume that he has some sort of formal training for evading capture."

"What about his AI?"

"What about it?"

"Can't that help him, like, survive and hide and stuff?" I asked, feeling like I was grasping at straws.

"There is only so much his Clepsydra would be able to assist with if he is untrained, but I think you might actually be right. Especially if he only needs to hide for a few days to allow the exotic matter contamination to dissipate."

"How long do we have before Retnuh finds us after we send out your energy signature?"

"Tough to say," Tim replied as he brought up a map of the greater Houston area. There was a dot in The Woodlands where my house was, and another at the neighborhood we were pulling up to where the killer had jumped the fence. "If he came straight here, less than an hour."

"Why wouldn't he come straight for us?"

"If he suspects it's a trap."

I swallowed as I prepared to ask a question that felt surreal.

"Did any of the other, um, *Andrews* . . . leave a trap like this?"

"No. I can confidently say that we will be the first to take this path."

"Then he won't be expecting a trap then, will he?"

"I suppose not," Tim replied, impressed. "You are definitely not like the others, Andrew."

I ignored his statement, not wanting to dwell on the implications of how many times I had died trying to save my family; or at least the other variants of myself, plucked from the timeline ahead of where I was found.

"This is going to work," I said as I parked the truck on the street and looked out the side window at a drainage path at the edge of the neighborhood. Behind it was a clearing of tall grass, followed by a landscape of trees as thick as a mountain around three hundred meters past.

"Send out the signal."

"Are you sure?"

"No. But what choice do we have?"

"Alright. If you say so," Tim spoke with a noticeable amount of confidence lacking in his tone.

I audibly swallowed, feeling my heart begin to race, and repeated, "This is going to work."

# CHAPTER 38

walked along the outskirts of the field, heading toward the fence that the killer had jumped over, all while knowing that Retnuh Ordune was on his way to hunt me down.

My vision flashed with a kaleidoscope filled with all the colors of the rainbow, and I dropped to my knees as ethereal electricity flowed through every cell in my body. My skin informed me that it was boiling, while my bones felt as if they had been replaced with perfect replicas made of ice. Bile bubbled at the back of my throat as tears streamed down my cheeks, and I realized I was looking up at the afternoon sky.

Grayish clouds that held a small swelling of water from the Gulf of Mexico drifted overhead, obscuring the intensity of the sun while still letting the light shine through, like a lampshade over a powerful bulb.

I lifted a hand to wipe at the warm tears on my face and gasped in utter surprise as I was able to see *through* my hand.

I stared at it, wiggling my fingers while my brain tried to comprehend what it was looking at, and then shook my hand back and forth several times. When I was done, I checked again, letting out a sigh of relief that my flesh was whole once more.

*Are you alright?* Tim asked with concern in his voice.

"I . . . I thought I could see through my hand for a minute there."

Tim didn't say anything, and I managed to push myself to a seated position, a scowl etched into my forehead.

"Tim?"

*You are being* erased, *Andrew,* he reminded me softly.

"So I . . . I *could* see through my hand? I wasn't imagining that?"

*I think it's best we carry on with the mission. We don't know when another episode might occur.*

My lip quivered, and I didn't know if it was from the fear of my impending, unescapable death or just a twitch left over from having every literal part of my body yanked toward oblivion.

With a groan of uncomfortable pain and exhaustion after such an attack, I got to my feet, held out my hands to make sure I wasn't going to fall over, and just breathed in and out for at least a minute.

*I know you need a moment to catch your breath, but may I remind you that Retnuh is on his way?*

Taking a step forward, I let my hands drop back to a neutral position once I thought I wasn't going to lose my balance, and continued on with the mission. As we moved, the trees began to inch closer and closer to the row of expensive-looking houses, until we finally came across what we were looking for.

*Here!* Tim exclaimed. One of the back fences lit up in my vision, slightly startling me.

"I'm never going to get used to that," I muttered to myself as I approached the fence and stopped.

*Why? Because you'll probably be dead?*

I let out a sharp sigh and ran a hand down my face. "Tim . . . you don't need to be literal with me *all* the time."

*Whatever do you mean?*

"I *know* I'm probably going to die. Either from the bastard we are hunting, Retnuh ambushing me, or if I manage to survive them both, from the Temporal Sickness."

*But your family will live on. And this timeline's version of you will carry on to give them a lifetime of love and support.*

My vision blurred as my heart sunk, but my resolve was reinforced by the idea of making sure Sylvie and Alison got to live.

I lifted my chin, wiped at my eyes, and then clenched my fists.

"What now?" I asked with as strong a voice as I could muster. I would do whatever it took to save my wife and daughter. Not even God would be able to stop me.

*Look at the ground, starting at the fence line.*

I did, and two deep prints were highlighted in my vision.

*This is where he landed from the six-foot drop.*

I didn't need Tim to tell me what to do next; I kept looking at the ground as I moved toward the thick trees.

"Hey," I spoke, following the tracks Tim was illuminating for me. "Why is one of the prints staggered?"

*It looks like he hurt himself when he jumped over the tall fence.*

"Good," I said darkly. "It'll make it easier to catch the bastard."

*I don't suppose you've ever heard the adage about injured, cornered predators, have you?*

"He doesn't know he's cornered."

*Fair enough. Oh, and you might want to hurry along. I calculate Retnuh is less than thirty minutes away. Perhaps even less.*

I froze midstep and asked a question I already knew the answer to.

"Why are we bringing him here again?" Now that it was time to act, it was as if I were trying to avoid evolving the plan from a simple idea to reality.

*If we manage to kill your family's murderer, and you survive the Temporal Sickness long enough so we can leave, we won't be able to escape with him hot on our heels.*

"But if we enter the wormhole, he'll be able to follow us anyway, right? You said we leave some sort of signature like a computer visiting a website, and they can trace that in the future."

*Right. Unless we get access to his Clepsydra, and I copy his signal blocker.*

"Why would he have a signal blocker?"

*The same reason your local police station has computers with firewalls, server rooms with backups, and IT personnel—or third-party companies—on payroll.*

"I don't—"

*For protection, bonehead.*

"Protection? Against what?" I asked, mind whirling with the beginnings of several ideas that would never materialize into full thoughts. "What would someone like Retnuh need protection from?"

*If someone had the gumption and comprehension to print their own Clepsydra, who's to say they wouldn't come up with a nefarious idea to counter other people using them? People who think they are right don't like to be challenged, Andrew.*

"You mean some sort of virus or something?" I asked while I resumed following the illuminated footsteps deeper into the forest.

*Correct.*

"How would a Clepsydra get a virus?"

*Think about it, Andrew. I am able to interact with the world around me, am I not?*

I nodded as I thought about the credit card readers, security cameras, and even the rental vehicles' GPSs.

*Having the ability to interact externally means the doorway is open—both ways.*

The last piece clicked into place, and I was able to see the picture as a whole.

"We can travel without being seen if . . . " I whispered to myself, the power of the realization getting hold. "So if I fail . . . "

*You would be able to try again, yes. But . . . that's assuming you survive the Temporal Sickness.*

"What if he finds us first *before* we discover where the killer is hiding?"

*Retnuh might actually find him before us, in the likely event he decided the killer was a bigger threat. Then you could deal with whoever was left standing.*

"And what if he finds us in the middle of battle?"

*That would be the inherent risk, wouldn't it? However, I am banking that Retnuh would choose to target the Tick, or the other way around.*

"What other way around?"

*The Tick didn't kill you when he had the chance. As a matter of fact, he saved your life.*

"Maybe he just really hates the Clockmen . . . or-or sees them as a bigger threat."

*Hmm . . . that does seem to add up. Either way, we can hope for a repeat and have the leader of the Clockmen draw the Tick's full attention.*

"This all sounds really hopeful and not at all tactical."

*Pfft. You wouldn't know tactical if it was tattooed on your forehead.*

"That doesn't make any se—" A branch cracked somewhere nearby.

*Thirty yards to the east.*

"I'm in a forest!" I harshly whispered. "I don't know where east is!"

*To your slight right, dummy, behind the big tree.*

The tree in question lit up in my vision, and I crouched down behind one of its fallen brethren with a large amount of its roots sticking up from the ground, offering adequate cover.

Peeking over the top, I let out a quick bark of laughter at seeing an adolescent deer come from around the highlighted tree.

*I'm picking up something . . . something odd.*

"It's just a de—"

*DROP!* Tim shouted, and I flopped to the ground just as the root system to my side went up in a bloom of white fire, flash frying the moisture beneath my skin. Hitting the ground hard enough to rattle my teeth,

I scrambled away from the tree, feeling like the forest floor had been replaced with slick ice.

"What the hell was that?" I panted while clamoring around a particularly thick tree.

*I . . . I don't know. I've never seen that type of energy be used before.*

"Is it him?"

*Him who? Retnuh or the killer.*

"The killer, goddamn it!" I blurted in a harsh whisper as I peered from around the trunk.

*I can only assume that it is,* Tim admitted. *Oh, and Retnuh is sure to be on his way now, even if he thought it was a trap before. That blast lit up my sensors like the Fourth of July.*

"Why didn't you see it coming?" I whispered while moving to the other side of the tree trunk and carefully peering out again. "I thought you would be able to track the buildup of energy from the Clepsydra."

*That's what worries me, Andrew. I believe he has some sort of suppressor hiding his signature.*

"And why does that worry you?" I asked in a prone position and squinting at a bush that I thought had moved.

*Because that means he is working with, or for, a powerful organization that is* not *the Clockmen.*

"Who wou—"

*Duck!* Tim shouted, and I bashed the side of my head into the dirt as the tree I was hiding behind erupted into white fire. My reeling brain clicked as to what would happen next, and I rolled onto my back with my hands up toward the sky in a wishful hope of stopping the top half of the giant tree from crushing me.

"Huh?" I exhaled as I was met with a blue sky in the clearing between tree canopies.

*MOVE!* Tim bellowed inside my head, and I felt a surge of jet fuel light my muscles. With a primal scream that I didn't even realize was coming from me, my body shot up and began running through the dense forest, right as another blast of blinding white light rocketed past me.

A thick specimen of a tree went up in a bloom of white fire just ten yards in front of where I was sprinting. I was in awe watching the entire thing get consumed into nothing. Not even smoke was left; the wood was just erased from existence.

*Oh, my science,* Tim drawled. *He has an antimatter adapter!*

"What the hell does that mean?!" I shrieked, dodging through the forest at erratic angles.

*It means that if you get hit by a blast of antimatter, no matter where it strikes on your body, you will experience the inevitable conclusion of Temporal Sickness, but all at once!*

I wanted to ask if he meant it would erase me from the face of the universe, but I was too busy sucking in deep, frantic breaths that had an alarming taste of blood in them.

Instead, I managed to ask between sucking gasps, "What . . . do we do?!"

*I'm getting a lock on his position. Around eighty yards behind you . . . at your five o'clock.*

"Are we charged?" I asked as I skidded to a halt and turned in the direction Tim had indicated. Through the trees, I could see a rough, bright outline of where the AI thought the killer was coming from.

*We are,* Tim confirmed with a smile in his tone.

I lifted my glowing fist toward the area he was highlighting and waited.

A warm breeze glided over my skin, bringing with it the scent of oak. My heart pounded in my chest so hard that I thought I was moving in place, like one of the old American football toy games that had figures placed on a vibrating board. I could feel the adrenaline-laced blood coursing through my veins, making swishing sounds in my ears.

The highlighted image coalesced into a man as the killer stepped from behind a tree. He was now a black man with a long, thick beard that went down to the top of his chest while the rest of his head was hidden by the hoodie. But something was off. His hands w—Tim fired from my fist without waiting for my input, sending a blast of blue light straight at him.

For the briefest of moments, I felt a surge of hope as I saw that the attack was going to be a bull's-eye. But the killer simply opened his glowing hand and absorbed the blast, sucking every last bit of raw energy into his Clepsydra.

"Shit!" Tim and I both yelled at the same time, right as the killer sent a blast of return fire our way.

I froze in terror, watching the antimatter streak toward me at chest height.

Something happened to my knees because they went numb and my legs buckled under me, collapsing my body to the ground. As my back struck a protruding branch that punched into my right shoulder blade, the blast of white energy flew overhead, nearly blinding me with its brilliance.

*Move!* Tim cried out right as the feeling in my legs came back like a breaker had been thrown.

Rolling to my stomach, I scrambled forward on hands and feet, looking like some sort of newborn deer.

"You shouldn't be here!" the man called out, though his voice sounded . . . odd, like it was being ran through audio filters. "It's not your time yet!"

I barely registered he was speaking to me, as I kept falling while trying to run on all fours.

My hand slapped against something that my brain alerted me should *not* be found in the forest, and I slowly turned my head to see a shiny black dress shoe.

The world became silent; I could only hear the beating of my own labored heart and follow the black pants up to a damaged suit and tie, where a man in a fedora looked down at me—a glowing fist pointed at my head.

# CHAPTER 39

A laser three feet wide shot out of Retnuh Ordune's fist, and he ran the beam down my entire body. Relief washed over me as I saw it was harmless, only to be replaced with the realization that I was a large fish in a small barrel.

Looking at his Clepsydra, Retnuh read something that I couldn't see, then looked back at me.

"I'll deal with you soon enough, Frost," he said in his Spanish accent, sounding to me like he might have hailed from somewhere in Spain.

He stepped over where I was cowering on the ground and strode toward the killer. He had a faint scent of leather about him that stuck in my mind for some reason.

"Ordune!" the killer cried out, eager for a fight. "We meet at last!"

"I've met your type before, Tick," Retnuh responded stoically. "You're all the same to me."

*We should, perhaps, find a place to take shelter,* Tim spoke, though I could hear the undertone of his message that suggested he, too, wanted to watch what was about to happen.

Pushing myself up, I jogged in a half-crouched position to a particularly thick section of forest with bushes that came up to chest height between trees thicker than I was wide.

"Leave it to a dog like you to think we are allllll the same," the killer said with a malicious smile in his voice. "Tell me, did the other *Ticks* you've hunted have this?"

I peered over the bushes while the bulk of my body stayed hidden behind a tree, just in time to see the killer, who now appeared to have Asian features, lift his glowing left hand toward an unfazed Retnuh.

A part of me wanted to shout *watch out!* but confusion as to my choice of who I was rooting for caught me off guard.

Retnuh lifted his own left hand right as the white light streaked across the distance between them. A half sphere of blue light caught the anti-matter and sent it flying back at the killer, reminding me of a skateboard park's half pipe. The attack went down one side and was flung in the opposite direction, using its own power against it.

The killer did something I wasn't expecting and barked out in laughter as he dove to the side. Where I would have screamed in terror, this guy seemed to be enjoying the battle.

Retnuh followed up the reversal with a blast of his own, aimed at where the killer with the shifting features was diving toward.

In midair, the laughing man pivoted with his left hand out and caught the blue energy, absorbing it before hitting the ground and expertly rolling to his feet. I did, however, notice he winced at putting pressure on his hip from where he had jumped over the fence, and that gave me hope that he could be stopped. An idea came to me that was more of an instinct than a fully-fledged thought, and I bent down to grab at a baseball-size stone protruding from the dirt.

The killer swung out his left hand in an arc and sent a wide, thin blast of blue light resembling a saw blade toward Retnuh.

The bald man left his left leg in place while his right shot out, and he crouched onto that side while sticking his left hand above him, unbeliev-ably catching the saw blade. Immediately, he straightened himself, took a step forward like a baseball pitcher, and sent the saw hurtling back at the killer.

The man braced himself and extended his left palm out as a wall of white light formed just in time to catch the blue energy, though he was flung backward with the transfer of momentum. However, the saw had been reduced to nothing more than a split second of wavering air before fading into oblivion.

The killer was gone from sight, swallowed by the thick foliage; the only trace of him was an eerie cackle that seemed to come from everywhere.

"He he he heeeee. Is that the best you can do, *Tock*?" the killer chal-lenged, using Retnuh's title as a seemingly pejorative descriptor.

The bald man, who didn't answer, simply looked at his Clepsydra, nodded once, then reached across his chest and under his coat. What he pulled out defied physics as I knew it.

A handle was in his right hand, silver *fuzz*, for lack of a better term, growing around it, forming into what I knew to be some sort of gun.

*Oh my . . .* Tim gasped.

"What?" I whispered, lifting myself further up over the bushes to better see.

*It's a nanite gun.*

"The tiny machines?" I asked, calling on every sci-fi movie I had ever seen that dealt with nanotechnology. As I squinted, I recognized it wasn't fuzz I was seeing, but a mass of microscopic robots that were forming into a gun.

Tim ignored my question, and I took that to mean I was mostly correct.

The tiny machines formed into a weapon that looked reminiscent of a Desert Eagle mixed with a hyperdramatized gun one might see on an anime.

"Is that going to be any better than the Clepsydra?"

*The Tick is able to cancel Retnuh's attacks while using the Clepsydra. However,* nothing *can counter a nanite gun.*

I was about to ask *why* when Tim continued.

*Each machine is powered by exotic matter, with countless billions of particles to use as ammunition. This basically provides an endless source of power to be used at the wielder's discretion.*

Though I couldn't see the killer, he apparently had eyes on Retnuh because he called out in a stone-cold voice, "You . . . wouldn't . . . *dare!*"

*We can't let him shoot him!* Tim cried out.

"What? Why the hell not?"

*Be-be-because the chain reaction could take us with it, Andrew! Anything caught in the radius of the blast will be erased from existence across the entire timeline!*

I could feel my left hand begin to hum with power as Tim readied my attack.

"Should we just run?" I asked, feeling the moisture in my mouth suddenly vanish like the after shot in a movie that showcased an apocalyptic landscape.

*It's too late!* Tim exclaimed with an alarming amount of panic in his tone. *Stop him!*

I lifted the rock I was holding—rather, I *felt* my arm lift as if on its own—and I slung the stone at the man as he aimed his nanite gun into the forest . . . and pulled the trigger.

# CHAPTER 40

Retnuh roared in surprise and rage as the rock struck him in the side of the face, but it was too late. The nano bullet powered by exotic matter streaked through the forest at nearly the speed of light.

I slammed my eyes shut and shielded my face, but I could still see the blinding light piercing through my flesh and burning my retinas. What was even more alarming was the fact that I could see the bones of my hands like some sort of X-ray.

There was no sound; rather, I felt a rush of wind pulling me toward the blast like the ocean seeking entry to a large ship whose hull had just been hit with a torpedo.

I screamed, or at least I think I did, as I pushed with all my might against the tree in the absolutely most difficult push-up I had ever tried in my entire life. It felt like I had every weighted plate in a powerlifting gym stacked on my back. Panic began to take hold as the vortex pulled at my right side, and I began to slip toward the blinding light that promised nothingness where my life had once resided on the timeline.

My fingernails dug into the bark of the tree, first loosening, then beginning to pull both nails and bark free from their homes. The nerves at the ends of my hands tried to send a signal to my brain that they were experiencing an alarming amount of input, but the transmission was lost along the way as I was yanked free from the tree and thrown through the thick bushes.

Everything went black as gravity took back control over me, and I flopped to the ground where I rolled once before coming to a full stop, facedown.

My body quivered from the surge of adrenaline and the abrupt drop to the ground. Anyone over the age of twenty-five could confirm that the simple act of falling required more than a curse word and patting of the dirt from your clothes in order to recover. Costco-size bags of frozen peas and painkillers that had been saved up from a root canal four years prior were usually required for those of us who had used a VHS player in our lifetime and suffered a fall.

Something was in my mouth, tickling the back of my throat, and I gagged while moving a throbbing arm from under my body to pull at a blade of grass that had violated my oral cavity without consent. At least I think it was grass; I couldn't see, even with throbbing, wide eyes flicking all around.

A different type of panic, one that focused on the immediate realization of long-term ramifications from an injury, began to replace the existential one I had just experienced. A part of my brain tried to distract me from my blindness and suggested we debate how odd it was that negative emotions were so easy to replicate and overlap over one another, like fear and hate, versus more benevolent feelings such as love. It was hard to fall in love again after a hard breakup, and it took time. Hate, on the other hand? Hate was plentiful and—

I shook my head, not allowing the distraction.

Pushing the small patch of grass to clear my face, I moved my fingers to my eyes and began rubbing with a trembling hand, hoping the action would be similar to using windshield wipers after getting a thin layer of muddy water on your car.

No such luck.

"T-Tim!" I wheezed, trying to suck in a breath to expand my deflated lungs.

*Thank 01! We are still alive!*

"I . . . I can't see!"

*We need to get out of here.*

"Do you remember the part when I said I can't fucking see?!"

*Give me a moment,* Tim replied as something twanged in the back of my skull, making me wince in pain. *Oops. You weren't supposed to be able to feel that. I must have dug into your bone on accident.*

"My . . . my *bone*?!"

*Annnnnd almost done,* he said just as my vision returned. But something was very wrong. *There we go!*

I was staring down at a man lying on the ground who looked a lot like me. Then I realized it *was* me, and I was seeing myself from a third-person perspective.

"What the hell!" I babbled, waving a hand in the air to verify what I already knew to be true.

*Your eyes are burned, and they will take some time to repair. But in the meantime, we need to get out of here before either of them recovers!*

"Either of them?" I asked, pushing myself up to a seated position and feeling dizzy watching the man on the ground move. It was like viewing someone else from a few feet away, but *feeling* everything they did. The dirt and grass beneath their palms. The rock pushing into the back of one leg. And the apparently broken right arm that had waited for me to notice the slightly protruding skin before sending all the pain signals at once.

"Uhhh!" I inwardly gasped, clasping my left hand around the swelling right forearm.

*For the love of science,* Tim cursed as a flood of relief washed over my body. *Here, this will take care of the pain for the time being. Now, if you don't mind, CAN WE GET THE HELL OUT OF HERE?!*

"No! We need to kill them . . . *both* of them! That was the plan, right?!"

*That was before it became overly obvious that we are completely out-matched,* Tim countered. *I didn't know Retnuh had a nanite gun! And I don't even know what energy the killer was using!*

"We can do this!"

*Oh dear. I think I've given you too much of the good stuff, and now you are high as a kite with delusions of grandeur.*

"Tim . . . please . . . "

*Andrew,* Tim inhaled sharply, and I could hear the palpable frustration in his voice. *We only have* me *as a weapon. And both the Tock* and *the killer from the future seem to have no problems with countering our attacks. So we* must *flee and come up with another plan.*

"I'm dead no matter what," I drawled.

*You don't commit euthanasia by doing a cannonball into a swamp of alligators, Andrew. Now, we need to hurry! Retnuh is back on his feet, and it won't be long until he finds where we were thrown!*

"Fine, goddamn it!"

My arm stopped throbbing, as did the fingertips of my left hand that I hadn't even been paying attention to until the pain was gone. I carefully got to my feet, trying not to lose my balance as I watched myself move.

"Can you go behind my back? Over my shoulder, I mean."

*What?*

"In college, I played a lot of video games in the third person with the camera angled over the shoulder looking forward."

*Oh, that makes sense, I guess.*

The camera moved way too fast, and I nearly toppled over, as my body thought we had just physically spun in the same way someone in an intense VR game might experience.

I shot my legs far apart with my arms out in front of me, lowering my center of gravity until I could catch my bearings.

*I'm also going to control the signals to your muscles to act as a sort of autocorrect.*

"What the hell does that mean?"

*If you dictate where to go, I will control your coordination, considering you've never practiced moving your* actual *body in the third person. It'll be just like playing a video game for you while your dad bod sits on the couch and makes* oh *and* ah *faces at the screen.*

"Okay, I guess," I replied, feeling my body sort of disappear in much the same way as if I'd been put under anesthesia. I was left with only my third-person perspective, and I mentally commanded my left arm to lift. The body did as instructed, and I repeated the process with my right.

*Shit!* Tim cried out inside my head.

Before I could ask what he was shouting about, the camera slightly zoomed in about twenty yards in front of me, highlighting Retnuh Ordune like some sort of video game boss. He was reaching up with his free hand to wipe at the blood seeping from a large cut at his temple. Examining his black gloves to see the dark crimson reflected in the sunlight, Retnuh shifted angry eyes from his fingertips to where I was speaking out loud, without whispering.

"What the hell did I do now?" I mumbled as I told my body to get off my knees and stand up. To my delight, it did as instructed, much more smoothly than I could have managed.

*We hit him in the head with that rock.*

"Oh . . . wait, *we*?"

*Oh is right. And if you don't mind, I'd like to flee, please. Like . . . now, maybe?*

Retnuh raised his glowing fist toward me, and I took off in a sprint.

"Highlight any obstacles," I ordered as I focused intently on not tripping or running into anything while Tim fed some sort of camera stream directly into my brain.

*Got it.*

I didn't have to worry about feeling or controlling each of my muscle groups, simply relying on my input of where to go. It was like being behind the wheel of a car. By using the steering wheel and pushing on the accelerator, you told the vehicle where to go without having to worry about combusting the fuel and spinning the axles.

A group of trees exploded to my right, and I pivoted to the left at a wide angle in an attempt to throw off my pursuer. At that moment, it did feel like I was playing a video game, and the part of my brain that had spent thousands of hours competing against other players online kicked in, granting me a degree of control that filled me with confidence that I didn't deserve, considering it was a life-or-death scenario with no checkpoints or saves.

"Are we charged?" I asked over labored but controlled breaths.

*Yes. But can I suggest that we keep moving away from the danger?*

"I am the danger," I whispered as I jumped off a large rock and spun in midair with my left fist pointed to where I knew Retnuh had been.

Tim highlighted the Clockman, who was only a few feet to the side of where I had originally aimed, and everything moved in slow motion while I oriented on my target . . . and fired.

# CHAPTER 41

**R**etnuh was in quick pursuit, fully intent on capturing his prey, when he rushed from between two thick bushes obstructing his view and was met with a fully charged blast to his unprotected torso.

The man didn't even make a sound as he burst into a pink mist while his arms, legs, and even his head continued forward, tumbling on the ground with surprisingly heavy thuds. The black wide-brimmed fedora, which had somehow stayed on during the entire fight, now fell away as the detached head rolled violently.

*Nice shot, Andrew!*

I landed on my feet from my jump, but Tim apparently lost my balance because I began to fall over backward. My body reacted and lifted my right arm up to shield the back of my head from any potential rocks on the ground.

Boy was *that* a mistake.

Though the ground was blessedly free from sharp stones or pointy roots sticking through the dirt, my head *did*, however, hit something vital—my broken right arm.

"Aye-aye-aye," is what came out of my mouth as I sharply sucked in air from the sudden bloom of intense pain. I could see my jaw flapping open and closed as my blind eyes bugged out of my skull, and I realized I was looking down on myself.

*Oooooohhhh . . . that* had *to hurt,* Tim said helpfully.

A twig on the ground *cracked* nearby, and Tim pivoted the camera toward the sound, once again making me dizzy and nauseated with the swift movement.

A man in a black hoodie stopped where Retnuh's bald, fedoraless head rested.

"Fuck," I mouthed.

*It's him!* Tim croaked inside my head, disbelief energizing his words to near frantic levels.

"Can we shoot again?"

*No. It's going to take another forty-five seconds to get a full charge. And the closer we get, the easier it will be to get notif—* The killer looked at a notification on his Clepsydra, and then up at where I was lying. *Shit!*

"There's no need for that, Andrew," the killer said as he leaned down to pick up Retnuh's head. He stood up straight and held it out while placing his other hand over his heart. "To be . . . or not to be."

He giggled to himself and then let the lifeless head drop to the ground with a sickening *crunch* as it landed nose first.

"This guy is insane . . ."

*Thirty seconds.*

The man pulled back his hood, and I was surprised to see a cascade of different features rolling over his skin and hair. In one instance, he had a wide nose with large nostrils before it shifted to a long, narrow, protruding version. The color of his eyes flowed like they were testing all shades of the rainbow. His lips varied from plump to pencil thin and back again while his hair grew, thickened, shrunk, or banded together in dreadlocks before fading completely. It was the same with his facial hair.

"What the hell is that?" I whispered to Tim.

*Twenty seconds.*

"He's gone, Andrew. You can relax," the killer spoke with a casual tone as he bent down and picked up the detached right arm. "At least for now." He switched to an Alec Guinness impersonation from *Star Wars*, and said, "But they'll be back, and in greater numbers."

The killer with the shifting features pried the handle of the nanite gun free from Retnuh's grip and smiled as the weapon came to life in his hands.

*Oh no . . .* Tim said with serious concern in his voice.

Then the killer did something I wasn't expecting. After dropping the empty arm, he bent down again and picked up the other one with the Clepsydra still intact. Looking at me with a wide smile, he tossed the arm over to me; it landed only a few feet to my side. "You're gonna need that."

The killer then let the nanomachines retreat back into the handle and put the grip into his hoodie pocket before turning and limping away.

He paused, looked up at the sky, and did something I never would have anticipated—he appeared to cry. His shoulders bounced up and down in quick succession as his hands went up to cover his face. I could hear the galloping moans just as he began to shake his head back and forth, throwing his hands away and then screaming to the forest, "I can't do this anymore!"

Though I was confused by how the killer was acting toward me and how he was attempting to make himself seem like he wasn't a threat, I still felt the awful pain in my heart of finding my wife and daughter murdered in our own home. He had killed them. And he had his back to me right now.

*Charge ready!*

"Rah!" I bellowed, pointing my glowing fist toward the man and firing.

With surprising reflexes, the man smoothly crouched and let the rushed blast fly over him, where it obliterated the trunk of one of the largest trees in the immediate area. The killer righted himself once more and slowly turned to look at me with a scowl as his features continued to shift and morph.

"You're starting to piss me off, Andrew," he declared darkly as his left fist began to glow. No longer did his voice hold the chaotic enthusiasm as when he had hoisted up the skull of his enemy, nor did it carry with it the brief bout of sorrow and rage at a universe that was indifferent to his plight.

"Oh shit," Tim and I said in unison as we realized the game was up. Had I only taken an extra half second to aim, I might have hit my target. This man, however, knew he had all the time in the world to take aim and remove the threat.

The enormous tree I had struck began to snap apart, sounding like shotgun blasts as the bark crumpled and split. The killer tilted his head to the side in confusion and slowly turned around, right as the top half of the tree smashed into him. I couldn't see through all the branches if he had been hit dead-on, but I could feel the impact as the enormous tree smashed into the ground.

*You got him!* Tim shouted in glee. *Ha haaaa!*

From where I sat in the dirt, I could feel my eyes begin to water and left arm tremble as relief washed over me in a landslide of emotion.

Retnuh was dead, for now, and the killer was crushed under a tree that could have turned a full-size car into a thin sheet of aluminum foil on impact. Not only that, but I had Retnuh's Clepsydra and would be able to hide my signature as I utilized the wormhole. That was, of course, if I survived the Temporal Sickness long enough for the contamination to fade so that I could even use the tunnel again.

*You did it, Andrew. You did it!*

I dropped my left arm to my lap and let the flood of emotion flow through me in body-wracking sobs. The emotions that had stacked up since the day of the funeral were just too much, and now that I didn't need to suppress them, they wreaked their havoc with a vengeance . . . and I let them.

I sobbed.

I sobbed from the pain over my entire body. I sobbed from the relief of having done the impossible. And I sobbed from having saved my family from their murderer.

I sobbed . . . and it felt good.

# CHAPTER 42

After ten minutes, I stopped weeping and just lay on the ground, feeling a sort of vibrating numbness that could only be experienced after letting the cleansing of a good cry run its course. Ten more minutes of staring up at the sky, and I was ready to move. I was thankful to Tim for letting me have my time.

Pushing myself up, I wiped at my eyes with my left hand, and then looked to my side to see Retnuh's Clepsydra lying on the ground with his arm still inside. With a long sigh, I reached over, careful not to hit my broken right forearm on anything, and grabbed the device.

After getting to my feet, I examined it and asked, "How do we get it off?"

*Touch the device to me.*

I did, then stared in mild amazement at all the flashing lights that came to life for a few seconds before fading away. The arm seemed to wiggle as I held the metal device before the flesh slowly slid free to plop on the ground at my feet. I glanced down by chance, but stared by choice, at the rows of tiny holes in it. And at that moment, my own left forearm itched like a person in a cast unable to reach the source of discomfort.

"That's what you've done to me?" I asked, kicking at the appendage more to signal the topic of conversation than as a means of disrespect for my fallen enemy.

*Hmm? Oh, those . . . um . . . don't mind those.*

His refusal to answer my question . . . answered my question. The itching on my arm grew more prominent.

*Almost . . . done . . . aaaaannnnd got it!*

"Got what?" I was ready for nothing more than to take a hot shower and get a full night's sleep before figuring out how to return to my wheren . . . and my family.

*I've managed to unlock the Clepsydra, and I'm scanning for anything helpful.*

"Like what?" I asked, feeling how both comfortable and weird it was to be seeing everything from a third-person perspective.

*Like how to mitigate your Temporal Sickness symptoms long enough to be able to portal away from here.*

I simply nodded rather than using the energy necessary to form words.

*Boy, there is a lot to unpack here!* Tim informed with evident excitement in his voice. For some reason, I pictured Indiana Jones coming across an ancient, untouched temple full of goodies just waiting to be explored.

"I need to rest," I sighed as I began walking in the direction I thought would take me to the parked truck.

*Oh, right. Of course,* Tim replied as a path was highlighted in front of me.

I followed it, feeling like it was taking four times as long to make the trek back to the truck than it had taken to get to the forest.

I held Retnuh's Clepsydra between my left forearm and stomach, allowing Tim to do whatever he needed while letting my broken arm hang loosely at my side. Something caught my attention, and I looked down with a face-contorting cringe after seeing I was missing three of my five fingernails on my left hand.

I wanted to ask Tim if he could grow them back, but decided I didn't care at that moment. All I wanted to do was make it back to the truck, and maybe rest my eyes for a few minutes.

Sirens wailed in the distance, and I paid them no mind. Living in a suburb of a big city like Houston, I heard them all the time.

*We should probably hurry.*

"Hmm? Why?" I asked, seeing the edge of the neighborhood come into view.

*Where do you think those police and firefighters are heading to?*

I did a mental forehead smack as I remembered all the explosions that had been in relatively close proximity to the neighborhood.

Picking up my pace, I made it the rest of the way to the truck in just under five minutes and climbed in with a grunt.

I moved Retnuh's Clepsydra to the passenger seat before using my left hand to press the vehicle's Start button.

*Hey! I wasn't done with that!*

"I can't drive with my right hand," I groaned while I gently set my broken arm on the center console, thankful for the ample room provided by the truck.

*Grr*, Tim growled, but I could hear he was accepting of the situation.

Using my left hand to shift the truck into drive, I said, "You could spend this time fixing my arm and eyes."

Tim mumbled something under his breath, and then I felt a tingling in both of my eyes and my right arm. I could only guess that was him getting to work.

Using the third-person view Tim was providing directly to my brain, I did an awkward U-turn, and oh so carefully made my way out of the neighborhood.

# CHAPTER 43

Using the service and back roads, because I was uncomfortable with driving on the highway while using Tim's borrowed vision, I pulled into a hotel parking lot and threw the truck into park.

Leaning back against the headrest, I let out a long breath as I felt an exhaustion I had never experienced before creep up on me.

I had won.

I had pushed myself beyond the limits of what should have been physically or even mentally possible and come out the other side victorious. And now . . . now I wanted nothing more than to shower and sleep.

After making my way to the hotel room that Tim had booked, I did just that.

The water was hot enough to leave red streaks where it ran down my body, until all of me resembled a human-shaped lobster. Normally, I preferred a warm shower—or even cold—but right now, I needed the heat to cook away everything I had gone through during the past couple of days.

It was funny, how I didn't even feel the pai—

My body collapsed in a heap as ethereal electricity ripped at my very soul.

From the third-person perspective of my body, I could see every muscle twitching and writhing beneath my skin as my jaw stretched open far enough that I thought it was going to snap off.

Noises streamed from my mouth, but they were incoherent and devoid of any structure.

*This is a bad one,* Tim said apologetically while my organs seemed to ripple and my skeleton felt like it was trying to tear itself free from my flesh.

Then it was over, and I was left watching my red-stained body quiver in a heap on the shower floor. I was, however, thankful it was a walk-in and not a bathtub combo, or I might have broken my neck when I fell.

*Tim?* I mentally asked, not knowing if he could hear me or not.

*Y-Yes, Andrew?* a surprised Tim responded.

*Am I dead?*

*Um, not yet. I am working to slow your heart before scanning your brain for any damaged neural pathways.*

*I feel like I'm dead,* I admitted, staring down at my body.

*Oh, it's because of the perspective I am sending to your occipital lobe. I can change it if you'd like.*

*Just help me get to bed,* I replied, defeated. I didn't have it in me to fight the Temporal Sickness anymore, and was content to just let it finish me off.

*Give me another minute,* Tim said.

Five minutes later, and I was slowly crawling toward the bed, not caring to towel off.

*Make sure I'm in contact with the Clepsydra.*

I slipped onto the mattress and somehow managed to perform a miracle and roll myself onto my back before moving my left arm to touch the stolen Clepsydra with my own.

*Okay. You get some rest, and I'll continue to decipher what I can while you sleep.*

"Sounds . . . g—" Unconsciousness took me with swift, eager arms.

# CHAPTER 44

I awoke with a jerk, as if someone had jammed a taser into my chest, but there wasn't the usual ethereal pain that was becoming all too familiar. Instead, it felt like my body was being invigorated in what I could only guess was the opposite effect of having the universe try and erase me. For some reason, my brain equated the sensation to a coloring book with the pages being filled in rather than being bled dry.

"What's happening?" I sucked in at the uncomfortable feeling of having my body manipulated. But at least it didn't hurt.

*Oh no,* Tim gasped. *That* caught my attention.

"What?!"

*We have to get up. Quickly now,* he instructed. *I've repaired your eyes, to the best of my abilities in the limited time, and have set your broken bone, though it is not, in the least, secured.*

"Secured?" I asked as I all but fell out of bed and stumbled to the bathroom. The remnants of the episode still lingered, leaving me with a tingling sensation just beneath my skin.

*Just don't hit your arm on anything,* Tim blurted out, and I could tell he was focusing on something else that he wasn't telling me.

This felt like the complete opposite of the previous times I had been attacked by the universe; like I was being charged instead of drained.

"Tim . . . what is it?"

*Please hurry. Skip the shower . . . we don't have time.*

I looked down at my hands, feeling the tangible energy that had been inserted into my being, and a sickening feeling began to rise from my guts, building in intensity as a horrifying idea formed. If I wasn't being erased any longer . . .

"They killed me . . . "

Though he was speaking inside my mind, I could hear Tim actually let out a long, stressed sigh just before he said, *That's what I'm afraid of.*

"Who did it? Who would have wanted the past me . . . dead?"

*I can only surmise it was one of the Clockmen. Since they failed in capturing or killing you . . .*

"They thought they could erase me . . . the *real* me, I mean," I flatly finished as I looked up at the mirror and poked and pulled at my face with my fingers. "But I'm still here."

*That only means that whoever did the deed didn't have a high enough impact on the Chronos Scale,* Tim explained. *They probably knew that would be the case but tried anyway, having run out of more viable options.*

"Why?"

*Why, what?*

"Why did they run out of options? Couldn't they have just waited for me to die from the Temporal Sickness?" I gripped the cool stone countertop and continued to stare at my reflection. "I mean, all they did was help me survive long enough to escape, right?"

*Yeah . . . that doesn't make sense, does it?* Tim thought openly. *Unless . . .*

"Unless?"

*Unless they know you have Retnuh's Clepsydra and are assuming that if you were to survive the Temporal Sickness somehow, then you'd be able to slip away through the wormhole, and they'd never be able to track you.*

"How do they know I have it?" I asked, my mind straining to comprehend the cause and effects of time travel. "If I understand this, and I'm sure I don't, they wouldn't be able to know anything in the future until after the-the-the contamination thingy passed. Right? Because I'm Jupiter or something like that?"

*Very good, Andrew,* Tim said with approval. *You are close. Because of your impact on the timeline, which is similar to the largest planet in a solar system having the most pull of gravity besides the sun, of course, events do not unfold in the future until a threshold has been crossed in your present.*

"Then I'll ask again. How do they know I have the Clepsydra?"

*Best guess is that they prepared for this unlikely scenario and acted on it when Retnuh didn't check in by placing a speck of radiation deep below the crust at a specific point. He probably was tasked to do that every hour or so.*

"And when he didn't report in, and I crossed the threshold of when he was supposed to do that . . . "

*It could have alerted the future that something was wrong.*

"Then that means the Clockmen are here? Right?"

*I didn't want to mention it earlier, seeing as how we were busy stalking the killer while Retnuh was hunting us . . . but I didn't see the shorter Tock die after the tall one's Clepsydra contaminated this wheren.*

"But he blew up with the Tannerite stuff, right?"

*He did, yes. But if you recall, I also said that I registered that the replacement versions of both Tocks had come through before the contamination.*

I played back the chaotic scene and latched onto a particular part just before Retnuh had pummeled me with his bare fists.

"I remember I shot him!"

*You're right. He did fall over with blood seeping from his stomach, but he might not have died. Retnuh could have easily rendered first aid.*

"I don't understand," I groaned, letting unfocused eyes drop to the countertop.

*If I had to guess, I would theorize that Retnuh recognized that you are different from all the other Andrews he has hunted and moved the chess piece—that is, the shorter Tock—to another part of the board just in case he was to fail in capturing or neutralizing you.*

"So he killed the past me as a last-ditch effort?"

*On this timeline, the critical moment of Alison and Sylvie's, um, removal has already passed. You stopped the killer before he could get to them on this wheren. Which means the Clockmen might have no compunctions about trying to remove the current you by killing the past you.*

"That doesn't make sense."

*Which part?*

"Wouldn't they be altering Ali and Sylvie's future? I mean, if they kill this timeline's version of me."

*That's the part that isn't adding up for me either, Andrew,* Tim admitted. *Please keep in mind that I am only providing best guesses . . . but something doesn't feel right about all of this . . .*

"Well, I'm still here, damn it. They tried—and failed—to take me out. And now I'm going to make that little Tock pay," I growled.

*You're right! The pull you have on the Chronos Scale does appear to be very much in your favor!*

I thought for a moment, feeling a sense of power as the odds shifted in my favor, similar to how the casino would always have a slight advantage over the players.

"How can we use that to our advantage?"

*Now you're talking!* Tim exclaimed. *We can discuss that along the way. For now, I think we need to head toward Houston.*

Another, darker thought replaced the feeling of confidence I had briefly experienced, and my mouth went dry.

Unable to fully speak, I squeezed out a question in what could be described as a memory of a whisper—faint and with the barest semblance of volume.

"Sylvie . . . Alison . . ."

I could hear the wince in Tim's voice as he confirmed my darkest fear.

*I didn't want to say it, but that's what I'm afraid of, Andrew. If they got to you . . .*

"Does that mean . . . the Clockmen *want* Alison and Sylvie . . . de-dead?" I whispered, unable to give full strength to the words that represented everything I feared the most.

*I don't know. But if they are going scorched Earth with trying to kill you . . .*

"No . . ." I said with a little more umph. "No!" I repeated in a full-on shout as I glared at the man in the mirror. "I did *not* go through hell and stop the fucking murderer only to have those government bastards kill my family anyway!"

*There's one other pos—Actually, never mind.*

I ignored him, no longer caring to talk. Now was the time for action.

Without another word, I grabbed the Clockman's Clepsydra and rushed out the door.

The clerk tried to wave me down as I stomped through the lobby and toward the parking lot. I barely registered they were anything more than wallpaper, as nothing else in the entire world mattered at that moment.

Jumping into the truck, I slammed the door shut, tossed the Clepsydra in the passenger seat, and smashed the Start button with bared teeth. Doing so reminded me that my right arm wasn't fully healed yet, but I ignored the twinge of pain that shot up my elbow.

With a trail of white smoke that billowed like a wildfire, my tires eventually caught traction, and I was rocketed forward with an engine that roared like a ferocious predator about to attack.

"I'm coming, Sylvie. I'm coming, Alison," I growled as I approached my destiny.

# CHAPTER 45

The GPS popped to life, and I glanced with scowling eyes to see Tim had entered a destination that was only fourteen minutes away. Fourteen . . . minutes . . . They had been so close to me this entire time, and that thought made my knuckles pop around the steering wheel.

"I failed them . . . twice," I growled as tears stung my eyes and my jaw popped from a clenching pressure that could have turned coal to diamonds.

*We don't know that they are dead, Andrew,* Tim offered, but I could hear the lack of conviction in his words.

"Why wouldn't he kill them?" I asked flatly. "He already killed me, right?! HA HA!"

I could feel my mind beginning to slip toward insanity. All the work I had done, had been for nothing.

*I . . .* Tim started to say before dropping his unrealistic point and letting silence be a consensus to my fears. *Can you at least put on your seat belt?*

I barked out another dark chuckle of disbelief that he would bother wasting words on something so insignificant at that moment.

With my foot pressed firmly to the floorboard and the gas pedal crushed between, we made it to a dirt road that led to a modern farmhouse on what had to be an acre of land. There were patches of gravel along the driveway as if the owner had paid to have the pebbles distributed once and then never kept up with the maintenance.

*It's an Airbnb. I thought it would be safer and easier to hide than a hotel with cameras,* Tim answered the question I had not asked, nor cared to ask. It didn't matter.

I took note that there wasn't a black Grand Marquis parked anywhere, drawing an even deeper scowl across my forehead.

"Did he leave?"

*Andrew . . . there's something I need to tell you,* Tim said with a sigh.

I barely heard him as I drove down the loosely graveled dirt road, the sound of my own rushing blood swishing in my ears, along with my pounding heart.

In front of the garage was the SUV that Sylvie and I alternated using whenever one of us had to run errands, transport items, or when the family went out for a night on the town. I parked just behind it, my eyes gliding over the farmhouse with rage bubbling just beneath my scowl.

*Andrew . . . please . . .*

I jerked the gearshift into park, punched the Start button to turn the truck off, and threw open the door. I *knew* I was going to be walking into a scene similar to the first time I'd found my wife and daughter dead. No, not dead . . . *murdered.*

Fury and anguish mixed in a vortex of emotion at the center of my chest, producing a soul-eating poison that surged throughout my being.

My boots crunched on the gravel and dirt as I stomped toward the front door.

*Andrew . . . I have to tell you something.*

"Shut . . . up . . . " I growled at the AI. I stopped at the threshold and looked down at the door handle. It appeared alien to me; a surreal feeling flooded my brain, making even the mundane seem extraordinary, such as a doorknob. A simple . . . metal . . . doorknob that was a steadfast guardian to the nightmare just beyond.

Baring my teeth, I wrapped a shaking fist around the handle and turned it with enough force that something broke inside the mechanism, but the door still swung open when I pushed on it.

The thick metal lightly bounced off the doorstop affixed to the baseboards, and an aroma of cleaning solutions typically associated with Airbnbs and hotels wafted out, along with the cool air from the central AC.

A bird chirped twice in a tree just outside, as if to remind me that it wasn't too late to turn around and return to the world of ignorance and bliss. Another chirp seemed to suggest that *maybe* Sylvia and Alison were just fine, and that I should just go about my business without having to worry about laying eyes upon the still warm husks that once housed my family's souls.

Something caught my eye, and I looked down at where I was standing to see several spatters of blood staining the welcome mat that read *Home*

*Is Where the Heart Is.* With a quivering brow, I followed the path that led deeper into the home.

A single, muffled sob came from somewhere inside, and all hesitation evaporated in a violent puff as I stormed toward the noise.

"Sylvie?! Alison?!" I bellowed, panic cracking my voice.

*I'm sorry, Andrew,* I think I heard Tim say softly from the back of my mind. *I was wrong.*

As I rushed from room to room, my hands shot out to catch the doorway that led to the kitchen and dining area. The sudden jolt in my right arm tried to remind me that it was broken, but I was only aware of the pain as an informative signal rather than a sensation.

My eyes attempted to pop from my skull as I sucked in a breath that was almost a scream and saw them sitting at the dining room table.

White dishrags stained in crimson covered the faces of my wife and daughter, who sat motionless with their heads slumped back.

"N . . . No . . . " I croaked while a war of emotion was waged inside me. Rage looked at anguish, who looked at terror, and they all shrugged at who should take charge. Instead, the three emotions decided it was best to work together, and all I could do was let out a single squeak as my throat tightened to the point of choking me.

Sitting at the end of the table, where the head of the household would traditionally sit, was the killer clad in his black hoodie . . . and he was crying into his own hands.

"You . . . w-why . . . I . . . " I tried to get the words out, but only semblances of the whirling questions I had bubbled out of my gaping mouth.

The killer heard my attempts at speaking and stopped sobbing. He let his hands drop from his face, turning to look at me.

What I saw threatened to rip the last fraying strand of sanity I had left.

Beneath the hoodie, familiar eyes stared back at me from a face I had seen a hundred thousand times in my life. Only, this wasn't the reversed reflection from a mirror . . .

"Thank God you're here," the killer said, wiping at eyes that belonged to me.

"I . . . " I tried to speak while a trembling finger pointed at . . . *me.*

My knees gave out, and I gripped at the drywall for support as my brain desperately tried to figure out what the fuck was happening.

*I'm sorry, Andrew,* Tim repeated, and as if for the first time, I heard him.

"S-Sorry?" I asked an entire sentence using only a single word, unable to find the strength for the rest.

*I had to.*

Drool slipped from my slack jaw as I struggled to breathe. Then my brain flashed with every time I had seen the killer whose identity had been obstructed with shifting features. Features I had seen with my own eyes . . . which Tim had direct control over. I thought about all the times he had illuminated things or had provided vision when my eyes had been burned. He had controlled everything I saw, manipulating what my brain processed at his will.

Red-rimmed eyes stared back at me from the far end of the table as I slowly pulled myself to my feet.

With all my will, I managed to take the few steps to where Alison and Sylvie sat motionless—their crimson veils looking toward the heavens.

The killer moved, and I drunkenly looked over to see him set a modern pistol with a long tube at the end on the table. The same silenced pistol the police had said had been used, taking into account that none of the neighbors heard any shots when I had been at the store.

He made a show of pushing it forward and away from his immediate grip before leaning back in his chair and staring at me with apologetic eyes.

"Why?" I mouthed as I hovered my hand over my daughter, unsure of what to do but longing to feel her beneath my fingers. Moving from her covered face, I gently glided my palm down her little arm, feeling that she was still faintly warm. There was a brief explosion of desperate hope inside of me that maybe she was still alive . . . until my eyes latched onto the bloodstained dishrag once more.

"You'll understand . . . one day," the killer spoke with my voice.

I glared at him with a hatred that could flash boil the ocean.

"What the fuck does that mean?" I growled; my face contorted with barely contained rage.

With a dark relief in his voice, the killer said something that shook me to my very soul. "It means . . . it's *your* turn."

# CHAPTER 46

Absurdity created a systems error inside my mind as the man wearing my face spoke. His message played back over and over, ricocheting off of my skull and creating a cacophony born from the words; some came as soft as a whisper and others louder than a jet engine, but they all said the same thing: *it's your turn.*

"My-my turn f-for what?" I breathed out on the verge of fainting as I braced myself on the dining room table between my unmoving wife and daughter. I could smell them, and my nose tried to fill my body with the feeling of love whenever I inhaled their scent, but the metallic aroma of blood tagged along with Sylvie's perfume and Alison's shampoo. My body didn't know how to react to the contrasting smells of love tainted by uncaring death.

"Tim . . . will explain . . . " the killer said as his eyes welled with tears and his face contorted. What was odd was that I could recognize relief in his features, which were almost completely overshadowed by anguish . . . but it was there.

"Explain?" I repeated in a quick, inward gasp, fighting the urge to allow insanity to take hold and reduce me to a sobbing mass on the tiled floor.

*Yes, Andrew. I can explain . . . everything,* Tim replied softly inside my mind. His tone strongly suggested he was completely aware of how difficult the situation was for me, but that he still had a mission to complete, regardless. *But first . . . you must kill him.*

"W-What?" I asked in building confusion as I used the back of my hand to wipe the dripping snot from my nose.

"He's right," the killer spoke, and I narrowed my eyes and tilted my head at how he had heard Tim inside my mind. Probably seeing that written all over my face, he smiled and said, "I was you, not long ago. And things are playing out precisely as they are meant to."

"I . . . I don't understand."

"Oh, *that's* an understatement!" the killer chuckled darkly. "But don't worry. You'll understand . . . soon enough."

"Understand what?!" I barked. "That some alternate version of me *killed* his own family?!"

"That is one of the questions that will drive you insane. For example, am I the past you or future you?" the killer asked. "If I were the *past* you, meaning I was given this . . . this *mission* before you were given Tim . . . then why don't you remember?"

"I . . ."

"Am I the past, the present, or the future? If I am one, then what are you? All I know is we are cyclical, brought to question what free will is . . . and is not."

"I don't know what you are trying to say . . . "

"It boils the brain, doesn't it?" the killer chuckled again, but I could see the pain in his eyes. "Let's say we are one person, no matter how many variants there are, because the universe treats us all as one, hence the Temporal Sickness."

"Okay?"

"I am from a future where this has already happened," he said, motioning around the table where the bodies of my family sat. "It happened in my past, only I was standing where you are now. *Then* it became my future, knowing it was my turn and not having a choice but to play my part."

"I—" I started to say, not liking his wording about not having a choice and wanting to argue the point, but he cut me off.

"JUST . . . just listen . . . please."

I closed my gaping mouth, if only to get to the end of the conversation.

"From my perspective, *you* are the future. But from where you sit, *I* am the future. So who is killing who?"

"Paradox . . . "

"Unless Tim is right about the alternate timeline theory."

Even though I was on the verge of either losing my mind or passing out, my brain still played for me the memory of Tim showing me a diagram of a splintered timeline.

"No one knows for certain," he continued. "But what we do know is . . . you have to kill me."

"Oh, I'm going to," I growled.

"I know . . . because I did the same thing. As did the Andrew before me . . . and the one before him." He looked around the Airbnb kitchen, and slowly shook his head. "Though the location is different . . . the end result is the same. Well, *mostly* the same. I had to kill this wheren's Andrew, or risk *you* dying."

I had to shake my head as my feeble, mortal mind tried to comprehend the intricacies of time travel and alternate timelines.

An idea I couldn't shake formulated in my head, and I remembered standing in front of the grill while holding the tray of meat.

"You took the lighter fluid . . ." I mouthed, barely above a whisper.

"I did." The killer nodded. "As did every Andrew before me, creating a reason for you to go to the corner store to allow us to . . . to . . ."

"Kill my family."

"Do what *must* be done," he countered, frustration leaking into his words. "But you . . . you've changed *everything*."

I glared at the man wearing my skin, feeling like I could burst him into flames with how much I hated him.

"He didn't tell you the whole truth, you know?"

"About what?" I asked, trying to stay upright, assuming he was referring to Tim, since he was the only sentient being I had engaged in prolonged conversation with. That, and I had caught him lying more than once, with the excuse of telling me what I needed to hear at the time.

"When he said that going back in time alone makes your Chronos Scale stronger, like folding steel. That is only half the potential," he explained. "Killing the other variants of *yourself* gives you the other half . . . and then some. Absorbing their energy . . . like I did to this wheren's Andrew."

Something that had seemed odd to me since arriving at the kitchen clicked into place. While I hadn't been able to focus on it with the glaring distraction that were the bodies sitting around the table, I now understood that I hadn't seen the corpse of this timeline's Andrew.

The killer slowly lifted his palm to face me and said, "After you kill me . . . touch my body . . . and you'll absorb my energy, along with all the other Andrews' that have come before you."

"W-Why?" I croaked, overwhelmed with everything that was smashing me in the face at once. What was the most eerie, however, was that this Andrew was entirely too calm about his impending death.

"I know," he said. "I can see it in your eyes. Odd, because I was where you are not that long ago . . . only, it wasn't in *this* kitchen. But your expression is just how I imagined it would look, almost like staring into a mirror."

"What do you know?"

"You are asking yourself why I want to die."

I didn't answer.

"The weight of what . . . what I've done," he choked up, " . . . it's too much to bear. And I want to be with my family again."

"And how will killing you do that?"

"I'll be with them, in Heaven."

"At this moment," I began with a flat tone, "I doubt there even is a God. But if there is . . . what makes you think he'd allow someone who killed his own family into Heaven?"

"What about Abraham? The Lord asked him to sacrifice his son, Isaac, did he not? Do you think *he* was denied Heaven?"

"You're saying God asked you to kill Sylvie and Alison?? To . . . to-to-to shoot them in the fucking head?!"

"To save all of creation . . . " he whispered back.

"I . . . I don't believe *any* of this! Hahaaaa! I'm—I'm insane! Talking to myself because a puppy from the future riddled my brain with holes!" I aggressively ran a hand down my face, stretching my skin to the point where it felt like it was burning.

"You aren't insane, Andrew."

"Then you *can't* be me! I wouldn't hurt my family for *any* reason! I don't give a shit what the consequences would be!"

The killer slowly took off his hoodie and tossed it at the center of the table. I let out a single moan at seeing what was hidden beneath.

Cloaked by the shroud he had worn was the outfit I had first put on before my first jump. The blue Dickies overalls stared at me as if to mock me and chip away at my fraying mind. I'd been half expecting to see the same black tactical clothes I had on at that moment, but for some reason, this felt worse. The same, but *different*.

"Oh God . . . " I wheezed. This small fact seemed to compound on the already gathering disbelief that was testing the very limits of my mental stability.

"It's your turn, Andrew," the killer repeated. Tears began to stream down his face, and his bottom lip quivered. "I'm so sorry for what you're going to have to do. But first, you have to kill me."

"Why?" I mouthed as my heart pounded and a cold sweat coated my forehead.

"So you can save the universe . . . "

I thought I felt a twinge inside my head as a floodgate opened inside of me.

"You took *my* universe from me!" I bellowed, marching around the corpse of my daughter and scooping up the pistol the killer had placed a few feet in front of him.

"You'll soon understand," he said, looking me in the eyes. His tears stopped flowing and his bottom lip stilled as I lifted the barrel to his forehead. "I can leave you with some hope, at least."

"Speak your last words, bastard."

"I think you might be the last of us. The Chronos Scale should be at its peak, if not really close. And this cycle can finally end."

# CHAPTER 46½

Andrew wanted to ask what the killer meant by that, but his finger squeezed the trigger as if on its own volition, and the murderer's head jerked forward against his gun, surprising him to the point that he had to wonder if it had been him who shot him or someone from behind. It wasn't like in the movies where the person getting shot was flung backward.

The brass casing tinkered on the tiled floor by his feet as the air filled with the pungent aroma of propellant, smelling to him like sweet charcoal smoke with a hint of sulfur. Then a wave that reminded him of hot rust smashed into his nose as the killer's brains and blood coated the now cracked window behind him.

The only sound that remained was that of trickling blood racing to the floor and Andrew's own labored breaths as he stood in his dining room filled with the bodies of his family and the still warm killer Andrew.

Tim pleaded his case, explaining in great detail why killer Andrew had had to go back in time to kill Sylvie and Alison. He delivered the message through memories and images, conveying several hours' worth of information in only a few minutes in much the same way one might remember a weeklong vacation with a few simple thoughts.

At first, Andrew had absolutely no desire nor comprehension as to why it'd had to go down like it had. But the more Tim spoke, the more Andrew began to understand.

"So if he didn't go back in time to kill them . . . then the universe would collapse into another Big Bang?" he asked, trying his best to summarize the hours of technical jargon and holographic demonstrations.

"Which would result in them dying across *every* timeline," the puppy added as he floated above Andrew's left arm. Behind him was a blackboard filled with complex mathematical formulas and diagrams.

"And it is supposed to stop with me?"

"Either you or the next variant at the most, yes."

He thought about his lecture, remembering a particular part, and stated, "Because we are increasing the Chronos Scale with each event . . . "

Andrew hated that he was beginning to see the dead body wearing his skin with understanding and even sympathy.

"So . . . so I have to . . . *do it* now?" he asked, unable to say the words *murder my family*.

"I'm afraid so, Andrew," Tim replied as the blackboard slowly vanished, leaving only the puppy with knowing eyes staring at me.

"And . . . and if I do this . . . if I am the-the last . . . the other Andrews will get to live with Sy . . . *them*?" he asked, incapable of speaking their names while discussing their murders.

"Both your time variants and your family will get to live on in peace within a stable universe."

With a dark feeling of understanding, unease, and dread, Andrew picked up the hoodie, slipped it on, and pocketed the pistol.

"Touch his body, and then take his Clepsydra," Tim instructed. "We are running out of time."

"But I thought I couldn't touch him without being absorbed or something. Because his Chronos Scale is higher?"

"*Was* higher," Tim said. "You killed him, making his Chronos Scale drop to a zero. And now, you need to absorb his energy and every other Andrew's that came before you."

"If there's no other Andrew on this wheren . . . that means I won't die from Temporal Sickness?"

"Correct."

Andrew could hear the relief in Tim's voice that the *new* killer was apparently going along with the plan to save the universe . . . by destroying his own.

Andrew reached down, grabbed the Clepsydra from the dead man's arm, and allowed Tim to do his thing. He could hear wires moving, almost sounding like a fishing line being reeled in, and then the device was loose.

He slipped it off, examining it with narrowed eyes. Andrew could feel himself frowning.

*What is it?* Tim prompted inside his mind once more.

"The same thing is going to happen to me . . . isn't it?" he asked, looking down at the Clepsydra that he had just pulled off of his own corpse.

*Yes,* Tim answered honestly. A part of Andrew appreciated the AI giving it to him straight. *But hopefully, you'll be the last.*

He stood there for a moment, not daring to look at the bodies around the table because of the guilt he felt at knowing what he was going to have to do.

"What now?" Andrew finally asked, setting his chin.

*We take the wormhole to our next destination.*

"To the day they died."

*The day they* will *die, Andrew,* Tim corrected. *You are now the strongest version on the Chronos Scale, which means no other version of you will have traveled back in time. What you do determines the future.*

Andrew looked down at the time travel device he had just slipped off his dead body and understood he was going to be the one to leave the box and note for the next Andrew to find . . . after he killed his wife and daughter.

"I hate you," he said just above a whisper.

*I know.*

Reaching down, he touched the dead Andrew's skin and watched in horrid wonderment as he began to fade from view like some sort of CGI effect.

Energy rushed into him while he felt every cell of his body invigorating with the energy of countless variants who had made the ultimate sacrifice. Then he was alone in the kitchen, standing next to the bodies of his wife and daughter, and a pile of clothes left by the vanished killer. Only they weren't *his* wife and daughter. This wheren's Andrew was at the store right now, buying candy and lighter fluid. But the pain remained, all the same.

Grabbing the clothes, Andrew made his way outside and asked, "What now?"

*Now comes the tricky part.*

"What's that?" Andrew asked, looking all around to see that the coast was clear.

*Are you ready?*

"Ready? For what?" he asked again, knowing the answer but desperately trying to avoid the reality of what he must do.

*The funeral.*

"The funeral . . . " he repeated as his chest started heaving in quick gallops. "Oh God . . . it's happening . . . "

*Get yourself together! This is to save the damn universe!*

Before Andrew could hyperventilate, he took in a long breath, held it for a ten count, and then nodded.

*You'll have to drop the Clepsydra off in the box with the note.*

"Right." He loudly exhaled the air he had been holding. "The note. Where's a pen?"

*No need.*

"Huh?"

*Check the pocket of the hoodie.*

He reached into the big front pocket of the hoodie he had slipped on, and had his mouth drop open at feeling the letter inside.

Pulling it out, Andrew gasped when he saw the word *Daddity* written on it.

*Now all we need to do is wrap the box in the same brown paper and twine that Sylvie uses.*

"Why do we have to wrap it like Sy . . . *she* used to?"

*Otherwise, he would tell the receptionist to throw it in the garbage before he could even get a chance to see the note,* Tim explained. *It's an important step that must be replicated to catch his attention.*

A car pulled up to the driveway that Andrew was standing on, which made him nearly jump out of his skin.

*I ordered the supplies and had them delivered here,* Tim informed me.

"Don't *do* that!" he loudly whispered before quickly regaining his composure and making his way to the car.

A Hispanic man in his early twenties was loudly chewing some gum as he lazily held out the bag through the window, not even bothering to get out of the car. Andrew grabbed it, thanked the delivery person, and walked back to the garage that this wheren's Andrew had left wide open. At that moment, Andrew decided it was a bad habit and would always make sure to close the garage door when he left.

*Does customer service not mean anything anymore?* Tim complained. *I mean, did you see his face? Not even a* fake *smile.*

Andrew ignored him as he opened the bag and saw the paper, thin folded box, and twine from the local crafts shop.

*I'm adjusting his tip,* Tim mumbled, still on the issue of the unenthusiastic delivery driver.

After placing the Clepsydra in a foldout box and wrapping it in the paper and twine, they were set.

*You can put the rest on the shelf.*

Looking to his side, Andrew saw where Sylvie kept her excess supplies, and he slowly slipped the extra paper and twine among the others.

"Why do we have to deliver the box first?"

*Oh, um . . . because . . . uh . . .*

"Because once I . . . *do what must be done* . . . the next Andrew will kill me, too."

*Y-Yes*, Tim admitted. *But remember! It is to save the entire universe, including letting your family live on a different timeline!*

Andrew sighed as a single tear rolled down his cheek.

"I don't want to do this."

*I know*, Tim said softly. *Are you ready?*

"No. Not really," Andrew admitted, wiping the tear away with the back of one hand.

Tim opened a portal, and Andrew hesitantly stepped through.

With Tim's guidance, they freely moved down the wormhole.

Coming out the other side, he saw we were just outside of the funeral home. The bright sun beating down on him hurt his eyes, which were accustomed to the low levels of light from the night.

*Go through this door and wait fourteen seconds.*

"Okay?" he hesitantly said but did as Tim instructed. Ten seconds later, at the end of the hall, Andrew saw someone walk past.

*Move down the hall and around the corner.*

He did.

*Wait here six seconds, and then move ten paces forward. The reception-ist is just on the right.*

From inside the cathedral, he could hear himself scream out, "They can't breathe!" and felt a wave of sorrow at the pain this man had experienced . . . that *he* had experienced. And that he was going to cause to another version of Andrew who would then, in return, kill him to keep the cycle going.

*Move forward! We are almost there!*

He did exactly as Tim instructed, eventually coming to stand just behind the receptionist.

*Wait one second.*

The phone began to ring, and the young lady pivoted to the side in her chair to pick it up.

"Hello? Helllooooo?" the receptionist said into the phone.

*Okay, now!*

Moving swiftly and silently, Andrew set the box down on her desk, then quickly slipped out the back again, using Tim to guide him so as not to be seen.

"Now what?" he asked, out of breath for some reason.

*Now comes the hard part.*

"I . . . " he trailed off, realizing what the AI meant.

It was time to go back through the wormhole to kill his family before letting the Andrew picking up the box from the receptionist do the same to him.

*You can do this, Andrew. To save the universe, and eventually, your own family.*

He looked up at the bright sky, once again unhappy that it was so chipper on an occasion that felt like it should be shrouded in darkness.

Then Andrew nodded once, and the portal opened.

He sat at the end of the dining room table, looking at the version of himself standing between Sylvie and Alison in the Airbnb kitchen instead of the kitchen at home.

*He's the last . . . isn't he?* he mentally asked Tim as he thought about all the things this Andrew had done differently. When it had been his turn, he had come back from the corner store and found the bodies of his family—thus beginning his turn on the game as the pursuer. He had received Tim after the funeral, just before being ambushed by the Clockmen. But they hadn't chased them after the initial encounter, allowing Tim to guide Andrew to the precise time he needed to arrive with the foolish belief that he would be saving his family, only to discover the truth. After the murderer had explained everything, Andrew had shot him in the head and absorbed his energy before continuing with the vicious cycle, becoming the killer and leaving the bodies of his family so that the new Andrew could become the protagonist . . . the pursuer . . . hungry to hunt the killer down.

But *this* Andrew had somehow drawn the attention of the Clockmen past the initial ambush after the funeral, prompting the chase to begin; that had changed everything. Hell, he himself had even thrown the other Andrew Retnuh's Clepsydra in the woods, giving him full, untraceable access to the wormhole.

*I believe he is,* Tim answered with a tone of awe and respect. *No other variant has done what he has.*

*Then the universe, and my family, are saved,* he mentally sighed in relief.

*I'm not entirely sure.*

*Why's that?*

*The Clockmen haven't hunted any of the other variants past the day of the funeral . . . something is wrong.*

*What do you mean?*

*I didn't tell you this before, Andrew, but I don't see a point in withholding it any further.*

Andrew mentally prepared for what Tim was going to tell him; the scene outside moved at a snail's pace while the pair conversed at the speed of thought.

*The Clockmen were sent to ensure that you went back in time because that was how it happened in the first place. It was their mission to follow the same steps and ensure the same outcome. But this Andrew . . . they are chasing him down, and I don't know why.*

*Always with the lies,* Andrew accused, but without any vigor left in his words as he faced certain death. Then he thought about what the AI had said, and added, *I think it means he is* the last one.

*You may be right.*

*And if I am right? What happens if he is* the last of us?

*I . . . I don't know, actually.*

*Well, I guess you'll find out, won't you?*

*I suppose I will when I merge my consciousness with his Clepsydra.*

*That sounds fun.*

*It isn't.* Tim chuckled, and then a few moments later said, *And, Andrew?*

*Yeah?*

*Rest easy. You've done your part.*

*Hey, before I die . . . how many of us were there? Andrews, I mean.*

*Three thousand, one hundred and forty.*

*I . . . I-I-I . . .*

*You will be forty-one.*

Something clicked in killer Andrew's head, and he said out loud, "Pi?" right as the other Andrew lifted his glowing fist and—

# CHAPTER 47

Everything above the sternum of the killer exploded, leaving behind a smoking stump as both arms flopped to the floor. The left one clattered as the Clepsydra clanged off the tile.

*That . . . that wasn't supposed to happen,* Tim said, disbelief slipping into his tone.

I lowered my arm and willed the muscles that had fired the blast to relax.

"Fuck your pie," I spat, not caring how odd it was the man had said the word seemingly out of nowhere.

*That wasn't supposed to happen,* Tim repeated, but with more concern in his voice. *First the damn Clockmen hunting you . . . now this?!*

"What wasn't supposed to happen, Tim?" I demanded, confused and angry that killing the bastard responsible for the deaths of my wife and daughter hadn't been met with cheers and verbal pats on the back.

*You really are the last . . . after all this time . . .*

"The last *what*?" I growled.

*Never mind that for now. I have to think,* Tim hastily said. *Grab his Clepsydra and let's go.*

"Why?" I coldly asked. "I did what I was meant to do and killed the bastard. I didn't fail. So that means I don't need to take his Clepsydra and go back in time to deliver it to my past self, does it, Tim?"

*Um . . . well, you don't want anyone else getting a hold of it. They would be putting themselves in danger if they used it.*

"Hmph," I let out, reluctantly acknowledging his point.

Reaching down, I lifted the arm off the ground by the Clepsydra, feeling movement happening somewhere beneath. Then the device came loose, and I let what was left of the killer slip free and flop to the ground.

"What now?"

*Touch his body.*

"I don't want to," I said with foolish pride, wishing to be contrary to whatever Tim asked of me.

*If you don't, all that energy will fade away, drifting into the universe, and leave you with half of what your Chronos Scale should be.*

"So?"

*So?! So you won't be able to save your wife and daughter!* Tim replied with urgency in his voice. *Now hurry, before the energy fades!*

Thinking of my family, I reached down with gritted teeth and gripped the bare left arm of the bastard, squeezing it as hard as I could, even though I knew he could no longer feel anything.

Energy rushed into me, making me gasp, and my mind played back the memory of when I had witnessed the Big Bang while in the wormhole. I didn't know why or what the connection was, but it *felt* appropriate at the moment.

The flesh of the killer completely vanished, leaving behind the blue Dickies overalls, white shirt, gym shorts, and hiking boots, all while I seemed to vibrate with powerful energy.

*At least this time we don't have to worry about another Andrew coming back from the corner store.*

"Now . . . what . . . ?" I growled, feeling both euphoric and disgusted as the stolen energy from countless other Andrews flowed throughout every cell in my body.

*Now we wait for the contamination to dissipate, and then travel safely away from here before the Clockmen find us.*

"And then what, Tim?" I asked, remembering how the other Andrew had said it was *my* turn.

*I . . . I need to think about that,* he replied, unsure of what to say. *For now, let's flee the scene and travel as far from Houston as we can.*

"I'm not killing my family, Tim."

*Andrew! Please! Give me some fucking time to think!*

At the AI fully losing his composure and cursing so strongly, I decided that what I had said was enough for now. What's more, I meant it. Nothing in the universe would make me kill my own wife and daughter . . . nothing. No matter what the consequences, I wouldn't do it.

Holding the Clepsydra in one hand, I left the hoodie and pistol sitting on the table and made my way to the truck outside. Unbeknownst to me, the letter written in my handwriting sat in the pocket of the hoodie, never again to be used to trick another Andrew.

Without knowing where I was going, I pointed the vehicle north and drove, content that I had avenged my wife and daughter. No future harm would ever come to them. I was going to make damn sure of it.

# CHAPTER 48

I pulled into the Buc-ee's in Madisonville and parked the truck at one of over a hundred gas pumps. The further I was from Houston, the better I felt.

Tim had been silent the entire time, and I was just fine with that because I needed time to process everything that had happened. I was also formulating an argument that equated to a verbal beatdown as to why he had changed my vision when looking at Andrew.

He had wanted to tell me something before I had entered the house, but now I knew what it had been.

*I can sense your blood pressure spiking.*

"I'm not ready to deal with you yet," I grumbled as I opened the gas tank and looked at the pump.

*Do . . . do you want me to pay?*

In answer, I held up my left arm to the card reader and waited until the prompt said to select an octane. I jammed the nozzle into the tank loud enough that the person in front of me turned and looked at me with a nervous expression.

Ignoring them, I made my way inside, mind flying with different obscenities I wanted to scream at Tim.

After using the bathroom, I bought enough food to last me a few days, the largest coffee they had, and a twelve pack of water, along with some travel-size toothpaste and deodorant.

The crowds at Buc-ee's were always thicker than the humidity in New Orleans, and I just wasn't having it. Though I didn't do or say anything aggressive to anyone, I still received more than a few double takes, presumably from the anger radiating off of me. It could have also been the impossible amount of energy coursing through my body. Either way, it probably didn't help that I could feel all the muscles in my face contorting while I grinded my bared teeth.

*Do you want me to give you something to relax?* Tim asked in a timid voice that leaned toward subdued, which was a stark contrast to his normally brash, authoritative tone.

*Fuck you,* I mentally said. I didn't know if I was attempting to be tactful and not seem like some sort of crazy person, or if the muscles in my face and jaw were simply too busy flexing at that moment.

*I'll just be quiet, then.*

*Wait . . .* A dawning revelation distracted me from the bubbling hatred. *You can hear me?*

*Yes,* Tim answered, suspicious of my question.

*You can hear . . . my thoughts?*

*If you direct them toward me, I can.*

*Why didn't you tell me sooner?* I asked, willfully letting my focus shift away from the shadows and feeling the muscles in my face relax as I did. Tim was still going to get an earful, but it was exhausting to hate at peak levels.

*You . . . you don't remember us mentally communicating after you fell in the shower, do you?*

*No, I don't remember because I had just been electrocuted by the damn universe, Tim!*

*Your blood pressure is dropping to nominal levels,* Tim informed. I couldn't tell if he was trying to change the subject or felt it was simply that important to announce.

*I don't care about that,* I mentally grumbled before stepping up to the counter.

"Did ya find everythang ya need, hun?" a young lady with a thick Southern drawl asked.

"Yes," I muttered, trying to fake a smile that I think came across as creepy, judging by the change in expression of the employee.

Dropping my smile, I ran Tim over the credit card reader, and the transaction went through.

"Whoa. How'd'ya do that?"

"Do what?"

"Ya paid without a card or nothin."

"Oh, uh . . . smartwatch," I offered before grabbing my white plastic bag with the smiling beaver on the front along with the pack of water—which I slung over one shoulder—and quickly walked out the sliding doors before any more questions could be asked.

After putting the supplies in the cab, I moved to replace the gas nozzle, and then I was ready to go. But to *where* was the question.

"How long until we can leave?"

*I assume you mean this wheren and not the gas station.*

I didn't dignify the weak question with an answer.

Tim continued, assuming what I had meant.

*My best guess is a time window of sixteen to twenty-eight hours from now. Give or take a ten percent margin of error.*

I grunted in acknowledgement as I started the truck, pulled out of the mega gas station, and headed north on I-45 to lie in wait for the last part of my journey.

Tim wasn't going to be happy with what I was going to do . . . and I didn't fucking care.

# CHAPTER 49

Once we made it through the chaotic nightmare that was Dallas, we were on I-35 heading toward the more docile country between DFW and the Oklahoma border.

Tim spoke up, apparently unable to hold it in any longer.

*Andrew . . . can we talk? Please?*

"About what, tin can?" I said coldly, knowing full well what the topic of conversation was going to be and dragging it out to force the AI into an uncomfortable position. No one liked starting critical conversations with a listener who was already a primed nuclear bomb ready to explode.

*About preventing the next Big Bang and destroying the universe as you know it.*

His choice of words gave me pause, and the rational part of me urged the emotional side to listen.

*I'm going to speak, now, and I want you to listen without flying off the handle. Can you do that for me?* he asked tentatively as he carefully maneuvered into the conversation.

"What, Tim," I demanded without the inflection indicating a question. I could feel myself preparing for the utter bullshit that was about to come spewing out in an attempt to poison my mind. But my resolve was unyielding. I would *never* kill my own family.

*What if I told you that Sylvie and yourself are quantumly entangled.*

"The fuck does that mean?"

*It means that when your universe was formed in the most recent Big Bang, that there were particles that split apart to form space dust that, if we skip forward to the day you and Sylvie were born, created the two of you. Where most particles remained whole after the explosion, there were an infinitesimal few that split, similar to how twins are formed in the womb.*

"What does that have to do with anything?" I asked with a tone that was growing less brittle and harsh.

*It means that you two weren't made for each other, as the saying goes . . . you were made from each other. The odds of which are so spectacularly incalculable that no one thought it was possible . . . until you two had Alison.*

"Ali?" I breathed out, feeling a stirring inside my heart that I didn't like.

*When the two of you procreated, a new life that hasn't been seen in this cycle was formed. A life born from quantumly entangled particles that split at the dawn of the universe. A life that, if allowed to bloom, could bring about the next Big Bang.*

"That doesn't make any sense. I thought quantum entanglement involved two atoms or something that moved and reacted to stuff as if they were one, even if they were across the galaxy from one another," I said, thinking about the few YouTube videos I had seen on the subject after getting sucked down a rabbit hole of streaming whatever videos popped up after the last. I remembered a small part of one of the clips, and added, "Like if an atom on Earth is moved and its entangled counterpart is on the Moon, it would move the same amount, even though no one touched it up there."

*Close . . . kind of,* Tim replied. *At this point on your timeline, the basic theory is that if two particles—not atoms—are entangled, then we would be able to accurately guess the spin of one based on the other. It's really quite rudimentary because our understanding has been vastly expanded upon in the future. Where once we had the barest semblance of a theory, mankind eventually discovered the fullest extent . . . which is what leads us to this critical moment.* He said the last part carefully, as if watching and judging my reactions as he neared to the major point of the conversation.

"What moment?" I asked, feeling my hands begin to sweat around the leather steering wheel while I shifted uncomfortably in my seat.

*The moment I have to tell you . . . that you have to save the entire universe.*

"By killing my little girl?" I hissed out in complete disbelief.

Tim continued onward, deflecting my emotionally charged statement.

*Right now, you are in a superposition, which is the ability to be in multiple states at the same time until measured.*

"What the hell does that have to do with anything?"

*It's just a basic explanation that would require at least an entire day to dive into, complete with PowerPoint slideshows and diagrams.*

"Then cut to it, Tim."

*You and Sylvie were born from the same particles from the Big Bang. And being quantumly entangled means you share equal and opposite spins.*

"What does that have to do with Ali?"

*No one could have predicted two humans with perfect entanglement having a child, because it was thought beyond improbable.*

"How improbable?" I was growing more curious as the conversation went on. Then again, most humans craved to be told they were unique and special, and that their spouse was *literally* meant for them. "One out of a billion? Trillion?"

*It would require a blackboard thirty-two meters long to showcase it as an actual number. That's including the entire surface, from top to bottom and side to side.*

"Okay . . . once again, I ask what the hell it has to do with my daughter."

*The pull that you and Sylvie had on the Chronos Scale, which at one point was even, resulted in an offspring that could eventually lead to the collapse of the universe into a singular point in space,* Tim explained just before his hologram came to life and showcased the familiar gas giant in our solar system. "Where you have the gravitational pull of Jupiter and can directly impact the future, Alison is more like a combination of every black hole in the entire universe forming one *scary* supermassive black hole." The hologram showcased his point by dragging swirling black vortexes from across the universe into one spot, resulting in what looked like a drain in a bathtub. Every star began to slip toward the hole in space; even the farthest, trillions of lightyears away, felt the pull.

After the last bits of light were swallowed, there was a moment of absolute nothingness before a bright explosion happened, sending clouds of particles in all directions.

"When is this supposed to happen?" I asked, watching the Big Bang give birth to a new universe before my very eyes. Though it wasn't as impacting as when I had witnessed the literal Big Bang outside of the wormhole, it still created a pit of dread in my gut knowing that Ali was directly involved.

The hologram faded, leaving only Tim's avatar.

"We don't know, exactly. But it is a risk that we cannot take."

A question that needed to be asked leaped to the forefront of my mind.

"Why don't you just go back and prevent me and Sylvie from ever meeting? Give me a flat tire or something on the day we met in college, making me late so someone else takes the seat next to her. Spare the past me from the pain of knowing true love . . . and having it taken away." My voice cracked at the end, and I had to fight back the tears that wanted to run free down my cheeks. I was praying that Tim would convince me this wasn't the right path, because life had been a hollow existence before her. It hadn't been a bad life, but it'd been missing something almost tangible. And no matter how hard I'd tried, nothing could fill the hole inside me, until the day I had met her.

On the other side of the coin, there was only one thing scarier than forgetting a true love that could *literally* be described as your soulmate . . . having it, creating an offspring that brought a previously unfathomable joy and completeness . . . and then violently losing them both.

At that moment, the phrase *damned if you do, damned if you don't* came to mind like a whisper from the shadows, almost mocking me with how perfectly the phrase fit my situation.

But at least Sylvie would live . . .

"We need to go back and stop me from sitting next to her that day."

"I was hoping to avoid this conversational path," Tim sighed, shaking his head.

"Why?" I inquired, feeling both dread and hope teeter on a scale. On one hand, my heart wanted nothing more than to remember my family and have them *exist*, even if only for what could be described as a limited time on this Earth. On the other, my brain suggested that *if* they were destined to both die, we could sacrifice our own happiness if it meant at least Sylvie could survive.

"First of all, there's nothing in this world that could keep you and Sylvie apart. You could try putting obstacles in the way, then record the absurd methods that love wins out every time to the point that you could sell the footage to Hu-Flix, or whatever they're called right now, and have a hit show on your hands," Tim explained as he created a scene above his head. It showed me driving, and I correctly guessed it was a representation of me on the first day of class, when I had met her.

The tire popped, and I cursed while smacking the wheel with the palm of my hand before pulling over. Another driver had seen what had happened and decided to pull over behind me. It was Sylvie. I couldn't help but smile, watching the hologram display the incalculable odds of me running into her at that moment.

The scene vanished into TV static before another image replaced it. This time, I was lying in bed with a perspiring brow and a greenish undertone. I had to choke back a gag as I watched myself suddenly roll over and throw up into the small trash can sitting between my bed and modest desk. The scene changed, and I was sitting in a pop-up ER, clutching at the same trash can, as a woman entered.

It was Sylvie.

She had the same greenish undertones, along with a similar trash can, though hers was pink where mine was a generic black.

The receptionist checked her in, and then pointed over to the small waiting room.

Our eyes met, and even in our sickness, we both managed a smile.

The scene dissolved into TV static again, only to be replaced by the image of me sitting in a park and reading a book, right as a violent explosion happened somewhere in the distance. The mushroom cloud of flame reached up into the sky, almost blinding me, and everyone in the park screamed before beginning to run around like frantic chickens.

The scene fast-forwarded to a version of me with tattered clothes, a red bandanna tied around my head, and dirt obscuring every inch of my skin. I was holding a black semiautomatic rifle while giving a speech to a group of scared but determined survivors.

I watched the hologram and smiled as my warrior leader's eyes locked onto a disheveled woman that I knew to be Sylvie.

Then the hologram faded, leaving only Tim, who said, "Okay, that last one was a little bit of Hollywood magic, because *pfft*, when have you ever read a book in a park? But you get the idea."

My mouth flapped a few times as I tried to come up with something to say. Luckily, Tim continued on.

"You two weren't just *meant* for one another . . . you were *made from* one another. Nothing would keep you two apart. Ugh." Tim gagged. "It's like some cheap romance story on basic cable."

"I knew it," I mouthed, remembering all the times Sylvie had looked at me with eyes filled with palpable love radiating from them. Each time we locked gazes, my heart would flutter in a nonmedical emergency sort of way. Hell, we even seemed to get sick at the same time, leading me to believe it was only sympathetic symptoms, but now I wasn't so sure.

"Which leads to the next problem," Tim inhaled. "And you aren't going to like this one."

All the feelings of joy from remembering how much I loved my wife faded like an eclipse over my heart.

"Alison *must* be born."

"I . . . I don't understand. You just said she can't live without destroying the universe . . . "

A hologram of space appeared, with distant galaxies dotted about like freckles on a redhead.

"Right now, the universe is constantly expanding. Eventually, and we are talking billions and billions of years from now, entropy will play out, and all energy in the universe will be stretched thin until there is nothing left." The hologram once again showed a expanded view of the universe before each of the stars began to fade, including our own sun, which Tim zoomed in on. "All heat that gives life will spread out until everything freezes, and all mechanical motion will cease. No stars will be left, and no new ones will be able to form. Only a frozen universe in a perpetual state where nothing ever happens."

"How does my daughter play into this, Tim?" I asked, growing frustrated at the overly scientific explanation.

"Alison *has* to be born and survive long enough to slow the expansion of the universe. If done properly, she could prevent the Big Freeze and provide a sustainable existence for all of mankind."

"And if she lives out her life?"

"Then the Big Crunch will eventually occur as she pulls everything back toward her, resulting in another Big Bang." Once again, Tim showcased his point by bringing up a hologram of the universe and collapsing it all into a singular point before a mind-bogglingly massive explosion happened, sending matter out in all directions to start anew.

"She *is* the center of the universe," I mouthed.

"You aren't wrong, Andrew. And as such lies the critical importance of her existence."

"How do you even know, for certain, that it *will* happen?" I accused.

"In the time from which I come from, it was discovered that the expansion of the universe had started to slow at an alarming rate thanks to the new, more efficient ways of measuring the distant galaxies we created. Before, we had been reliant on things like light and radiation to determine the distance between us and objects in space, such as stars and the like. The only problem is it took thousands to hundreds of thousands of years for the light and radiation to reach us, which meant our data was severely out-of-date. *But* once we figured out subspace, where the wormhole was created, we then started to develop new methods of measuring the distance between galaxies. And boy, you should have seen the faces on those first scientists."

"They saw that things weren't rushing away from them . . . "

"Correct, Andrew," Tim confirmed. "Galaxies had been racing *toward* Earth. The idea was laughed at in the beginning, until more and more in the field recorded similar findings. *All* matter in the universe was approaching Earth, which, as you can imagine, was statistically impossible."

"How does Alison have anything to do with that? It sounds like you are referring to hundreds of years into the future. Wouldn't she have already lived her full life and been long gone?"

"Yes. Which leads me to the next part." The hologram appeared again, showing Earth as a tiny speck, and an exaggerated collection of galaxies all slowly moving toward it. "After decades of research and testing of countless hypotheses, they discovered the reversal had occurred during a specific time frame, and then stopped all at once."

"Stopped? As in everything stopped moving toward Earth?"

"No, no, no. I mean stopped their acceleration, but kept their current momentum. Sort of like speeding down an icy road and then losing traction. Even if you hit the brakes, you aren't slowing down."

"I see," I said as I let my gaze go unfocused and tried to process his words.

"To make matters worse, the closer the galaxies drew to one another, the stronger the pull of gravity became. So even though the unexplained acceleration had ceased, a new *gravitational* one that could be quantified occurred. Which would lead to—"

"The Big Crash," I whispered, trying to remember a particular video on the subject of how the universe could end.

"Big *Crunch,* actually. But yes."

The puzzle began to show itself as more pieces were set in place.

"You need Alison to be born . . . to slow the expansion . . . but not live long enough to fully reverse it . . . " I concluded weakly, my head becoming light.

"That is exactly the point, Andrew," Tim spoke softly, knowing it was an impossibly large pill to swallow. It might as well have been a suppository to go along with the undeniable feeling of being fucked.

"Why . . . "

"Why what?"

"Why is this happening?"

"Some theories suggest it is the universe's way of hitting the reset button. Initializing another Big Bang in the process before repeating it all over again."

"Like a fail-safe?"

"That could be one way to describe it. But what no one can figure out is *why* the function exists," Tim said. "As far as I can tell, the future is prosperous, and everything is going great for mankind and the handful of other alien civilizations we have encountered."

"Aliens? For real?"

"Not to get off topic, but yes. There is life in the universe. And that life is probably wanting to continue to exist."

I didn't like his tone or his choice of words.

"Well, I want my *daughter* to live, Tim!"

"If the universe collapses to a singular point in space . . . then how would she be able to live, Andrew?"

"You're telling me . . . that no matter what . . . my daughter dies . . ."

"I'm afraid so, yes. But only *after* she is born."

"Then what about Sylvie? Huh? Why does she have to die?!" I asked with a cracking voice as emotion rocked me. "Why do I have to lose *everything*?"

"Once your entangled partner is . . . is . . ."

"Killed!" I spat out, saying the word he was trying to avoid.

"Once you are no longer tied to her energy, you cease to be in a state of superposition. And with each iteration of the events, your pull on the Chronos Scale becomes stronger and stronger, until we get to you, Andrew. You are the last."

"The last what, Tim?" I asked with a heavy exhale. My head hurt from trying to fathom all the impossible things the AI was attempting to convey to me.

"You are the last . . . *killer*."

"I . . ."

"After you go through the wormhole and complete the mission, the pull you have on the timeline will ensure no other variation of you will have to go back and do it again."

"Which means Sylvie and Ali will be dead . . . forever."

" . . . yes," Tim hesitantly answered.

"If I am the last, then why do I have to kill Sylvie?" I demanded with a scowl marring my face. "If no other Andrew has to go back, then why would I need to take his entangled spouse?"

"So he does not reproduce again."

"You would have me leave him in utter darkness, with no mission that could give him hope of seeing his wife and baby again?"

"Because of your Chronos Scale, you could touch him, Andrew. Spare him the pain you endured and then take his place on the timeline, knowing there *is* a timeline because you saved the universe."

"Touch him . . . you mean *kill* him?"

"It's hardly murder, seeing as how you *are* him, just from the nearby future."

"Fuck you, Tim," I blurted out, taking both of us by surprise. I hadn't meant to say it, but I sure as shit felt it in my heart and didn't mind it being said.

*I suppose you could just sit back, have a beer, and wait for the end of all existence,* he countered coldly as his avatar vanished from above my left arm.

"Which might never come," I replied.

*Is that a risk you are willing to take?*

Silence filled the cabin, leaving me with a nauseated stomach, dizzy head, and dry mouth.

I was the last. The only question left was, what would I be willing to do to save all of existence?

# CHAPTER 50

Full night was upon me as I pulled off the road toward the modest cabin in the woods that Tim had rented out near the border of Oklahoma.

The dirt road was shrouded on the top and sides by a thick canopy of green that waved in the wind, seeming like a haunted dance in the headlights of my truck.

After parking, I lugged in the supplies I had with me, dropping them off in the kitchen, and immediately went to the master bedroom for a shower. Not only did I want to rid my body of the filth that had accumulated, but it was also a period at the end of what could only be described as a bullshit day.

As I let the water run over me, I thought about everything.

I had won. The killer was dead, and by my own vengeful hand. The Clockmen were nowhere to be seen, *and* I had Retnuh's ability to use the wormhole without anyone being able to track me. But I didn't have my wife and daughter with me.

*You promised,* I said mentally.

*Hmm? Promised what?*

*That I would save my family.*

*No,* Tim replied with an air around him that reminded me of a lawyer about to drop a bomb on the courts. *I said you would* see *your family* again *and* avenge their deaths by killing the murderer. You did both of those things, just as I said.

My fist slammed into the shower wall, cracking the subway tile in a spiderweb around the point of impact.

*Careful, Andrew! Your right arm is still very much broken. I'll need at least another day to fully mend it.*

"Stop manipulating me, Tim," I said out loud, hearing my furious voice echo off the bathroom walls. "And I *haven't* seen my fucking wife and daughter again! Because you lied! You *keep* lying to me!"

Water spilled down my face while I stared forward, unblinking, feeling my eyes agitate and uncaring of that fact.

*Andrew,* Tim started with an inhale. *I did what I had to do. The truth was revealed to you when it was necessary to do so. Keep in mind you aren't the first Andrew Frost I've been assigned to.*

"I don't care if there have been a *hundred* other Andrews! You've never worked with *me!*"

*Pfft. A hundred,* Tim mumbled under his breath.

"Goddamn it, Tim!" I roared.

After a few moments of heaving breaths, Tim backed off.

*You are right, Andrew. There hasn't been another variation quite like you. It is an anomaly, but one that gives me hope.*

"Hope for what?" I exhaled, pulling my throbbing fist away from the wall. I was having trouble keeping my cool, but given the circumstances, I think I was handling it better than most would have been able to.

*Hope that you are the last, Andrew. That everything will be okay after this.*

"After . . . what . . . " I said, knowing full well what the answer was.

*Try to get some food in you before you go to sleep,* Tim ignored my question. *I have some calculating to do.*

As I shut off the water and felt the immediate rush of cool air glide over my tired body, I told Tim, "I want to see my family. Just like you said I would."

*I think that can be arranged.*

"Think? You *think* that can be arranged?" I indignantly barked. "How about this . . . if you don't let me see them again, I'll put a bullet in my head, and then all this would have been for nothing. Do not doubt what I would be willing to do to see them again."

*Okay, Andrew,* Tim replied hesitantly.

"No, not *okay,* Tim. I want to hear you say it."

*I'll take you to see your family.*

"No more games, tin can. No more manipulating me," I sternly ordered. "I will *not* hurt my family for *any* reason."

*Very well, Andrew. Get some rest. We'll talk in the morning.*

I spent the rest of the night in blissful silence as I numbed my brain with TV, filled my belly with gas station food, and drank four of the water bottles. It didn't take long before I regretted not buying some beer . . . or maybe straight-up moonshine. Anything to dull my thoughts more so than whatever basic cable show was on.

With a stomach stuffed with artificial flavors and other ingredients that could survive long past the point where humanity went extinct, my body assured me that the old, stale-smelling recliner was the most comfortable thing I had ever sat on . . . and sleep took me with a promise of bad dreams.

# CHAPTER 51

An infinite expanse of nothing encompassed everything around me. A perfect void with no beginning or end. The ideal housing for a universe comprised of hundreds of billions of galaxies, each with a hundred billion stars contained within. Around the countless stars, gravity formed solar systems made up of a vast collection of planets, some made entirely of dense gases held in place by their own enormous mass, others nothing more than world-size clumps of space dirt, content to exist without any further meaning or desires. Still others were just far enough away from their stars that life could form. Life in a universe where once nothing had existed.

The scene around me zoomed out at impossible speeds until the countless galaxies began to form a silhouette of a woman.

Sylvie stared at me with eyes made of supernovas. She smiled, and her teeth were formed from white dwarfs. I blinked, and she was floating in front of me, completely naked and with palpable love in her eyes.

We embraced, and I could feel her kiss even in my dream state. My body, which knew it was asleep, wanted to sob at how real Sylvie's touch was . . . and how much I missed her.

Pushing the feeling aside, I allowed the euphoric intoxication from the dream to fully take me, and we made love. I looked into my wife's face, and lightly kissed the tip of her nose. We were the only two beings in all of creation, and it felt . . . *right.*

She smiled at me once more, moving her hands to her belly. I looked down to see it was full and round, with a glowing light visible beneath her skin made up of galaxies.

I blinked again, and Sylvie was holding a baby girl.

Alison.

The center of my universe.

My sweet, beautiful child, whose giggles melted my heart.

Closing my eyes, I kissed her forehead while a little coo of fulfillment escaped my lips. I had never known such joy and happiness than while holding my wife and child in my arms.

Opening my eyes, I saw Alison as a young woman, just before the age where adolescence stole the innocence of youth. She strongly resembled her mother, though our families would say they could see a perfect balance between mine and Sylvie's features.

The grin that had been permanently affixed to my wife's face as if she were a marble statue standing against the march of centuries faded. I tilted my head in confusion, just as the galaxies that made up Sylvie's flesh began to fade one at a time.

Her beautiful, thick hair began to thin while her skin drooped.

"S-Sylvie?"

Alison remained unmoving as I watched her mother continue to fade. I could see the pain in Sylvie's eyes, but she tried her best not to show it in front of our daughter.

A bright light flashed, and I shielded my face with both hands.

Not wanting to lose sight of my wife, I dared the brightness and opened my eyes while lowering my hands to see Sylvie was gone. Only Alison remained.

She stared at me with a body made entirely of light. A young girl who entered into womanhood . . . and swallowed the universe.

I looked around and saw nothingness surround us. The universe had become a void once more, devoid of all energy and life. Only the light of Ali remained affixed at the center of the abyss.

"Daddity," she whispered before closing her eyes, leaning her head back, and exploding into a new Big Bang.

# CHAPTER 52

I flung myself awake, feeling the heat of the blast beneath my skin and hearing the remnants of Ali calling my name, *Daddity*.

The chair toppled to the side, and I instinctively shot my right arm out to catch my fall. There was a slight surge of pain where the bones had mended, but that was it.

*Andrew?*

"I'm . . . I'm fine," I panted as I awkwardly maneuvered out of the sideways chair and climbed to unsteady feet.

*Bad dream?*

"I don't know," I admitted, not having time to process what had happened just yet. Now that I was awake, the intensity and strong emotional feelings of the dream began to fade while my mind assured me it hadn't been real.

*Well, I have some good news to share with you,* Tim informed proudly.

"I could use some right about now," I muttered as I made my way to the kitchen to make some much needed coffee. The morning light spilled through the windows, warming my skin where the rays touched.

*First, my analysis shows that the exotic matter contamination should be cleared up enough to portal out in about three hours.*

"Okay," I said indifferently while I grabbed a mug from the cabinet and set it under the coffee machine that used capsules instead of grounds.

*Second, I think I have a solution to our little, um,* problem.

"You mean the fact that I won't kill my own wife and daughter," I asked in a statement.

*Y-Yes,* Tim stuttered, apparently not liking the unshakable will I was emanating with my words. If the universe was to die because I refused to kill my baby . . . then so be it.

*There is a man, in the fut—*

"It's me, isn't it?"

*I, uh . . . yes.*

"And he will probably tell me that the only solution to saving every-thing is to kill Alison."

*And Sylvie,* Tim confirmed. *But! After witnessing the things that you can do, no matter how seemingly impossible, I'm certain that if anyone can convince him to find another way,* you *can.*

"What do you mean, 'the things that I can do'?"

*Andrew, I have witnessed these events folding in on one another over three thousand times. Not once has a variation of Andrew Frost been able to catch on so quickly or change important details in his favor. I mean, the events with the tall Clockman alone prove how unique you are.*

"Three . . . thousand . . . ?" I mouthed, feeling the inside of my skull be replaced by what felt like dryer lint. Luckily, the aroma of freshly brewed coffee brought me back to reality before I could pass out, like a ship's anchor in an angry bay.

*That's not what is important, Andrew,* Tim quickly said, sensing my slipping sanity. *For me, it has been like watching the same movie over and over and over again, knowing exactly what is supposed to happen. And then one day,* bam! *Key scenes are changed, which should be impossible.*

"I think I'm going to be sick," I gagged. My gaze slid to the sink as if ask-ing my reeling brain if that would be a good vomit receptacle.

*Andrew. You stopped the Clockmen. Something that* no one else, *not just the previous iterations of you, has ever done or even* had *to do. You also avenged your family's murder. You literally accomplished the things you set out to do!*

"So what are you saying now? I don't have to become the killer anymore?"

*I'm saying* maybe *there is a chance for a happy ending, after all. But it won't be easy.*

"Nothing ever is," I muttered. Willing my stomach to settle, I took a slow sip of the piping hot coffee. I could feel its warmth sliding down my throat and radiating outward from my stomach, feeling like the physical manifestation of hope inside me.

*I've never said this to an Andrew before, but I* believe *in you,* Tim said. *I believe that you can both save the universe* and *your family. However, I would be remiss if I didn't point out that this will be the most difficult mis-sion yet.*

"When do we leave?" I asked after taking another sip of my coffee, allowing more of the warmth to flow through my body.

*As soon as the exotic matter contamination has reached safe levels. But we will have to move quickly. The Clockmen are not going to be happy once they discover you stole Retnuh's Clepsydra.*

"Good. Fuck that guy. I'm glad he's dead."

*Weeeeellll . . .* Tim drawled out. *Technically, he's not* dead.

"Oh, right . . . shit."

*Shit indeed, Andrew. Shit indeed. They are going to come at you harder than before, especially after witnessing the anomaly that you are compared to your previous iterations.*

"What do you mean by that?"

*I mean, they initially only made sure that the Andrew who received the Clepsydra would go back in time and start the process over again.*

"Why?"

*Because the governments of the future wanted to make sure everything happened exactly as it had before. But then you came along and triggered something that I couldn't have foreseen, making them pursue you with vigor.*

"Bastards," I grumbled.

*Indeed. And now those* bastards *are going to come at you even harder in an effort to preserve the future.*

"Which means they are going to try and find a way to kill Alison and Sylvie anyway . . . aren't they?"

*That would be a safe assumption. But not at first.*

"Why's that?"

*They will first try to anticipate your next move and probably set up a trap of some kind for you.*

Sylvie and Alison flashed through my mind, and I felt love reinforce the determination in my heart.

"Then we'll do something they aren't expecting," I stoically claimed. "Let's bring the fight to their front door."

*That's what I'm talking about, baby!* Tim exclaimed, briming with the excitement of change intermixed with danger.

An unshakable idea came to me, and I knew, before even fully realizing what the plan was, that I was going to act on it.

"Tim."

*Yes, Andrew?*

"I want to go back. To the night of the murder."

*W-What? Why?*

"If what I do directly changes the future, then I want to make sure they are going to live."

*I don't believe there are any other Andrews that will be going back in time,* Tim said. *At least not anymore.*

"Then it won't hurt anything to go and make sure," I spoke with a degree of finality.

*Very well,* Tim agreed with a sigh. I couldn't help but feel like I had just caught him in a lie.

Two hours and fifty-five minutes later, I was fully cleaned, fed, and geared up.

*The portal is ready to be opened,* Tim announced. *I have the energy suppressor from Retnuh's Clepsydra installed, and the wheren is set for the night in question.*

"Do it."

The portal opened, and with a clenched jaw, I stepped through.

# CHAPTER 53

*For the record, I think this is a bad idea,* Tim whispered inside my head as we moved down the wormhole to the precise spot marking where my life had been forever changed.

"Noted," I dismissively said while glancing down either end of the tunnel, half expecting to see figures clad in black approaching.

The stars and galaxies outside the tunnel appeared to remain unmoving as we slowly walked.

*Here it is,* he announced, and we came to a halt.

After a few seconds, impatience burst from out of nowhere, and I demanded, "Open it!"

*Andrew . . .* he started, finding the strength to tell me what I knew I didn't want to hear. *If there is another Andrew . . . and you stop him before he completes his mission . . . if you interrupt the cycle . . . there might not be a future to go to. More specifically, it's entirely probable there will not be a future Andrew to help us solve this complex puzzle. Or if there is, he might not like that you broke protocol and risked everything for your own selfish interests.*

"If I am the last, then that means I exist in the future. Right?"

*I guess that makes sense. But we can't know for sure.*

"Only one way to find out," I said coldly, not giving the AI even the barest space to try and wiggle his logic like a bug slipping beneath a baseboard.

*As long as you understand the potential outcome . . .* Tim sighed, then the portal opened up in front of me.

One corner of my lips curved into a smile, and I didn't know if it was because of my foolish defiance or the fact that I was proving to myself that I would, in fact, do *anything* to save my family. Everyone said that, but no one had ever been faced with the obstacles scattered in front of me . . . or the ones behind.

Before stepping through, I focused on the portal and held an idea in my mind. The gateway rippled once, drawing a *What the . . .* from Tim, but I ignored it.

I finally pushed through the portal and stepped onto damp grass. The sky above was a blueish purple with thick clouds lazily drifting overhead. It took my brain a few seconds to figure out that it was my own backyard, and a feeling of familiarity washed over me. There was movement through the kitchen window, and I almost gasped when I saw Sylvie preparing a salad for tonight's dinner.

She was the most beautiful woman I had ever seen, and I longed to stride into the house and embrace her.

My foot lifted to do just that, but I froze as I saw a man come into view, holding *my* daughter and giving a small box to *my* wife.

Anger began to build until I realized the man was me. Then confusion intermixed with relief, followed by a pang of anguish, like watching old home movies of loved ones no longer with us.

I set my foot back in place, seeing as Andrew Frost hugged his wife and daughter, celebrating their ASA-Day. I remembered it clearly—the joy of preparing dinner with my family on such an important occasion, only to have to leave because a different version of me had stolen the lighter fluid, and then coming back to . . .

Turning to the grill, I could see the white container with the red lid sitting right where I knew I had left it on that night.

*Take two full steps backward, please,* Tim instructed, though his words sounded like he wasn't expecting anything to happen.

I did, right as a portal opened where I had just been.

*Oh . . .* Tim drawled in complete surprise.

As quickly as it had arrived, the doorway closed.

In front of me was a man wearing a black hoodie. His upper torso rose and fell with deep, ragged breaths while his right hand, which held a silenced pistol, trembled.

"O-Okay. G-Grab the lighter fluid . . . and then . . . and then . . . "

Though I couldn't hear the other side of the conversation, I knew *his* Tim was instructing him on what to do.

"I-I-I can't do this, Tim!" he whispered, shaking his head.

"You don't have to," I spoke flatly, and the would-be killer gasped and spun around, right as I grabbed his face with my bare hand.

*WAIT!* Tim shouted. But it was too late.

The man violently vibrated like he was being electrocuted, and his skin grew translucent, revealing a silently screaming skeleton beneath. Then it, too, faded, and I could see all the vessels and organs inside of him before the universe corrected the scales and erased him from existence.

However, I *didn't* absorb his energy like I was expecting. He simply vanished.

The flesh was gone, leaving behind a pile that contained a black hoodie, blue overalls, and hiking boots, along with the silenced pistol and Clepsydra.

*H . . . How?* Tim asked in utter disbelief. I could picture his avatar's lower jaw touching the ground as he spoke.

"How what?" I whispered while I gathered up the pile of clothes, gun, and Clepsydra before carefully making my way behind the moderately sized shed and dropping everything to the ground once out of sight.

*How were* you *not erased?* Tim breathily asked. *You didn't kill him first before touching him. And-and-and he* had *to have been from your future, meaning his Chronos Scale should have been stronger than yours . . . unless . . .*

"He wasn't from *my* future," I confidently said. "I told you, Tim, that I was the last. That I was going to break the cycle."

*Y-You're right! That Andrew barely registered on the scale . . . which means . . .* Tim thought for a few moments. *Please pick up the Clepsydra so that I can merge with its consciousness.*

I moved the device with my toe, letting it slip from the black hoodie, and reached down to grab the smooth metal sleeve.

Knowing what to do, I touched the apparatus to Tim, walked around to the side of the shed, and looked through the window at the past version of me reaching into the fridge to grab the tray of steaks. My eyes darted to the grill once more, and I saw the lighter fluid was still there.

*Oh, my science! He . . . he was the very first! The first Andrew!* Tim gasped. *You've stopped the cycle before it began! And, heh,* boy *is this Tim confused.*

On reflex, I lifted a hand to my chest to make sure I was still corporeal. If this were a movie, I would have expected to start vanishing after completing my mission.

"I'm still here," I said both to Tim and myself as I moved a few feet to the side of the shed and out of view once more.

*How extraordinary,* Tim drawled in amazement. *I . . . I can't believe you actually did it.*

"I told you there was nothing that could stop me from saving my family."

*Apparently not even the laws of time travel! Hahaaaaa! Wow!* Tim exclaimed. *I actually think we have a chance at this!*

"Glad to see you're finally on board."

I leaned from around the shed and looked through the kitchen window. It was empty, and my heart skipped a beat as my breath quickened.

*How did you even manage to change the wheren? I mean, it should have been your turn, if I am being completely honest.*

I ignored his comment about how he had, once again, tried to trick me into killing my family, instead focusing on his question.

"Before we went through the portal . . . I thought about the first time this happened. Not just *my* experience some three thousand Andrews later . . . but the *first*."

*You . . . you can do that?*

"I guess I can."

*01! That's amazing!*

Moving farther out, I heard the back door slam closed, like Alison always did, and saw my girls crowding around . . . me.

I was setting the coals, and then coated them in lighter fluid before igniting the flame to start cooking the steaks for our ASA-Day.

"Daddity!" Ali called out. She clutched at the air with both hands, which signaled she wanted to be picked up.

I had to cover my mouth as tears filled my eyes at hearing her say my nickname again. How I had missed it; more than a desert rose yearned for rain.

Andrew picked up his daughter and rested her on his hip while he carefully set the steaks with the long metal tongs.

By cosmic coincidence, Alison happened to turn her head toward the shed and locked eyes with me. She then raised a hand to point in my direction, and I mirrored her motion by lifting my own hand, as if I could touch her living flesh from across the backyard.

"Daddity!" she called out again, but this time, it was directed toward me, and my heart nearly melted out of my chest to pool on the wet grass at my feet.

*Um . . . Andrew?* Tim worriedly spoke, drawing me back to the now.

I quickly understood the situation and darted back around the shed before Sylvie or Andrew looked to where Ali was pointing.

*We have to go.*

With tears slipping down my cheeks, I could only nod in understanding while Tim finished charging another portal.

*I need you to know that there might not be a universe once we go through the other end of the wormhole, Andrew.*

"I understand," I replied. I wiped at my tears, picked up the clothes and gun to add to the Clepsydra I was already holding, and steadied myself. A question came to mind, and I asked, "Will his memories sear into my brain when I go to sleep?"

*Honestly, I have no idea at this point. This is all brand-new territory for me. But if I had to guess, I would say yes.*

"Good," I said as another tear ran down my cheek. "I want to remember this night, and how it should have happened."

*You ready for this?*

I thought about Sylvie and Alison, and how they would *not* be killed in this special night—the birthday that we all three shared. Instead, they would enjoy dinner with Andrew, who would remain blissfully unaware of the fate I had spared him from.

I thought about Retnuh, and how we had defeated him.

I thought about the killer and the fact I had stopped a vicious cycle of sacrifice from a man that thought he was doing what was right in order to save the universe. I was the last Andrew that would have to endure having his world taken away. No other *me* would experience the pain of immeasurable loss. I, alone, would carry that burden, like Atlas holding up the world.

But the story wasn't over. Now, I would discover a way to save *both* the universe and my family . . . and nothing would stop me from doing just that.

"I'm ready," I declared with my chin lifted high, prepared to face whatever came my way.

*Then here . . . we . . . go!*

The portal opened, and I stepped through into an unknown future.

# EPILOGUE

Retnuh Ordune stepped through the portal to the Clockmen HQ, where he immediately received a ping on his Clepsydra.

Lifting the sleeve of his black coat, he read the hologram that had appeared, a scowl increasingly etching into his face with each passing word.

"Traze?" he asked with an aggressive tilt of his head toward the man in all-white medical scrubs.

"He-he sustained grave injuries, sir. The contamination lasted for nearly three days, psychologically scarring his mind from the accumulated pain that his entire timeline experienced all at once."

"Don't patronize me, doctor. I am fully aware of the effects brought on by a Clepsydra breach," Retnuh growled, turning his full body toward the cowering man in white. "Will he make it?"

The pair turned to a hyperbaric glass room where what resembled a man lay in a medical bed. Tubes ran from every orifice of the sedated creature while multiple IVs with different colored liquids infused him with enough life to keep his heart beating.

"It's hard to tell, sir," the man hesitantly said. Slowly turning toward the field commander of the Clockmen, he asked, "The question is . . . do you want him to? The psychological damage is enough to drive anyone mad, sir. And, quite frankly, we've never seen anyone with this degree of damage."

Retnuh grabbed the smaller man by his collar, lifting him off the ground as easily as if he were nothing more than a tiny kitten.

Bringing the doctor close to his face, Retnuh declared in a dark voice that promised a world of untold agony, "You had *better* make sure Agent Traze makes it, or you will share his fate. Am I understood?"

"Y-Yes, s-sir!" the doctor croaked before Retnuh dropped him to the ground.

As the man in white scampered away, Retnuh turned his attention back to his loyal agent.

A shorter man—dressed in the same attire, complete with the fedora with a wide brim—limped next to the bald man.

"Is he gonna make it, boss?" Davix asked. He looked at his best friend, who was clinging to life via tubes and chemicals. As he spoke, the shorter Clockman gingerly touched his stomach, where a new liver had been grown and inserted after the old one had been eviscerated by a bullet from the Tick's primitive rifle.

"The doctor seems to think so," Retnuh replied with a wry smile.

"And what are we going to do about the Tick?"

"Once again . . . he'll come to us."

The wry smile Retnuh had morphed and mutated into a full shark's grin that seemingly stretched from ear to ear.

# ABOUT THE AUTHOR

Hunter Blain is the bestselling author of the Preternatural Chronicles, an urban fantasy series, as well as the Sol Saga, a superhero series. He also has no idea what to submit for a bio. So, let's start with *why* Hunter decided to start writing in the first place.

The story begins with two best friends who grew up together, breaking rules and raising hell as they shaped each other's personalities to become the shameless assholes they are today. Well, one of them at least, but I'll get to that in a moment. These two boys—let's call them Hunter and John—were all but inseparable. John excelled at creating music powerful enough to make angels weep and being the funniest asshole in Texas, while Hunter dabbled—poorly, I might add—in his humble writings. Because they were self-declared brothers from other mothers, John respected Hunter's humble writings as much as I—I mean Hunter (stupid third-person perspective)—respected John's musical magic. John's tunes could have changed the world one day . . .

One fine day, after reading one of Hunter's horrifically detailed short stories about a serial killer, John asked Hunter to write a story about him.

"Hell yeah, dude! What do you want to be?" Hunter asked, brimming with honor and biting back a very manly *squee.*

"A vampire," John responded with a mischievous gleam in his eye. "But not one of those sparkly ones. A true badass!"

"Done!" Hunter crowed, with a smile and an accompanying high five.

"No, dude. Promise. Promise you'll write and finish a book about me. You are the most prolific writer of our generation!" John said. (Something like that. I might be paraphrasing a little, but you get the gist of it). "I would consider it an honor to live on for eternity with your words as my life's blood."

Hunter agreed, never to realize the weight of that promise until one Sunday morning when John's mother called, crying incoherently.

John . . . had died.

Hunter was left in a cold world without his best friend and doppelgänger. He still thinks about that moment to this day. How the morning light crept through the bedroom window while he stared at the ceiling, noticing how the popcorn texture created cruel, jagged shadows. How everything started to blur as his chest was crushed beneath the weight of what he was hearing, each word stacking heavily upon the other until only fitful, ragged gasps of air could escape his throat. Only fiery tears existed, especially after the horrific realization that Hunter now had to make some of the hardest phone calls of his life to the circle of friends who orbited around John's solar pull.

Their star was no more, leaving their universe a colder and darker place.

John left not only Hunter but a friend named Valenta as well. There were also Nathanial and Depweg. The friends were each stricken numb with the loss of such a beloved flare of life. But . . .

When the three found out that Hunter was keeping his promise to write the greatest story ever told—starring their dear friend John—they demanded to be a part of the adventure. Each of them immediately knew what type of supernatural character they wanted to play in this urban fantasy eulogy. It would be a funeral pyre of words, and their fictional personas would be John's pallbearers.

Fast-forward three years, and John Cook has solidified himself as one of the funniest, most human vampires in the literary world. Not only this, but he gets to live on in the theaters of readers' minds, giving him eternal life after death.

As it turns out, Hunter had a knack for using words real-good-like and has expanded into a full-time author. Heck, you just read one of his works a few moments ago! So, if you enjoyed the twists, turns, and feels brought on from this book, please dive into his other ones!

*—Dictated by Hunter, holding a cigar and wearing an ascot,*
*but not read, because I couldn't be bothered*